GOOD RED HERRING

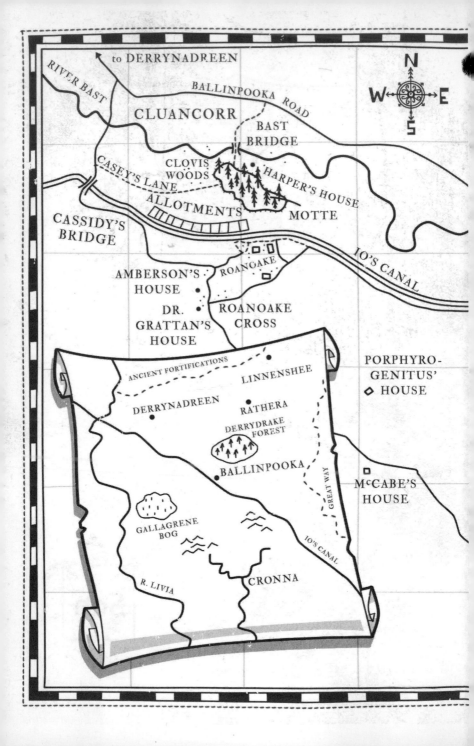

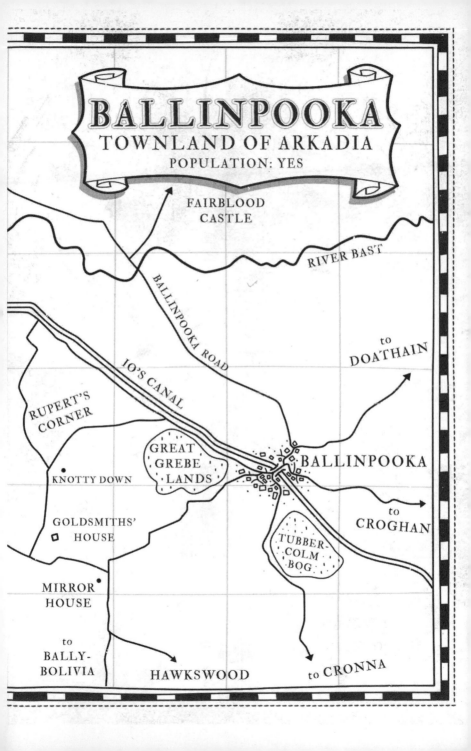

GOOD RED HERRING

SUSAN·MAXWELL

Little Island

GOOD RED HERRING
First published in 2014 by
Little Island Books
7 Kenilworth Park
Dublin 6W, Ireland

Copyright © Susan Maxwell 2014

The author has asserted her moral rights.

ISBN: 978-1-908195-93-7

A British Library Cataloguing in Publication record
for this book is available from the British Library

Cover design by Steve Simpson
Typeset and designed by Kieran Nolan, Oldtown Design
Printed in Poland by L and C Printing

Little Island receives financial assistance from
the Arts Council/An Chomhairle Ealaíon
and from the Arts Council of Northern Ireland

10 9 8 7 6 5 4 3 2 1

To Kathleen P Maxwell,
for whom the corpse can never appear too early on the page,

and to Anthony Maxwell,
for unexpected gifts

Dramatis Personae

Major characters are in bold. Note that characters only mentioned in passing may not be listed.

Albright, Coast *A senator*

Amberson, Mackerel *Brother of Shearwater Amberson*

Amberson, Shearwater (Shear), aka The Green Man *Friend of Fen Maguire's and a Ghillie of Demeter (defender of the environment)*

Benson, Deputy *A guardian, second deputy to McCabe*

Boru, Dr Copper *Deputy Khipu-Camayacos*

Brown, Honey *An amanuensis, a colleague of Fen's*

Bryce, Hopper *A fisherman*

Butler, Sand *An accountant who works at the senate*

Corbuse, Night *Velvet's brother, also fostered by Reed Cutler, a paramedic*

Corbuse, Velvet-Gem *Fen Maguire's apprentice, foster-child of Reed Cutler*

Cullen, Cedar *A master butcher*

Cutler, Reed *The Thanatos and foster-father to Velvet and Night Corbuse*

Darwin, Dr *A maths and physics teacher*

De Courcy, Bracken *An apprentice linguist whose family runs the Ravenous Raven Fooderie*

Donovan, Cotton *An investigative journalist*

Dunne, Bassett *A guardian, first deputy to McCabe and originally Salmon's despotes, later a werewolf*

Fallinish *A boxer dog in a former life, now reconstructed as clockwork by the Guild of Clockmakers; works with McCabe*

Farsade, Salmon-Grove *A teenage apprentice guardian, part-Outlander and refugee in Munibeo, has the ability to read auras*

Fenton, Bonbon *An apprentice archivist*

Finney, Perlucidas *Detective executive quaestor (a very high-ranking guardian), McCabe's boss*

Fitzwilliam, Marl (aka Boll Mason) *Undercover journalist and murder victim*

Fore, Conger *An apprentice engineer*

Gentileschi, Dr Ishka *The coroner*

Goldsmith, Archer *A master cardmaker and Salmon's foster-father*

Goldsmith, Marigold (Goldie) *An apprentice bookbinder and Salmon's foster-sister*

Goldsmith, Rainbow (Bow) *A schoolboy, later an apprentice journalist, and Salmon's foster-brother*

Goldsmith, Rose-Berry (Berry) *A master weaver and Salmon's foster-mother*

Grattan, Dr *A refugee from the Outland who teaches politics and ethics*

Gulliver, Madam *A sombrist abbess*

Harper, Imhotep (Immo) *Landlady of the Wooden O, a theater and residential arts centre*

Herbert, Waxie *An apprentice amanuensis*

Henry, Sugar *A physicist at the Possible Institute and a friend of Fen Maguire's and Honey Brown's*

Hobbs, Valerian *An environmentalist, member of the Ecological Assessment Committee, director of the Pachamama Institute in the Outland; person of considerable mystery*

Honeyman, Jeremy *Outlander and shady property dealer*

Hughes, Dr Silvanus *An academic historian and landscape archaeologist*

Inkster, Nefertiti (Nef) *An apprentice clockmaker with excellent organisational skills*

Johnston, Berberis *Factotum to Quaestor Finney*

Lake, Kale-Pearl *A microbiologist, expert in bog ecology, chair of the Ecological Assessment Committee, works for the Science Committee*

Logan, Geoffrey Ballantyne (GB) *A popular historian originally from Muinbeo but now living in the Outland*

Maccarrill *An African grey parrot who lives with Salmon Farsade*

Maguire, Badger, Fly, Heather, Holly and Sparrow *Fen Maguire's family*

Maguire, Persephone-Fen *Amanuensis to Senator Scarlet Woudes, despotes to Velvet Corbuse and murder victim*

Marten, Dr *A science teacher*

Martin, August-Joy *A friend of Fen Maguire's*

Mason, Boll *Real name of Marl Fitzwilliam*

McCabe, Hal *Detective Chief Inspector with the Muinbeo guardians (police force), appointed Salmon Farsade's despotes*

McKenzie, Butter *An apprentice archivist at the Senate Chambers*

O'Buachalla, Dr *A history teacher*

Paschalides, Frost *A veterinarian and a member of the Ecological Assessment Committee, an alien*

Peterson, Dr Silk-Joy *Deceased professor of history, whose bequest funds the Peterson Scholarship*

Porphyrogenitus, Heron *A lawyer, judge and legal historian, a friend of McCabe's*

Postmaa, Hellebore *A senator, chair of the Wildlife and Landscape Committee*

Pothinus, Theo *Director of the Apeteh Corporation in the Outland*

Richards, Berliner *A senator*

Sackville, Winter-Gold *Senior witch of the Smoke Coven, takes a particular interest in Salmon's welfare*

Sessaire, Hunter *An apprentice archivist and a sombrist*

Smith, Carbon *A portal engineer and a member of the Outland Watch*

Smith, Rabbit-Nut *A schoolgirl*

Tierney, Goose *A schoolboy*

Welsh, Puck *Maitre d' at the Hotel Grand Abyss and an elf*

Williams, Honesty *A musician, fosterlet of Winter Sackville*

Williams, Widow *A shopkeeper in Ballinpooka, mother to Honesty*

Woudes, Scarlet *A senator, to whom Fen Maguire is (or, mostly, was) amanuensis*

Vocabulary

If it is not defined here, you may find it in the footnotes. Otherwise, either we expect too much of you or we simply prefer that you don't know.

amanuensis A kind of high-powered secretary to a senator

aornis See footnote 15

arch-druid Religious leader

demonstration A kind of practical examination annually taken by an apprentice who wishes to graduate from apprenticeship to full adulthood

despotes Mentor or master, oversees and teaches an apprentice during their apprenticeship

dimorph A creature with a dual nature; dimorphs are distrusted and discriminated against by Muinbeo society, and for this reason tend to keep their nature secret, but see also footnote 46

EAC (Ecological Assessment Committee) On behalf of the senate, it assesses the impact on the environment of any new plan for development in Muinbeo

erratic portal A portal with a mind (a disturbed, confused mind) of its own

eolas A kind of search engine, a mechanism for finding information; pronounce *oh-less*

gairm Thanatos A kind of pre-funeral service, see footnote 47 for detail

Ghillies of Demeter Group of conservationists who take care of the environment and the wildlife of Muinbeo

guardian Police officer

Komnenos The sombrists' senior official

luchrupán One of the many species that inhabits Muinbeo; not exactly an imp, but close

Medon A very delicate, complicated structure on the top of the senate building; it looks a little like a very complex three-dimensional map of the stars. Like Ciplacti's Ear, the nature of the Medon is not understood but some people assume that the Medon is connected to the Khipu-Camayacos

motte See aornis (oddly enough)

Outland Foreign countries, under the sway of the Pharaoh

Patriarch Ultimate leader, see footnote 5

Pharaoh Despotic ruler of the Outland; not a good egg at all

portal A point of access between Muinbeo and the Outland

rogue werewolf A werewolf that does not conform to the usual rules of good behaviour among werewolves

senate Parliament of Muinbeo

sidh Other-world or fairy people, like elves and *luchrupán*s; also sometimes used to mean the places associated with them. Pronounce *shee*, of course (as in banshee, the loudest and best known of the *sidh*)

sombrist Member of a religious community, followers of sombrism. Among the mix of religious beliefs in Muinbeo, only the sombrists keep themselves a little apart from everyone else

Thanatos Official in charge of funerals and obsequies. It is partly a religious, partly a civic role (like the Patriarch)

Whedon Lights These are shimmering, sparkling lights seen at the edges of an erratic portal. They are very pretty but best seen from a (great) distance

Neither flesh nor fowl nor good red herring

Time and place?

Your guess is as good as ours

If you really want to hear a tale from Muinbeo, you have come to the right place. Come in, then, and shake the snow from your shoulders – that's both ends of a bitter north wind outside. Come right in – mind the door, now, it's heavy so don't get your tails or coats or anything caught in it. Leave your coat and boots in the porch. Through the door straight ahead to claim your comforts – a chair, a footstool, a warm fire, the welcome-glass upon the table. Don't mind the dogs. They certainly won't mind you. See? Better than a hot-water bottle. A story, is it?

All of you living in what we call the Outland – even those who refuse to believe that Muinbeo exists – will have heard the tantalising bits of gossip, the headlines of weirdness from beyond the Great Way. It's practically famous – the remnants of ancient worlds, the maps of Atlantis, the smorgasbord of races, tongues and species, the magic, the sheer peculiarity of the place. We like to make sure that the other stories are told, the tales from the shadows, from the edges of things, from underneath what happens in front of your face. Some of these stories really started decades, generations ago and now come to their close. New things begin to rise from the past, like phoenix feathers starting to separate from the flame. But be certain you want to hear. The winding down of the old stories and the starting of the new arose from a death; a murder, if you will believe such wickedness. We warn you. We are the last – eh – people to pretend that Muinbeo is some sort of Island of the Blessed. Bear that in mind.

And don't be misled into thinking we can really tell you the full story. Even all the information that we have to – um – *hand* in Muinbeo will never really tell us the whole truth. Stories flit into existence, between sighs and half-finished sentences, between rumours and muttered complaints; they are trapped by thoughts unspoken. But, sure, you're humans – well, most of you – so you will be accustomed to not knowing the half of what is going on.

Chapter 1: Thursday

First day of the January full moon

Swanhill Library, Croghan Hill, Muinbeo

Every window in the Swanhill Library was glowing like a jewel. Chandeliers and lanterns, gas-lights and torch-flames shining through thick glass littered the ground outside with copper, scarlet or emerald shapes. The broken earth, ploughed by hooves, wheels and feet and then jaggedly frozen, looked like the opening into an other-world. Wedged into iron holders spiked into the ground, big beeswax candles lined the avenue from the foot of Croghan Hill to the vast front door of the library. Braziers had been set up on either side of the door, and in the windless evening flames and sparks from the ruby heart of the coals flew straight up to the stars. The east pavilion door was open to ease the work of fetching and carrying between the great hall and the outside buildings, and down the glittering corridor, into the atrium, with its sparkling chandelier and mahogany tables polished to a deep, red glow, the place was alive with activity.

Busy occupants dashed to and fro and back again, carrying, lifting, seeking, finding, fixing, pursuing, fleeing and, occasionally – for it had been a long day and the ranks of food-trays were tempting – filching. The great hall where the lectures and the awards would take place, the atrium where the food would be eaten, the cavernous entrance hall and the anterooms where the guests could chat were seething with students, teachers, apprentices and librarians. Each one had at least a dozen tasks to perform, many at the same time, and usually in someone else's way.

Outside in the wintry dark, Salmon Farsade had stopped on the west side of the library and was standing still. As twilight drew down, the moon-shadows of the building were thickening, almost as monumental as the hexagonal towers that were the treasure house of Uisneach University's[1] earliest books. The walls of the library, built to withstand weather, time and even attack, were so very thick that from the outside the building seemed silent and only the dark shapes dashing past the windows gave a hint at the industry within. Salmon had another ten tasks to go, and the wheelbarrow in front of her was laden with boxes of crockery for which two fellow-apprentices were waiting, but they could, she thought, wait a moment or two longer. She set down the barrow and crunched over the uneven paths of the library's winter garden to climb up onto the walls and survey the countryside. Salmon was not looking for anything in particular. She just liked to know that things were still as she had left them.

From the height of the wall on the hill, Ballinpooka town was a great cluster of lights and shadows to the south. The

---

[1] A large and ancient university in Muinbeo, established probably before the library at Alexandria but privately owned first by the Lir family and now by the St Maur Kers, even though they mostly live in the Outland. The main body of the university was built on the Hill of Uisneach (pronounced Ishnac) and then the library and some of the smaller colleges were relocated to Old Croghan Hill, which they said was less dangerous than Uisneach. How we laughed! But no harm done. So far.

guardian trees that lit the road from the town to Marvaan, where Salmon's foster-family lived, looked tiny and bead-like. Lanterns lined the canal-banks through the town but petered out a mile or so into the countryside. Several boats, blazing with lights, were moored just outside the town walls. North of the town, lights were barely visible dotted along the banks of the river, and beyond that, the road vanished into the Doathain and the fringe of Derrydrake forest. Many miles north of the forest, near Linnenshee and far into the dark beyond the ancient trees, lived Salmon's remaining family, close to where her great-grandfather had had his home.

Salmon stood up, holding onto a giant beech tree for balance. East and west were blankets of violet twilight, a few scatterings of lights and the unearthly glimmer of the quartz statue of Pan at the edge of Tubbercolm Bog. Everywhere looked distant and restful. If there was strife or anxiety, or fear or conflict, it left no mark on the landscape. Salmon took a deep breath and blew it out in a frosted cloud. She began to slither and scramble from the wall – as always, easier up than down.

Hunter Sessaire, one of those apprentices who had been waiting for Salmon to return, came out from the east pavilion door and around the back of the library just in time to see Salmon scramble back down from the wall. She was short and made all the stockier by the layers of clothes under her thick coat – she was a cold creature, was Salmon – and her short hair was bright platinum blond. She stumped over the frozen ridges of the ground towards where she could see Hunter, his aura an occasional flicker of emerald-green, and grasped the handles of her wheelbarrow. Hunter, tall and thin as a scarecrow, was a year older than Salmon and an apprentice archivist. To lighten her load, he heaved the top box from the barrow and staggered off.

'Have you been vouchsafed any news yet?' he wheezed as they reached the library. 'About your new despotes?'

Salmon, breathless now as she struggled over the broken ground, shook her head.

'Not a bean. They will have to transfer me soon. But no-one even mentions what happened to Dunne, not since – well, since it happened.'

'How did they bend the rules to have you assigned to – Webb, was it?'

Salmon laughed and set the barrow down outside the open door. Catching her breath, she said, 'Webb thought of it – she's the despotes for our administrators. She said that since Dunne never did his paperwork properly, she'd mentor me for a few weeks while I did it instead. She got her paperwork at last and it gave the guardians a bit of time to see if Dunne would recover.'

'But he has not improved, I hear,' Hunter said, resting his elbow on the boxes in the wheelbarrow. 'If you don't have another guardian despotes –'

'I know,' Salmon said anxiously, 'I will be off the Register. I don't know who is available, though. Maybe Barton? Browne? They seem nice.'

'Browne's quite junior, isn't she?' Hunter said doubtfully, putting the box back on the barrow and wiping his brow. 'And Barton – well, the default gear is snail's-pace, so I believe. And the despotes are supposed to be – you know. Persons. Of. Standing.' He struck a mock-heroic pose as though he were about to grow a cloak and take flight.

Salmon laughed at him.

From the doorway, Conger Fore smiled and said, 'Will there be a repeat performance? I could sell tickets.'

'I am like the snows of yesterday,' Hunter said very solemnly. 'One appearance only.'

'We'll shortly be having the snows of today,' Conger said, looking up towards the sky and almost absentmindedly picking up two boxes of crockery. He was an apprentice engineer, short, blond and strong as a pit-pony. Conger didn't speak much; he always seemed to be listening to something. Salmon could see the air around him glisten electric blue.

Between the three of them they quickly unloaded the wheelbarrow and carried the rattling boxes into the bustling anteroom to the atrium.

As they set down the boxes, Salmon said in sudden alarm, 'Ye gods, I hope it is not Benson. I'd rather be an apprentice dancer.'

Hunter laughed without restraint.

'Salmon, my dear, you couldn't dance to a choir of angels,' he said. 'Benson must be pretty bad.'

Conger joined the throng in the anteroom, under the direction of the maths teacher Dr Darwin, while Hunter, wiping his eyes, went to the great hall. Salmon went as instructed to the atrium. At one end, Dr O'Buachalla was rewiring lights. At the other, Nefertiti Inkster, apprentice clockmaker, was perched on a ladder giving instructions to a dozen imps who were testing a vast mechanism, with seven different pieces of clockwork bristling with cogs and toothed wheels, at ceiling height.

'Chop, chop,' she was saying. 'This baby has to move two walls back in less than a minute. If more senators turn up than we expect, there'll be wigs on the green if their lord- and ladyships have to wait for a bigger room.'

'I thought they were supposed to reply to their invitation so we would know how many were turning up,' one of the imps grumbled as it swung on a pendulum back to Nefertiti. 'But that's senators for you. Just do what they please.'

'You forget our celebrity visitor,' Nefertiti said, adjusting a minuscule cog. 'They'll flock to see GB Logan. Move it along, imp.'

'Oh – clearly different,' said the imp sarcastically as the wall swung it safely out of reach. 'I wouldn't touch my cap to Queen Mab but Logan, now, is a different proposition.'

Nefertiti ignored the remark and clambered down the ladder.

'Isn't it exciting?' she asked Salmon, a question clearly expecting the answer *yes*. 'GB Logan coming here. Did you see him when you were in the Outland?'

Salmon was reluctant to disappoint her but had to shake her head. Nefertiti was about Salmon's height, and stout, with short, glossy black hair, a long pointed chin and a turned-up nose. Extremely long-sighted, she wore thick glasses with large metallic blue frames and, though her face was fat, her cheekbones jutted out, sharp enough, Salmon thought, to take the eye out of a spider.[2] Nefertiti's aura was very dark brown, like wet earth.

---

[2] What we have not mentioned is that Nefertiti also has an enormous head. Appearing simply very high-browed from the front, her head extends like a cone or a headdress at the back. Apparently when she was born, the druid could not help remarking on it, and her mother said, 'Honey, dolichocephalism hardly describes it.' We didn't mention it before because we are telling you things mostly from Salmon's point of view and, oddly enough, neither Salmon, the apprentices, nor any of the Goldsmiths noticed Nefertiti's head.

'I had heard of him, of course,' Salmon said, 'but the war made travel so hard, and the Pharaoh's army were able to spy on people when they used television – so we didn't have one.'

'Never mind,' Nefertiti said. 'Now you can, and without being shot at by the Pharaoh.'

Nefertiti consulted the notebook in her hand, her face solemn as a cliff once more as she concentrated on her work. Nefertiti was always in charge of the logistics whenever the apprentices – or the school – had a show of any sort to put on. She was fearsomely organised and had an impeccable sense of timing. She occasionally startled Dr O'Buachalla during class by describing how the losing side of historical battles could have been victors with only very few warriors but better strategy.

'Is it military strategy or lost causes that fascinate you, Nefertiti?' the history teacher had said once. 'I'm not sure whether you are to be admired or sent for counselling.'

Salmon weaved her way through the atrium, dodging the students as they carried tables, counted chairs, balanced glasses and arranged flowers.

The atrium was high and square and was entirely enclosed inside the library, its doors leading directly into the great hall, reception hall, reading room and keeper's office. The ceiling was mainly of glass and the stone walls of the atrium were riddled with odd little tunnels and flues so that such light as might be outside could come creeping in. As Salmon passed, a pale-furred beast, tiny as a fleeting light and with a line of coloured spots up its flank, darted out of one tunnel, looked round, and vanished up another. Only Salmon saw it. As in most of the other rooms in Swanhill Library, the walls were curved where they joined the floor, rather than straight. But that, of course, was not the strangest thing about the library.

'Any peep about who'll replace Guardian Dunne, Salmon?' said O'Buachalla as Salmon reached her. Salmon shook her head.

O'Buachalla was tall and 'built like a milestone', as she said, a phrase she borrowed from her great-grand-uncle's diary. She had large dark brown eyes with lashes as long as those of a camel[3] and tanned skin and she kept her brown hair tied back in a pony-tail, the ribbon for which had inevitably worked itself loose by the end of the day. Under her academic gown O'Buachalla usually wore clothes in various shades of brown, green and grey. She claimed that once she had been standing still on the bog near her home, and two birds, delighted at apparently finding an unoccupied tree, tried to build a nest in the crook of her arm. Hunter, who knew that Salmon could see auras, had been surprised when she told him that O'Buachalla's was violet rather than some shade of tree.

'Would you not speak to McCabe yourself?' O'Buachalla said.

Salmon swallowed and tried not to look as alarmed as she felt. Detective Chief Inspector McCabe was but one step down in the hierarchy from the quaestor. The quaestor was not only the chief of the guardians – Muinbeo's police force – in Ballinpooka, but one of just four quaestors in all

---

[3] Another of her own descriptions. Very little vanity in our Dr O'Buachalla.

of Muinbeo. Salmon had been apprenticed to First Deputy Inspector Bassett Dunne. Now Dunne, her despotes during her apprenticeship, was in a coma in hospital after an unexplained attack and the medics could only shake their heads when asked the prognosis. Salmon could not stay on the register of apprentices without a despotes and, so far, there were no volunteers.

'I'm not sure Inspector McCabe will be here tonight,' she said, more from hope than knowledge.

'He will of course,' O'Buachalla said. 'If you are going to award a prestigious scholarship for history, it makes sense to invite a vampire. Practically eye-witnesses, immortals are.'

'I often wondered,' Nefertiti said, 'why no one just asks the vampires what really happened in the past. Since they will have seen it all.'

'Nef,' O'Buachalla sighed, 'if I teach you nothing else, can I impress upon you that there is no such thing as "what really happened"?'

Salmon, who, as an apprentice guardian, was having it impressed upon her that her job in life was precisely to find out what really happened, said, 'But if there are eye-witnesses, would they not be the obvious – eh – people to ask?'

'But sure Salmon, even if McCabe and Heron Porphyrogenitus and all the rest of them sat down and talked for seven days and seven nights, you still wouldn't know what happened. They wouldn't agree with each other, the rest of the world wouldn't agree with them and none of them would agree with what was written down.'

'Then who puts it together?'

'Why do you think I teach you how to write history? Now,

I can see you don't cherish the idea of talking to McCabe. I'll try and catch him myself.'

'Thank you,' Salmon said, relieved.

'You're welcome. Nefertiti, there is a problem with the slide show for the third lecture in the great hall. And Salmon, could you be a star and help those young lads with moving Professor Peterson's portrait up behind the podium?'

Nefertiti and Salmon followed Dr O'Buachalla into the great hall. Nefertiti disappeared into the midst of a gleaming tangle of cogs, wheels and levers, and Salmon waited while the chief curator and six white-gloved apprentices removed the portrait of Professor Peterson from the wall. It was the professor whose fortune, after she died, had gone to setting up the much-sought Peterson Scholarship that funded research into any aspect of history in Muinbeo. Even in her painted portrait, Silk-Joy Peterson looked abstracted and faintly irritated, as though she had been interrupted in the middle of something she was unwilling to leave. Probably like the historian herself, the painter hadn't bothered much with the detail of hair or clothing and left these as hastily sketched clouds of white and flat planes of dark brown or red with flashes of gold. But he had painted in meticulous detail the papers that covered the desk and the books on the shelves in the background.

Reversing across the hall, calling instructions to the apprentices as they shuffled across the polished stone floor, Salmon recalled that when she had lived in the Outland, even she had heard of Professor Peterson. Peterson had worked for many years in the Outland and had been an outspoken and fearless critic of the Pharaonic Empire for the entirety of her academic career.[4] She had fought fang and claw against the attempts of the Pharaoh's exquisitely educated enforcers to turn countries into nations of philistines. Dead, she did the same, through the trustees of her considerable estate, despite the best efforts of several governments to stop it. Salmon wondered what the professor would have made of GB Logan.

Senate Chambers on Wolftrap Street, Ballinpooka

In the middle of Ballinpooka, between the old town walls and the Split Yew Tree, a by-gone Patriarch[5] had ordered that the Senate Chambers be built. The senate is the group of women and men and what-have-you that runs Muinbeo – politicians, administrators, the Registry of Records, the craft guilds, the hospitals and the lawyers – and the Chambers was their home. The Chambers evolved over the centuries and its

---

[4] A career that lasted for so long that even in Muinbeo, where people start being middle aged after about a century, it was widely believed that Silk Peterson must have slow-worm DNA.

[5] The person or entity with the last word of authority in Muinbeo. The Patriarch can be male or female and is elected by an operatically complicated procedure. Their job is to analyse and understand Muinbeo life in its totality so that when the going gets really tough and no one else wants to be in charge, the Patriarch (and some others, it's complicated) can make all final decisions. Deeply philosophical, rigorously intellectual and fiercely well-educated (especially in languages and farming), the Patriarch tends to speak in aphorisms and almost-riddles, and everything that they say is of monumental importance. Worlds have perished on less than the word of a Patriarch. This is why they spend most of their lives in silence.

current appearance is a sparkling melody of steel, glass and oak, six storeys high. At the summit is the Medon, coiled and gleaming, slowly spinning in a lambent halo. Now, in the dark of a mid-winter evening, the bright office lamps in the Chambers' windows seemed to have joined the stars of the Great Banb constellation hanging directly overhead.

But familiarity breeds, if not contempt, then at least an acceptance of the extraordinary. When Persephone-Fen Maguire tidied her desk on what turned out to be the last night of her life, she was not thinking of the antique mysteries of the building, the natural beauties of Muinbeo, the astrophysical wonders of the surrounding universe or the chanciness of her own existence. Rather, she was thinking about how much she wished she was going home. She wanted to have a cup of tea and sit down and think about that which she had been pushing to the back of her mind all day: the news, the life-changing news of yesterday. So far she had told only one person, the one who needed to know. Tonight she would plan the future. But first, true to her character, she would sort out the responsibilities of the day – she had to go to Cluancorr first, and once home she needed to clean the gutters and fix the bathroom tap. The huffy rattle of the machines and the irritated way they were ripping the paper from their carriages made Fen sigh. It would take days to woo the machines back to good humour.

She caught the eye of the only other person in the office, also looking sadly at the typewriters, and smiled. Her apprentice smiled back rather shyly and returned to her glimmering electrical pen and her sheaf of papers.

The door opened and the two cleaners came in – a natty green imp in a black suit with cloths hung like bunting over its arms[6] and a taller *luchrupán*[7] in crisp brown dungarees, with a broom and a feather duster.

'We'll be gone soon,' said Fen to the imp, which rolled its eyes in a burlesque of outrage. It jerked its head at the closed door and dark office of the cause of all the trouble, Senator Scarlet Woudes.

Most senators were easy to manage. Each one had an amanuensis, like Fen, who made sure that the office ran smoothly and – and this was the important bit – that the senator had all the right files, with the right contents, on their desk at the right time. It was the job of the amanuensis to know what 'right' meant. Most senators accepted the appearance of exactly the information that they needed when they needed it and they never interfered with the office in any way. In the office, they were expected only to do what was politely called 'high-level authorisation'. This was a fig-leaf for following the advice of the amanuensis when it came to agreeing to order new pipes for the letter-rockets in the senate's pneumatic postal system, approving orders for books or cakes for staff meetings, or signing the plans for the staff Shortest Day party. Senator Woudes, on the other hand, liked to draw attention to herself by deciding she needed her own copies of letters or memos so that she could work at home, thereby implying that she worked harder than anyone else. Often this meant that – as tonight – large orders were placed for copies, at short notice. This invariably annoyed the typewriters, which were, admittedly, a

---

[6]   Which numbered six.

[7]   Pronounced lu-krup-awn. Easy-peasy.

bit touchy and did not like inefficiency. They could sulk for days, working only if constantly supervised, sighing and whispering or claiming to be sick. Senator Woudes had more brass in her neck than the average human[8] and that her amanuensis and the apprentice were working late on an evening that Woudes was spending in a pub in Rathera did not cause her a moment's thought. The imp and the *luchrupán* got to work.

Fen spent a few minutes tidying her desk and making some notes for the next day's work. She reread these, marked the important ones with a blue dot and then closed her notebook. Rubbing her eyes, she went slowly to the window, staring out at the town lights and the stars on the canal as she took her coat off its hook. It had been a long day full of dramas and she had achieved little except soothing egos, patching up differences and untangling knots made by other people. To make matters worse she had lost a favourite scarf while shopping at lunchtime, she had dropped and smashed her watch, and later had knocked over her coffee reaching for the phone. The bright spot in the day had been when her friend Shearwater Amberson went to Hudson's Bakery and brought back not only another coffee but the last available slice of rich, treacly porter-cake.

---

[8] We mean this figuratively. Senator Woudes was not embarrassed about causing needless work or placing needless pressure on her staff. She did not actually have brass in her neck – it is always worth being clear about these things in Muinbeo, as you never know. Not that we object to metal necks. Dr Frankenstein's monster apparently was very good with animals when he lived here.

'Now, if porter-cake can't make everything better,' he had said, 'you may call it a day. But what a day!'

Fen turned down the flame on her desk-lamp. The neon glows from the apprentice's pen grew brighter and as she passed the desk, Fen said, 'Don't stay too late, Velvet. You are not Senator Woudes's secretary.'

Velvet Corbuse's head snapped up, and she looked anxiously at her despotes. With large round black eyes and a pronouncedly beaky nose, Velvet's overall similarity to a fledgling meant she always looked worried and much younger than her actual years. Fen felt protective of Velvet and wondered why she was so self-effacing and eager to please. Fen also wondered whether Velvet would be shocked or relieved when she was finally old enough not to care what other people thought about her. There were disadvantages to how slowly people aged in Muinbeo.

'Senator Woudes has more overdue files out from the Registry of Records than anyone else in the entire senate,' Velvet said. 'And she told Registry that everything would be back by the end of the week. But she didn't tell me until yesterday. And you know how long it can take. And I was supposed to be at the library helping Dr O'Buachalla get things ready for the scholarship awards. And Senator Woudes has hundreds and hundreds of files. And if it's not done by tomorrow, then Dr Boru will probably come around herself,' Velvet blurted out. 'And the senator will expect me to explain. And ...'

She trailed off, and Fen guessed that the unspoken sentence was, *And Dr Boru is too scary for me to be able to tell the truth.*

Velvet was looking down in something like despair at the disorganised papers strewn over the desk in front of her and at her own attempts to create and copy the proper list. Fen glanced towards the clock, which she could just see between the slender pillars that divided the office.

'Let me help you,' she said, turning back to her tidying. 'I have a bit of time.'

'Were you not leaving early today?'

'Chance would be a fine thing,' Fen said with a faint snort. 'I was supposed to … I had some things to collect from the canal-boat in Cluancorr. Until Woudes insisted I attend her *unofficial meeting* so I had to ask Hoprasinos to meet the boat for me. Not to worry,' she added, seeing Velvet's anxious face. 'No one's dead.'

As Fen approached the desk, the wick of the oil lamp flared a little and Fen turned. The sudden brightness glinted on the burnished colours in Velvet's hair, faint shimmers of blue and red and silver among the black. Struck by what, even after two years, she had not noticed before, Fen stopped and stared at Velvet's pale skin, the dim, dark markings under her eyes and along each side of her nose, her completely round eyes. Fen suddenly realised she knew exactly why Velvet was self-effacing and eager to please, and, looking up abruptly and finding her despotes staring at her, Velvet knew that Fen knew.

Back at Swanhill Library, Croghan Hill

The reception at which the Muinbeo Scholarships Committee announced the names of the few scholars to whom they would consider awarding the Peterson Scholarship was in full swing. There were more guests packed into the library than ever before, because such was the scholarship's worth now that included among the judges was a man who could fairly claim to be the most famous historian not only in Muinbeo but in the Outland – Geoffrey Ballantyne Logan. He was a constant presence in the Outland media – to whom he never mentioned that he had been born in Muinbeo – and wealthy enough and popular enough to disregard his critics or those who mocked his affected way of speaking. Logan was a heavy-jawed barrel of a man, but curiously restless even in repose, always turning, watching, pacing, smoothing his clothes. He was groomed until he gleamed and went to great expense over his wardrobe. Fame and importance acted as a sort of glamour, so that his expanding audience did not notice that the overall effect was of a mountain-dog dressed up as a Pekingese.

This was the last chance for the applicants to impress the committee and Logan. Each of the six candidates had fifteen minutes in which to summarise their entire body of research, and the rest of the night to sweat about it and eat too many canapés. The second candidate was at the podium, nervously checking his notes, while behind him imps pushed cogs and pulled down levers to bring a mechanical reproduction of the solar system into view. The audience whispered and settled themselves in their chairs or took another glass of mead. A few heads turned as a gust of icy wind announced a late arrival. Second Deputy Inspector Benson, followed by an orderly from Ballinpooka Hospital, slipped past the liveried attendants and made a bee-line for Detective Chief Inspector McCabe.

Cluancorr, about seven miles west of Ballinpooka, near Io's Canal (also called Cow Canal)

At such an hour, in so young a year, the air was virtually scoured clean of scent. A big wolfhound trotted along the grass verge of the canal towards Cassidy's Bridge. He stopped now and then to bury his snout in the base of the ditch or to leave his mark on a tree or wall. The verge opened out onto the bank of the canal, and the hound's paws crushed the frosty grass. Scents withered in such a bitter season, were worn to pieces by frostwork, and miles of blackness became hollow as a bird's jawbone. The dog snuffled at the reeds by the canal-bank. He overturned bits of litter and caught the stink of fish at the stall stop, where the boats stopped to deliver everything from apples to zithers for sale to the local population. He could smell dogs and calves at the Abelards' cottage, foxes and shrews in the hedgerows. His paws skidded where the ground changed to cobbles as it rose to the archway of the small bridge-tower. He emerged into the moonlight.

The air here was dense, almost like glass. Scents – a thin ochre from the warm flank of sleeping cattle, the fruity-red dust where a bone fell from a talon, the sulphurous honey from a bottle drained of whiskey – were patchy. Even the canal, crusted with winter, could offer only some fleeting threads of scent instead of the dazzle of summer. Cullen caught the scent of the silver-traced yew trees and turned his head. The sudden bellow of unfamiliar blood made him sneeze.

Spilled blood, heat vanishing as finally as the life that recently dribbled into the ground, was a stimulant and a warning. Cullen stood very still, watching, till he could make out a figure huddled on the ground. Cullen trotted across the bridge. Once over the treacherous cobbles, he ran into Cluancorr, clearing the gate easily and paying scant regard to the canes and cloches he disturbed as he ran over the allotments to what he now saw was a dead body.

He had not known Fen Maguire well during her life, so every breath he took at her warm corpse was a new word. She had been killed in the small crescent of yew trees that straggled from the edge of Chlovis Grove to the allotments, but had dragged herself a few yards along the ice-ribbed path, her hand stretched out towards Cassidy's Bridge. Cullen nosed about a bit, snorting out the pungent, spicy smell of recent blood, the unfamiliar smell of death. His amber-green eyes flicked over the body as he moved around it. Hard silver light caught in her dark hair, the moon shadows giving her pointed face a romance it lacked in life. Cullen wedged his nose against the clenched hand under the bent arm, against the blood-soaked earth where her life had finally trickled away. He sniffed the length of the overcoat. He rooted briefly in her pocket, finding only some crumpled paper, some coins and a silver pendant. He moved to the splayed, fleece-lined boots. Then he padded slowly round the body, sniffing the ground. The ghost of wind, which only he could feel, stirred, and he raised his head. He had learned the odour of her dead body and turned to inhale the story of her death. Somewhere he caught the wispy scent of the weapon, and he snorted gently and sniffed again, puzzled. The ice on the churned mud burned his nose as he hunted for a sustained smell-patch of the human that had killed her. This scent was exciting; it mixed a bitter fear with rage and an unquestioning power that Cullen recognised. He trotted a few steps, came back but instead before he could pursue the gamey smell of murder, a noise startled him. He hesitated for a moment. Another scent – a strong one, overlaid with a foul chemical, sharpened with sweat; then another, tangy with wine. Cullen fled.

Later, when he sat in his kitchen, breathless and confused in the moonlight, Cedar Cullen wondered what he should do. Now back in human form, he knew both that he should go to the guardians to tell them what he had found and that then he would have to leave Muinbeo. He felt guilty at leaving Fen lying there like a dropped fork for someone else to find. But he could not explain that his real reason for being in Cluancorr was to check out his territory. If he pretended that he had been there as a human, he would instantly become a suspect. To lie went against his character, and to lie and tell some truth at the same time was beyond his abilities as a diplomat. To admit that he was a dimorph would deprive him of his friends – he would be cast out by the community without which he would be nothing.

Back at Swanhill Library, Croghan Hill

The library had inadvertently been built on a loose thread of time, which glimmered, with infinitesimal slowness, through the building, providing the usually sea-sick visitor with a slide show of the library's past. Vanished times build and rebuild themselves like choreographed blocks. Candles, crinolines and codices appear, almost as real as the self-regulating oil lamps, sleek woollen chitons and the shining steel and quartz of the book-looms.

As Detective Chief Inspector McCabe hurried out of the crowded hall after the deputy, Salmon watched them go and berated herself for not having spoken up sooner. 'Never wait for a perfect time,' her uncle used to say, usually while sympathetically ruffling his niece's bright hair, 'because you won't recognise it till it has gone.'[9]

Her head was beginning to hurt from the combined auras of nearly two hundred people, and she inched her way out of the clapping crowd towards a window. Dr O'Buachalla had come whisking by earlier, apologising that she wouldn't be able to talk to McCabe after all as there was an unplanned meeting of the school commissioners and she had to attend.

'Do try and talk to McCabe yourself,' she had said, unexpectedly patting Salmon's shoulder. 'He's a decent old skin really. Look – if it's not you, it'll be the Witch Sackville.'

The idea of anyone from the Smoke Coven making the decisive move to settle Salmon's future filled her with determination and she had worked up her courage to approach McCabe. But she had missed her chance.

She folded up her thick woollen coat to act as a cushion between her and the cold whitewashed stone of the window-seat. Dr Chrysostom, mopping his face with the sleeve of his academic gown, had gratefully left the podium and his place had been taken by Dr Hughes, who researched early manuscripts of Muinbeo. Perched in the high window-seat, Salmon could see the senior witch of the Research Coven preening a little, with Hunter by her side.

---

[9] Another of the sayings that Salmon frequently quoted was her Aunt Bea's 'Everything is wrong unless it is the right time.' So you can take your pick, really.

Like Salmon, Hunter had changed his clothes and now wore the formal version of the apprentice uniform. These kilts were dark and ornately pinned, worn with double-breasted coats and pale leather spats. The only difference an apprentice could make in his or her uniform were the stripes on their charcoal-grey waistcoats. Hunter had chosen smoky shades of ruby and emerald and Salmon, who had as much sense of colour as a fish, played safe with ochre and cream.

Knowing that there were Outlanders in the audience, Dr Hughes made it a bit easier for them by explaining in summary what was known of Muinbeo's history.

'The Ancient Greeks were nervous of the apparent chaos of the sea,' he began, 'and huddled their cities and their lives around the coasts like, as Plato said, frogs around a pond.'

Salmon listened intently. She never quite knew whether she was an Outlander or a Muinbeon, so never felt certain if she was listening to what she already knew or to a new world. She had lived in Muinbeo, where her mother had been born, for only the last three years, and all the earlier part of her life she had spent in the Outland, where her father – who was half-Muinbeon – had been born. Her parents, like many people's parents, had been involved in the resistance against the terrible rule of the Pharaoh in the Outland, and they, like many people's parents, had been killed. Too young to live on her own, but too old to be considered a child, Salmon was sent[10] to safety in Muinbeo and

---

[10] When we say 'sent', we mean she was bundled, at great haste, under cover and in great danger, from the Outland into Muinbeo. No, we can't give you the details. Please. We have only just met you.

became apprenticed to the guardians. The ties of kinship and family in Muinbeo are very wide, and so rather than living with her closest relatives in Linnenshee, Salmon had been fostered by the Goldsmith family in Ballinpooka.

'None the less,' Dr Hughes was saying, 'many millennia before the fall of the walls of Jericho, a band of sailors set out and braved the threat of tsunami, shipwreck and sea-monsters to cross the seas to Ireland. They sailed from Athens, evidence suggests that they stopped along the north African coast, and they arrived on the east coast of Ireland, long before the Ford of the Hurdles was built. No record survives of whether it was curiosity or desperation that drove them, nor does any record survive sent from our wintry island back to Greece, though there are a couple of astonished letters from Strabo[11] in existence, having been accidentally stitched into a folio of The Book of the Rune. The explorers made their way past the ancient Hill of Tara before Fionn Mac Cumhaill had even been thought of, and settled in the river-lined, tree-ringed plain of Muinbeo, whence they never left.'

Salmon saw her foster-brother making his way from the refreshments table towards her, carrying a glass of lemonade in each hand. Rainbow was a few years younger than Salmon, whom he sincerely hoped he would soon outgrow, as being as tall as her did not make him very tall at all. Even though they were not related, there was a certain square-faced similarity

---

[11] Born in what is now Turkey, during the time of the ancient Roman Republic; he wrote seventeen volumes of geography and died when he was only in his eighties – cause and effect? We think so.

between them, despite Bow's generally shaggy appearance and his large brown eyes, which were very unlike Salmon's. But then, no one had eyes like Salmon's.

'I much prefer the bit about Odo of Alençon,' Bow whispered, slipping onto the window-seat beside Salmon, 'finding out that the local tanner spoke perfect French.' [12]

'All those years in his tower,' she whispered back, 'thinking he'd be murdered if he turned his back. Thanks, Bow.'

She took the glass from Rainbow's hand, and they listened to the rest of the story, losing interest only when the academic began to talk about his research into the Book of the Orchard and the fabled Dagda's Garden.

Bow said, 'Come on, Da said we'd leave as soon as we'd finished our drinks.'

Salmon was surprised that they had to leave so early, especially since Archer and Berry Goldsmith had been late in arriving. But as O'Buachalla was nowhere to be seen, Salmon

---

[12] Odo was a Norman, who was among those who arrived in Ireland to help the ousted King of Leinster; in the heat of the moment, neither himself nor several of his fellow invaders noticed that they were no longer in Ireland but had crossed the boundary of the Great Way. Eventually, most of them got bored because no one would start a fight and they all went off to get killed somewhere else. Odo settled where the Vikings previously had settled, on Chlovis Aornis, where he could keep an eye on everything. What he saw convinced him that his neighbours were all mad as a box of hair and his life was not worth a moment's purchase. How he found out about Muinbeo and how he married Esker Fairblood's daughter Arkadia is a long and, we think, quite funny story. But we'll tell you some other … time.

had no option but to slip off the window seat and begin to inch her way back out of the crowd after Rainbow. She stopped to say to Nefertiti that she was leaving, but Nef, along with most of the rest of the apprentices, was staring in such smiling rapture at GB Logan that no sense could be got from her, so Salmon hurried to the door and outside into the bitter night.

Archer drove the carriage to Salmon's house first, turning west at the boundary wall of the Hooke Estate and north again towards the secluded Rupert's Corner. From her front garden at night, Salmon could see the lights of McCabe's house about a mile across the fields to the west and those of her foster-family's house to the east, but her nearest neighbours were the Kingsleys, whose farmhouse was two fields further north and opposite the duck-pond, and Miss Aquinas, a music teacher in Killydanaan, a field away near the hermes.[13] Reluctantly Salmon pushed back the warm rug to clamber out of the carriage into the icy night air. She could see Bow's broad, good-humoured face in the darkness, grimacing as he looked out at the farm-cottage where Salmon lived. He was jealous, she knew, that she was allowed to live in her own house while he, so it seemed, was constantly either with his parents and his sister or in school.

'Good night, Bow,' she said, pulling her hat down over her burning-cold ears. 'See you tomorrow.'

---

[13] A small statue used to give directions and calculate distances, found at many crossroads in Muinbeo. It looks like a cross between a four-armed Cupid and a slide-rule. Hermes were also found in the ancient Outland, where they looked a little different.

'Good night, Salmon,' he said with reasonably good grace. 'Sleep well.'

Salmon had loved Knotty Down House from the moment she had seen it. Given to her by her great-grandfather when she had been brought, abruptly orphaned, to Muinbeo ('It would have been her mother's' was the reason he had given to the family), the house was close to Marvaan, making it easy for the Goldsmiths to be her foster-family.

Knotty Down was a small square whitewashed house with a garden of wild flowers and shrubs at the front, overgrown herbs and fruit-bushes at the back, and a small orchard. As soon as Salmon had walked into the small pale room at the front of the house, empty apart from a fireplace and some bookshelves built into the wall, she felt more at home than she had in any place she had lived in with her parents. She had followed Maccarrill, who was chirruping happily, into the kitchen and through the scullery and pantry. Even though she had arrived on a dark winter afternoon, even though there was hardly a smudge of daylight to alleviate the purple grey of the world, even though the house was empty and dusty, the garden overgrown, tangled and smothered in snow, Salmon loved it. She had wandered from room to room, touching the walls, staring from each window, certain that she was at last safe and had found sanctuary.

Maccarrill kept her company now in the kitchen while she pulled open the valves and spun the dials on the Spider, as Maccarrill had nicknamed the small long-legged copper oven that could reheat from frozen in ten minutes. Steam jetted out as soon as Salmon shut the lid on the iron pot of beef stew she had made the day before. Small sparks were spat out and thin rings of red, green and violet light shimmered around it as it heated. Salmon ate her meal while Maccarrill walked about on the table or perched on the chairs and asked questions.

'All the teachers were there,' she said in response to one, 'except Dr Grattan of course. Most of the apprentices. Velvet Corbuse was expected, but she didn't show up.'

'Was young Hunter there?' Maccarrill asked and gave a satisfied grunt when Salmon nodded. Maccarrill, an acid-tongued critic of the human race, especially its younger members, had taken a liking to Hunter. Salmon knew this by the approving grunts when Hunter came to visit. Maccarrill had suggested more than once that Salmon might adopt Hunter's more thoughtful approach to the world.

When Salmon had washed up, they went into the sitting room, Maccarrill enlivening the fire with some peat, and Salmon examining her bookshelf, reading out options to Maccarrill until he finally made a selection.[14] Salmon curled up in her big armchair, and Maccarrill perched on the chair opposite her while she read the story aloud. After almost as short a time as he had expected, the warmth and the effort of the ceremony won out, and Salmon fell asleep, her head on her shoulder and the book in her lap.

Later that evening

When the moon rose, it was a perigee moon, so close to the earth that it seemed within reach. The night nurses in St Brigit's critical ward in Ballinpooka Hospital were

---

[14] *The Iron Lily*. Maccarrill was fond of historical novels.

clustered, conferring anxiously with each other, at the foot of an empty bed. The warm silver light from the moon lit almost the whole room, and down the corridors and in the wards, all the patients were awake and those who could go to the windows stared up at the huge pale face of the satellite. On the pillow of the bed in which the nurses had placed the hospital's most recent critically ill patient was heaped a tangle of the shimmering cobwebs and seed-pearls with which nutrients had been supplied to the comatose man. The bands of magnetic quartz sensors, attuned to the slightest change in condition or development of disease, had been neatly unscrewed from across the bed. The brass bars, designed to keep a somnambulist from getting out of the ward and into danger, had been bowed down with immeasurable force, so that the door to which they were still partially attached looked like some vast metal flower blooming in the darkness. Despite restraints and monitors and alarms, First Deputy Bassett Dunne had responded to the full moon and, leaving only some long dark wolf hairs behind him on his pillow, he had quit his hospital bed and escaped.

Out on the Gallagrene Bog, under the cloudless indigo sky, trees moved uneasily. Animals tiptoed out from their shelters, sniffed the night air and licked their snouts, worried and confused. There was a taste on the air that should not be there. Near Ciplacti's Ear, plaintive droning was just audible, like a muffled swarm of distressed bees. Watchful fish circled under the ice of the lake and among the hazel trees a bittern boomed. The distant Tubbercolm Pan, the rose quartz statue that marked some long-forgotten boundary, resonated, and small pale sparks of electricity flickered and vanished.

When Salmon awoke to the loud knocking on her front door it took her some minutes to realise where she was, which was still on the settee, and what was happening, which was that she was hopelessly tangled in the blanket with which Maccarrill had covered her. Confused, she hurried to the kitchen, peering out into the back yard, until Maccarrill finally came after her and said, rather waspishly, 'This highly evolved brain you humans are said to have? Do you want to try putting it into gear and answering the front door? Or shall we just stand here gawking into the dark for no purpose instead?'

Salmon couldn't think of a suitable reply – and in any case, Maccarrill always had the last word – so she stumbled back and opened the front door.

After a few moments, during which Salmon merely gawked, Maccarrill said very politely, 'What an unexpected pleasure, Quaestor Finney. Please come in.'

The quaestor showed no surprise at being addressed by a large African grey parrot but pulled his cloak closer around himself and stepped into the hallway. His sky-blue aura shimmered intermittently in the shadows. Salmon pulled herself together, smoothing her hair, wiping the drool off her cheek, trying to think what in the world she could have done that meant a quaestor was calling to the house of an apprentice. Quaestor Perlucidas Finney was tall and thin, with large dark eyes, mahogany-coloured skin and great personal charm. He wore a pleated cloak of plum-coloured brocade, as was the custom for a quaestor, and under it he was dressed in a narrow, dark suit with a velvet collar, and a paler waistcoat beneath. A silver chain was attached to one pocket and from this hung a watch and a remarkable number of gadgets that allowed him to do everything from taking stones from hooves to predicting the weather. Remembering her manners enough to show him to a seat and stoke the turf fire, Salmon made some tea. She arranged the teapot, milk and crockery rather haphazardly on a tray, while Maccarrill made elegant small talk with their visitor. Salmon managed not to spill the tea or drop the tray and even unearthed some biscuits to take the bare look off it. Finney carried over a small table to the hearth, and Salmon felt a rush of relief as she sat down, despite the way Maccarrill, who was accustomed to more sophisticated society, was ruffling his feathers and flicking his crest up and down.

'You have a very charming house,' Finney said, taking his cup and saucer. 'I believe it has been in your family for many generations?'

Like all quaestors, Finney was also a diplomat and so, Salmon suspected, genetically incapable of getting to the point until extensive civilities and polite small-talk had been completed. Salmon fidgeted and nodded while Finney drank his tea and talked about the history of Marvaan. She was wiping a sweat of anxiety from her brow by the time Finney dabbed his lips (on his handkerchief; Salmon's housekeeping did not run to napkins) and turned to face her.

'Now – I have to admit that this is not a social visit. There is something I must tell you about your despotes, Dunne. There have been unexpected developments. Once the full moon rose – well, we know now what, even if not who, attacked him.'

Finney paused, clearly expecting Salmon to put two and two together. But Salmon, clever as a bag of cats, was polite and literal-minded. Finney had said there was something he should tell her and she would wait, till the crack of doom if necessary, for him to do so.

'Perhaps,' Finney said reflectively, 'I should put it another way.'

Salmon smiled encouragingly, wishing he would spit it out. Finney picked a minuscule crumb from his cloak.

'We have assigned you to another despotes,' he said.

Salmon's heart soared and then dropped anxiously.

'Is Dunne not going to recover?'

'Dunne is – not exactly sick. But he will need a lot of time to adjust.'

'Adjust?'

'To what he has become. To how his life has been changed by the light of the moon. Why don't I tell you everything on the way?'

Chapter 2: Friday

Second day of the full moon

Not in Cluancorr, as you might expect, but rather in the Wooden O Artists Community, over the (haunted) Bast Bridge

When Detective Chief Inspector McCabe stopped, as Finney took tea with Salmon, to look at what he already knew was a corpse, he did not do so from Cassidy's hump-backed bridge over Cow Canal – as Io's Canal was tactlessly called – but from the path at the foot of the hill that led up to Chlovis Motte.[15] He stopped his horse and his hound at a small gap in the knotty ash trees that lined the path, where he could see the crime scene before he reached it. Chlovis Woods was dense on the horizon from there. The sinking moon sparkled on icy trees and the crooked block of the motte with its ruins was silhouetted against the twilight sky. The log cabins of the Wooden O settlement were like beacons among the black trees and the shadows. Windows lit up and the glow spilled out of doors as the artists who lived there got up, came out to help and enquire and, McCabe thought grumpily, trample all over the evidence.

The River Bast cut the settlement in two and the theatre itself was built over it. The south-side cabins were bounded

---

[15] Sometimes called the motte, sometimes the aornis, the place where no birds fly. Both are accurate, both probably best left alone.

by Chlovis Woods and the aornis and, on the north side, by the less decorative Ballinpooka Road. The Wooden O theatre was a sooty, squat shadow, untouched by the flickering street lamps. Near the orchard at the edge of Chlovis Woods there was a shifting glow as civilians and guardians moved round. A horse snorted and pulled away, and McCabe's horse snorted in reply. In the distance, McCabe could see the ambulance rise from the horizon, pulsing lights and gleaming pipes hurtling through the sky.

Fallinish barked once. He was accustomed to McCabe's unpredictable working hours and to the nature of the work requiring a lot of hanging about. Fallinish had been a patient and temperate boxer dog in life, and his personality had survived his reconstruction in the various metals, precious stones and pieces of quartz in his clockwork. But he did like to be told what was going on.

'I am getting the lie of the land, Fallinish,' McCabe said. 'Because a lie there surely is.'

He clucked at the horse and they trotted up the riverbank onto a small gravel path that led into the Wooden O settlement. McCabe dismounted and handed over the reins to a police stable-girl. He could hear someone sobbing. The sound came from the porch of the communal kitchen that stood between the artists' cabins and the landlady's house.

McCabe looked round to see who was already there. Second Deputy Benson was keeping civilians away while sending off iris after iris. These messenger birds looked like tiny smudges of rainbow and disappeared so fast that not even a vampire's sharp eyes could read them. It was one of these message-bearers that had caused the ambulance to roar into sight through the cinder-dark sky, another had woken McCabe himself, and apparently – McCabe and Benson both turned in astonishment – another had gone to the Quaestor Finney. Benson automatically walked towards the quaestor. McCabe, who knew Finney on much more friendly terms, waved and turned to the person who had found the body, knowing Finney would join him.

The light in the kitchen was on and, as McCabe approached, he saw a figure emerge with a steaming bowl and sit beside the hunched woman, who was now whooping rather than sobbing. McCabe recognised her as Carbon Smith. She was part of the Outland Watch Committee which also had many guardians in it.

'A guest of the *Beansidh*,[16] that is a sight to destroy your rest,' he said, patting Carbon's arm. 'I hope you are not too distressed.'

'I'm OK, thank you, guardian,' Carbon said, controlling her whoops, though under his hand he could feel her shaking. The woman who had given Carbon the bowl of tea stood up and McCabe saw that it was the landlady of the Wooden O, Imhotep Harper.

'Perhaps I had better show you where it is,' she said. 'Carbon's too upset.'

McCabe patted Carbon's shoulder once more and got up. Benson strode up and grabbed McCabe's arm.

---

[16] 'A guest of the *Beansidh*' is a kindly way of saying 'a slaughtered corpse'. Vampires are quite genteel, and don't like to draw attention to gore. Oh, yes, and *Beansidh* is of course the same as banshee, only different.

'This is bizarre,' Benson said angrily. 'This is just completely bizarre. I've never heard anything like it in my life. Why did Dunne have to go and get bitten by a werewolf? This is going to ruin everything.'

Even for Benson those were strong words. His face was red with annoyance and his bushy eyebrows, always resembling the wing feathers of a landing eagle, were almost vertical.

McCabe led the way towards Finney, and he now noticed that behind him stood an adolescent girl he recalled as being the apprentice of First Deputy Bassett Dunne. Finney got to the point.

'McCabe, this is Salmon Farsade, Bassett's apprentice. As Bassett is – *indisposed*, she will now be your apprentice.'

His voice invited no contradiction or debate, so McCabe closed his mouth. He took a closer look. The apprentice, her blond hair almost glowing under her hat in the last of the moonlight, moved forward a little. Salmon smiled. When McCabe didn't smile back – because he was thinking – and Benson positively glowered – because he was very annoyed – she removed the smile and looked solemn instead. McCabe was examining her. With one part of his brain he was totting her up, like a bill, reading what signs he could see.

Disposition: Hmmm. Wants to be liked, but will grow out of that. Determined to be competent. Has a pet. Is not gawking at Fallinish, so not easily shocked.

Intelligence: School of Hard Knocks rather than Groves of Academe. Would rather apologise later than wait for permission now.

Heritage: At least one parent from Muinbeo. Will probably have a strange sense of humour.

Age: Adolescent. Very young, even for an apprentice. A Capricorn – no,

I lie, Gemini. Libra. Well, now. Perhaps it's a little early in the morning.
Something more simple.

Species: Human. Well, mostly. Oh – hang on just a second …

'What did you say her name was?'

There was a very slight pause and Finney caught McCabe's eye.

'Her name is Salmon-Grove Farsade.'

'Farsade,' repeated McCabe and took a closer look.

Well, now. That explains it. I remember this – the coven will not be happy. Well, now. I wish Benson would stop huffing like a train.

Belatedly, he noticed that the apprentice looked anxious. Benson, appalled at the proposal of expecting his chief – the *chief!* – to look after an apprentice, started an apparently endless stream of administrative and ethical objections. Now the apprentice appeared distinctly despondent. Finney was expertly parrying each of Benson's objections, directing him to obscure rules and regulations of the senate that gave Finney the authority to move apprentices around if necessary. Of course McCabe was very senior and very busy and, for that reason, Finney would occasionally lend him Berberis Johnston, his own factotum,[17] during the investigation of this

---

[17] The quaestors are all given a factotum, which is like an amanuensis, but the factotum's job is more vague and random. A factotum can be asked to do anything from making the tea and sharpening the pencils to designing buildings, writing political speeches or engaging in scientific research. It depends on what the quaestor needs and – very importantly – what the factotum is able to do. It is not easy to know why some people are factotums – quite often not even the quaestor knows. But a quaestor has to take whoever they get.

shocking murder. Benson – here Finney's voice became very slightly less agreeable – was simply going to have to accept the inevitable.

Salmon looked up at McCabe, who seemed to be eyeballing her from a great height. His tall black hat disappeared, so it seemed, into the night sky, its outlines hinted at only by the gleams of artificial light on the various cogs, gears, wheels and buttons through which the hat functioned. His form was swathed in the thick wool of his cloak, from the folds of which one hand emerged to greet Salmon. His skin was brindled, she thought, astonished. It looked whiter than pearls but up close it was flecked like a moth, with barely visible light grey and brown. Everything in the world appeared to Salmon with a narrow border of refracting light, as though encased in a clear gem whose angles gleamed colour as they shifted restlessly; since infancy she had called this 'aura'. McCabe, though, seemed to actually scatter lights, tiny atoms fluttering about him like dust, minuscule sparks of sapphire-blue, of bright green and scarlet. But his hand, when she shook it, was firm and strong, and his smile, when it finally came, seemed genuine and entirely without fang. She was closer to him now and familiar with his appearance, so his aura began to solidify and the colour – a metallic red – emerged. Now that he had registered her details in his mind, McCabe noticed Salmon's appearance.

Why do we make the apprentices wear those kilts? The poor babes must be famished with the cold on nights like this.

'It's OK, thank you, sir.' Salmon smiled politely. 'The coat is very cosy and there's lots of room under the kilt for extra layers.'

McCabe and Finney stared at her. Benson's bright green eyes popped unexpectedly into view from between his baggy lids, as his eyebrows shot up towards his hair. Salmon went pink. McCabe inclined his head to look more closely at her. Salmon knew that vampires' eyes were the reverse of human eyes, but somehow having the dark sclera[18] and the pale iris, with the diamond-bright spark deep in the pupil, concentrating so narrowly on her made her nervous. If his skin had an appearance of fractured shades of earth, his eyes overall were a smoky, steely shade of green. Or maybe they were blue. It was hard to say really. She swallowed. They seemed such a very long way away.

'I thought you knew I could see auras, quaestor,' she said to Finney.

'I did,' said Finney, recovering himself and looking at McCabe. 'I do.'

'I knew you could see auras,' McCabe said, 'but for one thing, vampires have no aura.'

'And for another thing?' Salmon asked cautiously

'It doesn't explain how you can answer a question I did not ask aloud.'

He turned away, telling Benson to talk to the pathologist. Benson rubbed his hand in irritation over his sandy poll, glowered once morc at Salmon, who could see his darkened aura throbbing with annoyance, and stalked off to where the ambulance was due to land. McCabe beckoned Salmon towards the kitchen of the Wooden O.

---

[18] Well, we can't very well say 'the whites of his eyes' when they are, in fact, a smoky green shade of grey, can we?

The landlady was patiently waiting in a pillar of shadow that made her almost invisible. Her neck-to-ankle amethyst overcoat, her crown-to-chin grey hat, her cloud of twilight-coloured scarf meant that even when she stepped into the light to lead the way, she was still practically invisible. She led them off the path, towards the glowing lamps that Benson had had driven into the ground, and stopped. At her feet lay the body.

McCabe approached and frowned. He could tell by inhaling that the body was dead, but he leaned down anyway and checked, then looked up at Salmon. He could see her frowning, looking at the bent, upright arm, the curled legs, and knew she knew that the body had been moved.

The ground immediately around Fen was hard but the surface was covered in leaves, twigs, fallen branches, all rendered fragile by the frost, and all undisturbed except for those actually touched by the corpse. Away from the street lamps and the open doors, the darkness sharpened McCabe's eyesight so much it disoriented him. He lost his sense of perspective. He could see, with needle-sharp clarity, individual details, like the threads in the wool of the single red glove that Fen wore, the scratches on the toes of her boots, each individual hair on the side of her head that was visible, shaved up to her top-knot. But though he saw the exact shape of the particles of dirt and of the crystals of ice on her coat, the details did not come together to make a coherent whole. McCabe gathered the copper-coloured cloth of his cloak close about him so that he could squat without disturbing the frozen grass and brambles, and leaned forward as far as he could go, stretching closer to the head of the dead woman, inhaling, leaning down to look into her face. He sat back on his heels and took off his black velvet top-hat. Pressing a small button on the underside of the brim opened a panel in the side, and from this McCabe took a gadget that, once in his palm, blossomed into a lantern. He held it up over the body of Fen Maguire.

The heat he could normally see from a human body was absent, and he guessed she had been dead for about ten or eleven hours, allowing for the freezing temperatures. One hand was under her body but he could see the bare fingertips. There were no marks on her face, no disturbance to her clothes. Her velvet scarf was still tied, her bright striped hat crooked but still on her head, nothing badly out of place, apart from one missing glove. Her waxy face seemed astonished but showed no pain and no fear.

Salmon was a better judge of human ages than was McCabe, but still she thought the dead woman looked very young. Probably because she looked so surprised, so open, Salmon thought, and then thought, *She must have known her killer.* Fen's eyes were wide open and navy-blue, her skin unnaturally pallid so that the freckles, perfectly round brown dots like a naive drawing of freckles, stood out disconcertingly. Her clothes were unremarkable: a well-made cashmere coat, a knitted hat, a green and red velvet scarf, thick gabardine trousers, boots. She wore a little jewellery, which seemed to have been chosen from personal taste and was not symbolic that McCabe could see.

He was inching his way around the body, keeping his cloak out of the way, the lights from his swaying lantern washing over Fen like the sea. Fallinish was sniffing circles around the body, padding to and fro, till he eventually picked up a scent, and Salmon looked up as Fallinish began to follow it back into the woods. She saw him stop, moonlight gleaming on his metal body. He trotted about, puzzled. Now a second scent. Salmon got up and went to him. They both went in among the trees. When McCabe looked around, to dutifully explain to his apprentice what it was that he was doing, he found that his apprentice was off finding out by herself.

'Never mind me,' McCabe grumbled when she returned. 'I'm only the despotes.'

His aura – or whatever it was she could see – was now a kind of pale, glittering green that she was not sure how to interpret. Being Salmon, she didn't dither.

'Fallinish looked confused,' she said, 'and you didn't, so I thought I'd be more use to him. I don't think you are too annoyed, though, are you? Do you want me to do something different next time?'

McCabe was a little startled, being accustomed to a bit more deference. After a moment's thought, he said, 'I am not so easily annoyed as that, but in future tell me where you are going. I do not expect to have to look for you. Did Fallinish find anything?'

Salmon shook her head. 'Scents, but we will have to wait till the other dogs get here.'

McCabe nodded and turned to the landlady, who was standing behind him, holding her arms across her stomach.

'Do you recognise her?' Salmon asked.

'Her name is Persephone-Fen Maguire,' the landlady said. 'I'd like to go inside now – this is terribly shocking.'

McCabe nodded. 'We need to speak to you,' he said. 'May I come with Salmon up to your house?' he added.

The landlady nodded and started to turn away.

'We will be with you in a few minutes,' McCabe said.

Salmon and McCabe, with Fallinish trotting between them, picked their way back past the frozen bushes and churning roots and followed the landlady at a distance up the path to her house.

McCabe said, quite without truth, 'I cannot for the life of me remember the landlady's name.'

Salmon said, 'Imhotep-Damson Harper, sir. She trained as a chef, so she runs an inn from the house as well as running everything else.'

'How long has she lived in Ballinpooka?'

'Um – strictly speaking we are not in Ballinpooka,' Salmon said, unsure if McCabe would take that as attention to detail – good – or pedantry – bad, especially so early in themorning – but he just nodded.

'Once beyond the motte,' she said, 'we are in Hephistu. Madam Harper came back eleven years ago, when the job of landlady came up.'

The wide rectangle of a house that Immo lived in was eerily pale in the pre-dawn darkness. The windows were darkened and the garden sculptures mere milky gleams among the trees and shrubs. The front door was open wide enough to let a blaze of light out onto the broad, shallow steps to the house, and over a small patch of the gravel path. At the top of the house, in a window shaped like a rising sun, Immo – like all landladies – kept a night-light lit to guide travellers.

The Harpers of Hephistu were of Viking stock, and Immo looked very like her grandmother, tall and long-armed.

Approaching middle age with no great haste,[19] she was still a strapping girl. She wore her hair long, in a single plait, and the strands that escaped she tucked behind her ears, which were pierced with such large discs that they made McCabe discover his squeamish side. Under her woollen bathrobe, Immo was dressed in a dark grey jumper with white around the neck and cuffs, and dark grey jeans.

She led them down the bright hallway and into the huge kitchen, where they could hear the sizzle of the water heating in the kettle. She put down a bowl of oil and metal shavings for Fallinish. Immo's house was blessedly warm and McCabe began to unpeel his scarf and gloves. Contrary to popular understanding, the undead could still feel the cold. Salmon removed her dark blue beret and rolled it up so it could fit into the pocket of her coat, which she hung on the back of a chair.

Once the tea was poured, there came the inevitable questions and McCabe was relieved that Immo didn't seem to be too much in shock. From his hat, he plucked a small red bead that unfurled into an Official Witness Report, and Immo waited calmly while he also fished a stylus out from his hat, and with the glowing end he wrote down her name and address. He made himself look as genial as possible and let her tell him what she knew.

---

[19] We probably should mention that, in Muinbeo as in the war-torn Outland, most species including humans now usually live to be two hundred years old, so middle age can take a while. Things might have started getting crowded in the Outland, but there are far fewer people there now because … well, let's not go into that just now.

It was not very much. She had been alerted at four in the morning by Carbon Smith pounding on the door of Immo's house, screaming, literally, blue murder. Carbon was one of the Outland Watch Committee, who regularly checked the skies to make sure that spy-crawlers, kamikaze planes or other war craft from the Outland war were not making use of Muinbeo's unique airspaces to hide. Immo awoke immediately and tumbled into her clothes, and, leaving her door on the snib, followed Carbon down the path between the houses, and around the back to the orchard. Carbon was talking ceaselessly, gabbling about how she always came home this way but if the Bast wasn't haunted beforehand, it certainly would be now. Immo and Carbon stood for a moment and then Immo had stepped cautiously forth. It was she who had confirmed that Fen was dead. She had brought Carbon to the communal kitchen, which was close, and which had a little bank of irises, one of which she sent to the guardians. Another she sent to Carbon's husband Gossan, expecting that Carbon would shortly start crying and would be best off with her own kind.

'Her own kind?' McCabe said, wrinkling up his face in thought. Immo thought to herself, *Man looks like a shar pei dog.*

'What is she?' McCabe said. 'Lycanthrope? She is not a banshee, is she? Or we will be in sore need of a gagging order.'

'No, the family has sprite blood. So emotional over any death.' She shrugged, indicating that was all she had to say.

McCabe nodded at her words. He would compare notes with Salmon later. Immo tipped the dregs of her tea mug into the glass bowl in the centre of the table and frowned briefly at the leaves.

'Anything of interest?' McCabe said politely. The natural world, in his view, kept a great deal up its sleeve, with only glimpses reflected in tangible things.[20]

'Not really,' Immo said. 'A change, perhaps a visitor. I'm so distracted, I can't read the leaves.'

'*Tia feliĉego estas kompreni*,' said McCabe reflectively. 'Will I pour you another cup of tea?'

Salmon, who was the only person in Muinbeo who spoke only one language, said, 'This is a bit embarrassing, but I don't speak any other language. What did you just say?'

Immo and McCabe glanced at each other. Why did Salmon strangely insist on saying exactly what was on her mind? Had she never heard of reticence?

McCabe said, 'A quotation from a poet. It is Esperanto. It means, "What bliss it is to understand."'

When they had finished the tea they went out to the back of the house and Immo showed them around. The Wooden O was a small complex of houses that sprawled, as though spun by centrifugal force, around a large new theatre,[21] which itself surrounded the remains of a very, very old temple. The cottages, thirty in all, were rented by the theatre trust to temporary residents, who might be artists in need of an escape from the distractions of everyday life, visiting acting companies performing in the O itself or locals needing a temporary shelter between more permanent homes. Everything was

---

[20] Some of us doubt that 'tangible things' include soggy tea-leaves. But we won't argue.

[21] Fewer than two centuries old. That is very modern for Muinbeo.

administered by the trust's landlady, currently Immo Harper. The title brought with it a good income, a spacious and comfortable house and an enormous amount of work.

'Was there anyone already in the kitchen when you arrived there, Madam Harper?' Salmon said, as they went back into the house.

Immo, surprised, said, 'No. Who would be there?'

'You are not wearing your chatelaine,' Salmon said. 'If someone comes to your door shouting about murder you will hardly stop and take one key off the chain. So you must have known that the kitchen was already open. I just wondered if that meant that the staff had already arrived.'

Not a bad start, McCabe thought.

'We leave it open at night,' Immo said. 'The artists work such hours, they might need food or drink. Sometimes there are very late visitors we need to feed.'

'Who?'

'Well – there's a pub a mile in each direction from here. Sometimes we get people too drunk even for a bicycle. That's the most usual one.'

'You had an erratic portal nearby, didn't you?' Salmon said, looking up from her notes.

Immo shook her head. 'Centuries ago. There are accounts of people popping up here who thought they were on their way to Ballybolivia, or Rathera – even Outlanders. But so dangerous – they shut it when people were killed.'

Salmon and McCabe made notes as Immo spoke. The initial stages of an investigation involved sifting through piles of jigsaw pieces, testing which ones might go together, trying not to make decisions ahead of the facts. Facts might not reveal themselves to be relevant, in McCabe's experience, until you started looking at things upside-down.

His contemplation of the nature of detection was interrupted by the echoing roar of Immo's bewildered stomach, long deprived of its accustomed nutriment. Immo went pink and pretended to ignore it.

'Funny enough, the last time I spoke to Fen, we spoke of food,' Immo said, and abruptly went very pale.

McCabe watched her from the corner of his long eyes, but her colour returned quite quickly.

'Sorry,' she said. 'I've just realised again that she's dead. She was supposed to be here tonight, to make dinner. There were eight of us, you know, for a class reunion? So sad.'

The stables of the Smoke Coven's hall, Killchryso

By the time the morning sun was casting a halo over the black and icy trees and glistening on the moist bog by the Coven House in Killchryso, Winter-Gold Sackville was already making preparations to visit the Thanatos, to ask the coven's archivist to take out the rule books for ceremonies in the case of violent death, and to find a way of insisting that custody of Apprentice Farsade be transferred to the Smoke Coven. Winter had an admirable capacity to plan several things at the same time, all while doing something – in this case, saddling a horse – that had nothing to do with any of them. Strong despite her slight build, Winter heaved the saddle onto the horse's back and began nimbly to tighten straps and fasten buckles while the horse munched on, regardless. Winter ran her hand through her bobbed white hair and patted the horse.

Protocol demanded that it be Winter, the senior Smoke Coven witch, who informed the Thanatos of the death, and she did not look forward to the job, though naturally she did not shirk it. She was far too sensible a person to pretend that she did not need to get guidance from the rule books as to what she needed to do next – murder was not so common in Muinbeo that she had the progress of the ceremonies at the tip of her tongue. She did not mind, though she remembered with a sigh that since these books were kept in the Early History Archives, she would probably have to speak with Apprentice Sessaire. In her own mind she called him 'the unfortunate Sessaire', not only because he was a sombrist (of which she disapproved but without admitting it even to herself), but because he had too mannered and old-fashioned a way of speaking for her liking. She heard sarcasm in every word.

Winter took off her glasses and closed her eyes tightly so that she could think. She tapped the harlequin-patterned frame of her spectacles against her temple. She foresaw great difficulty on the matter of Apprentice Farsade. The quaestor – and others – had been incredibly stubborn about who was taking charge of Salmon when she came to Muinbeo. Winter still had difficulty accepting that Salmon had really been permitted to join the guardians; she was far too young. The argument used against Winter, and the rest of the coven of course, was that Salmon's experience in the Outland, along with her quick brain, more than made up for her youth. But now that Dunne, Salmon's despotes, had become a werewolf, the question seemed to Winter to require a new answer. Winter sighed, rose gently into the air and landed neatly on the horse's back.

McCabe was trying to be fair to Salmon, who was, he knew, reasonably knowledgeable for an apprentice of her age, but at every turn he missed Deputy Dunne's competent presence. McCabe knew better than most the nature of Salmon's disrupted childhood in the Outland that made her so well suited for being trained in observation, deduction and dogged pursuit of clues. But McCabe had never had an apprentice before now. He was accustomed to people who were grown, experienced, even cynical. He was not used to working with a novice. It was as though, after many decades with clockwork Fallinish, someone had handed him a bright-eyed, inquisitive, wriggling bio-puppy and expected him to know what to do with it. Salmon worried McCabe, not because she might make mistakes, but because *he* might. Besides, he had to admit, up to now he could always expect his deputies to relieve him of the unpleasant duty of interviewing the bereaved. McCabe and Salmon looked at each other in some alarm, and McCabe could see, from her careful polishing of her toe-cap against the back of her leg, that she was as uncomfortable as he was with other people's strong emotions. In the same way that a vampire had an exaggerated sense of each second of time, so too was their sense of emotional

---

[22] Baile Bhéal an Libhia (Town at the Mouth of the River Livia). The River Livia is one of the boundaries between Muinbeo and the Outland. Very close to the Shannon River, it is also known as the Great River. (We thought you might be wondering if the road actually went to South America. Though it ... no. That's enough for now.)

experience very heightened, and McCabe had to deliberately rest his mental weight on the least human, most undead parts of his abilities, or he risked being overcome by the grief of others. But Salmon, he suspected, had no such defence. He would have to be the grown-up.

Pulling up the hood of his aluminium-lined cloak, he strode the few yards between the mouth of the access tunnel and the Maguires' front door. Salmon hurried behind him. As she caught up with him, Salmon hissed an instruction to him, and McCabe hastily yanked down his hood, just as Fen Maguire's brother Fly opened the door, so he would not look like the Grim Reaper in person. Three years younger than his sister, Fly looked nothing like her, having hair of almost Scandinavian fairness and blue eyes, now, predictably, red-rimmed.

'Hello, Mr Maguire,' McCabe said. 'I'm very sorry about all this.'

Fly nodded and turned away. Halfway down the hall he turned in surprise when he noticed McCabe was not following him.

'Detective McCabe?' he said.

McCabe hesitated and Salmon said, 'You have to invite him in, Fly. Vampires can't come in unless …'

Realisation dawned on Fly's face and he hurried back and led them into the scullery where his mother Sparrow was sitting by the window, blankly rubbing her hands together. McCabe made his way over to her and held out both of his hands. Slowly, Sparrow Maguire stood up. McCabe took her hands and, as was customary, kissed her twice on each cheek. Sparrow was as pale as linen, and Salmon could barely see any aura at all.

'I'm terribly sorry about this, Madam Maguire,' McCabe said, 'and I regret that I must question you now, but the demands of investigation ...'

'I understand,' said Sparrow, nodding, and going on nodding as though she had forgotten what she was doing. She ran her hand over her dark hair, which she would later crop in mourning, glanced at Salmon and said, 'Are you all right, alannah?'[23] But apart from this brief speech, Sparrow seemed to move in a shell of silence and emptiness.

The house was full of people, rushing about sending iris-messages, crying, making food, making tea, feeding dogs, comforting the weeping, making plans, moving furniture. Fen's sister Heather was as loud in grief as her mother was silent, and their youngest brother Badger was distracting himself with making travel arrangements for family.

Looking around at all this, Salmon remembered the way that the silence and disbelief that followed the news that her parents had died clashed with the noise and demands of the lives that continued. Death, it occurred to her, brought with it a huge surge in living; death was an end, but a dead body was the start of a great many things. Some were profound, like the Witch Sackville calling by to pay her respects on her way to the Thanatos and Fen's friend Autumn Martin speaking to a hologram of the Abbot Job about the funeral service.

---

[23] Just in case you were not brought up with relatives who ruffled your hair and said things like 'Haven't you grown very tall, alannah? Hasn't she, Maggie?' *alannah* is a term of affection (applied, oddly, only to girls).

Some were prosaic, like Shear Amberson and Cedar Cullen unpacking an extra room for guests[24] and Sparrow's sister Holly making industrial amounts of tea. All around, the living hurried to accommodate the dead. This mixture of speed and shock, of noise and silence, reminded Salmon forcibly of her parents' death. She did not hear McCabe speak to her and was startled when he touched her elbow.

'Are you all right?' he said.

Salmon nodded. She was uneasy, and was not sure why.

'Too many auras?' he asked. 'Need to nip outside?'

Salmon shook her head. The auras were not bothering her. The thought of going outside frightened her, though, which puzzled her. She said as much.

McCabe said, 'You are in no danger. The Pharaoh's army cannot find you here.'

She looked up at him, startled. She knew that she was safe in Muinbeo – that was the reason that she had been brought here the day her parents were buried. She knew that the army, even in their relentless pursuit of anyone with any connection to the Resistance, could not come into Muinbeo and could not know Salmon's hiding-place. She knew that she was safe, and yet being reminded of her parents also reminded her of the fear. She had come to Muinbeo to escape the fear. And now she felt afraid again.

_____

[24] One of the advantages of Muinbeo having a unique place in the Time-Space continuum is that people could, in effect, keep an extra room or two in their attic and take it out for use when they needed it. Designing such a room is one of the first lessons taught to magicians.

'You have seen a dead body,' McCabe pointed out. 'Murdered. And now you are surrounded by grief and loss. Not surprising that you are thinking the way you used to think in the Outland.'

Salmon nodded slowly, thinking, *I thought I was the one who could see auras?*

'In the Outland I was used to fear,' she said. 'Everyone knew that if not now, then soon, they might have something of which to be afraid. You get used to it being around.'

'Muinbeo is a sanctuary,' McCabe said, very quietly so that no one else could hear him. 'And we will keep you safe. The best thing to do is concentrate on your job. Come on, now.'

He turned away and she followed him into the shadowy corner of the room so they could speak with Sparrow Maguire.

'When did you last see Fen?' McCabe asked Sparrow softly, as though lowering his voice would somehow help her.

'Monday,' she said. 'She comes to see me every few days, she only lives up the road at McNaspy's Cross. She seemed her usual self. You know. Just – Fen.'

'What did you talk about?'

Sparrow shrugged and looked at Winter for inspiration. Winter stood beside Sparrow, her pale rose jodhpurs and jacket contrasting strongly with the crumpled black shirt and trousers that had been the first thing Sparrow found to wear when the quaestor had come at dawn to break the news of her daughter's death. Absent-mindedly, still standing, Sparrow picked off the dog hairs still attached to her sleeves and flicked them in the general direction of the fire. She sat down again, moving as though she was suddenly incredibly old.

'What did she say?' Sparrow asked of no one in particular.

McCabe waited. Sparrow sighed. Salmon was beginning to wonder whether the question had been forgotten.

'There was not anything in particular,' Sparrow said eventually. 'We talked about her job. She was having trouble with her senator. Fen was the committee's amanuensis, and they were very busy. She was going to do dinner for some friends on Saturday night – she was cooking for them. I think that was why she was at the Wooden O. Her own kitchen was too small, and she was bringing what she needed to the kitchen there.' Sparrow shrugged.

Salmon said, 'Do you know who was going to be at the dinner?'

Sparrow was frowning in concentration, as though Salmon was speaking in an unfamiliar language.

'Old school-friends,' Sparrow said. 'I don't know exactly. Fen was a good friend, she kept up with people she met. It was important to her. Even in the Outland.'

'The Outland?' Salmon said, and Sparrow looked at her in surprise.

'Fen worked in the Outland for a few years, oh, years ago now.'

'Were any Outland friends going to be at the dinner?'

'Maybe,' Sparrow said, turning her palms upwards. 'I don't know. Maybe. Immo would know. Fen used to work – where was it she worked when she was in the Outland, Fly? Shear might know,' she added as Fly shook his head.

Shearwater, hearing his name, came over. He smiled briefly at McCabe and Salmon, and touched Sparrow's shoulder. He was a muscular, big-boned man with very thick short brown hair and, even in winter, ruddy-tanned skin. As Sparrow seemed to have forgotten what she was asking him, Shear squatted down beside her to ask her gently again. He had high, broad cheekbones, and always had an air of having just come in from a bracing outdoors. He asked Sparrow again, and she looked at him blankly. Shear uneasily rubbed his hand over his thick moustache and looked up at McCabe. Fly set down the cup and saucer he had brought for his mother and watched her while she drank some tea.

'Madam Maguire,' McCabe said, and stopped.

Sparrow turned in her seat and, with a flick of her wrist, threw away her cup, emptying her tea all along the floor as the cup bounced along the table like a stone over water, till it hit the wall, where it shattered. The clamour and noise in the kitchen and the scullery stopped. Winter Sackville moved forward and her purple eyes shone, about to magic away the debris, but Sparrow gave her a look that quite clearly said, *Don't you dare!* Winter stopped.

McCabe glanced at Salmon and they stood up and moved away from the hearth. Sparrow covered her face with her hands, and so it was to her children that McCabe said that the guardians would be in touch again.

'Don't take it bad,' Fly said to McCabe. 'Ma throwing the cup. She's devastated. She took a hammer to the pantry earlier, then she was in tears for an hour over a pendant. She's all over the place.'

'I am sorry,' said McCabe, and Fly said he was too. He went to sit by his mother.

Winter Sackville showed them to the door.

'When did you last see Fen, Madam Sackville?' McCabe asked as they walked, their feet echoing a little against the tiles and the painted walls of the hallway.

The winter sun had not yet reached the high fanlight and the windows, and pots of plants arrayed on every available shelf made the hallway dark.

Salmon could not resist looking sideways as they passed a mirror to see for herself that McCabe had no reflection. She saw what she did not expect to see – rather than no McCabe, she saw several. Salmon made a mental note to herself to ask Maccarrill about it when she got home. Maccarrill would know.

'Oh – goodness, let me see. I didn't know her very well,' Winter added, to explain her hesitation. 'It was in the bakery, I think it was, a few days back. We just chatted in passing. She mentioned she had a few messages to get for her mother, and for this dinner she was cooking.'

McCabe glanced at Salmon and, rather to his surprise, she did exactly what he wanted and handed to Winter the list of names Immo Harper had given to them of the friends who had been invited to dinner. Winter gave Salmon a huge smile that rather startled the apprentice and pulled her glasses down her nose so that she could read. She nodded as she read the names aloud, adding little bits of information about each one. Silver-Water Eustace was a daughter of Lily-Water, who taught young magicians with Winter, and Crake Bachelor, engaged to marry a Sutton girl from Hylabeg, had asked Winter's husband to the feast. August-Joy Martin now taught geography in the same school she had attended in her youth, and Sand Butler … . Here Winter trailed off. The name was familiar and she was convinced that she could see the boy's face, narrow and freckled, with dark brown hair sticking out all about. She knew that for some reason she had thought recently of Sand but could not now recall why.

'You have been very helpful, thank you,' McCabe said. 'If you remember anything else, could you let me know? For example, was she romantically linked to anyone? No.'

He paused, holding out his hand to take the list, but Winter hesitated and read the list a second time.

'I've remembered something. Sand Butler. He was up in court about six months ago on a fraud charge – minor stuff, comparatively. He swindled money out of the council. Fen gave evidence against him.'

'Did he take it personally?'

Winter wrinkled her nose. 'Hard to say. She didn't point the finger, but she is one of the people who authorises public funding forms. She queries – queried – odd things when she saw them, and so brought him to the management accountant's attention. It is conceivable that he would have associated Fen with the figure of Nemesis or retribution.'

McCabe translated this, as he always had to when speaking with Winter, into general terms. Witches and druids could see so many possible realities of equal value that it was very common for them to cope with the potential chaos by dividing people and their actions up into archetypes.

'I wasn't involved and don't know much about it,' Winter added, 'except that of course the Smoke Coven has to go over parts of the council accounts. Sorry, I can't really help, but that's what I remembered.'

'Thank you,' said McCabe. 'I recall that Madam Porphyrogenitus was involved in the case. Perhaps she will have more details.'

Winter escorted them to the door and opened it carefully to keep the sunlight away from the guardian. Fallinish had been waiting patiently outside, and he sprang to his paws as McCabe appeared. Winter turned and smiled at Salmon, holding out her hands.

'I was very sorry to hear about what happened to your despotes,' she said. 'I am sure it is very disruptive for you, as well as upsetting.'

'It's not been disruptive,' Salmon said truthfully. 'I am upset about him, of course, but I have been reassigned, so there is no disruption.'

'You will recall the conversations that we had when first you came to Muinbeo,' Winter went on, 'regarding the best place for you to do your apprenticeship.'

'Madam Sackville,' McCabe said rather sternly, 'we are starting a murder investigation. Please do not distract my apprentice.'

'A murder investigation? Is that a suitable place for a girl of her age?'

'Of course it is suitable – she's an apprentice guardian. And perhaps under the circumstances the appropriate place for you is inside the house, with the bereaved, rather than outside on the doorstep inviting in the east wind.'

'There is always opportunity to reconsider decisions,' Winter said softly to Salmon.

'Not in my experience,' Salmon said bluntly. Winter's silvery aura flared and her eyes went pale. 'Thank you for your concern about my welfare,' Salmon said, to try and be agreeable, 'but I am where I should be.'

'Of course, you think it is exciting,' Winter said with a sigh. 'You see Adventure, Glory. But remember, very soon you will need to go through the demonstration, and that failure leads to removal from your post. Since you, most unusually, have no second language you will have to be very impressive to convince the board. As I am on that board I know better than you do that for someone who is facing their demonstration shortly a change in despotes is an enormous challenge.'

'You told me yourself, Madam Sackville, when I first came to Muinbeo, that a challenge was only the left hand of an opportunity.'

Winter tightened her lips but McCabe said, before she could speak, 'Since it is now well after mid-day I will be failing in my duties if I do not get some food into my apprentice – will you be kind enough to open a tunnel for me? I think the Ravenous Raven Fooderie serves a good lunch. Come along, Fallinish.'

Winter put the matter out of her mind – she would devote the evening to planning what needed to be done – and quickly ran through a routine spell that opened a temporary tunnel in space to protect McCabe from the sunlight. When the light-ring at the entrance of the tunnel began to pulsate, and she knew it was empty, she closed it down and retreated into the Maguire house, shutting the door firmly.

By that time, McCabe and Salmon had emerged in the shadowy courtyard behind the Ravenous Raven Fooderie, and had followed Fallinish inside.

The Ravenous Raven Fooderie, Dalread Street, Ballinpooka

The Fooderie was partly underground, so very suitable for vampires and anyone who liked calm, quiet places. In fact the food was so good that even people who loved vibrant noisy places that were so jammed with people you needed a shoehorn to get in still went to the Fooderie to eat. Visitors took off their shoes at the entrance so as to protect the deep velvety carpet, and they sat in ornate, spoon-shaped wooden chairs at glass-topped tables. The light was provided by phosphorescent plants, including a magnificent bonsai landscape set into a niche in the wall. The walls were decorated with tapestries and hangings.

The Fooderie had been owned by the same family for many generations and Ethiopian fare was the speciality, but there was virtually no kind of food that a person could not eat there, provided they had sufficient time on their hands. None of the de Courcys[25] did *fast*, especially when it came to eating meals, which they considered to be the foundation of civilised life. One of the walls was decorated in writing: the phrase 'Nothing good ever happened quickly' written in a hundred and seventy-four languages.[26]

Second Deputy Benson had already ordered for McCabe, drawing some slight attention to the fact that he knew McCabe well enough to know that it was texture, not taste, that mattered. Beside him was the quaestor's factotum, Johnston, his expression as lugubrious as ever and his spiky thatch of grey hair tousled and on end. He was making his way methodically

---

[25] Quite right, well spotted. De Courcy is not an Ethiopian name. But the original Hephaestus and his family got on the wrong side of the Queen of Sheba due to an unfortunate misunderstanding about a cow. They unexpectedly turned up in Cronna due to the cow eating the map, and Hephaestus and other members of his family married local people (well, they were local by that time). Hence the name.

[26] This was the courteous and artistic way in which the current owner communicated to an impatient and unappreciative customer the concept that they were never again to ask for 'food to go'. The barbarians.

through an omelette, and he raised his fork in greeting. Salmon asked for a poached egg and some toast. Fallinish settled himself under the table with his snout on her foot. Benson himself did not often eat lunch. As soon as McCabe sat down to a plate of cucumber and lemon that would take away the heavy scent of clay, Benson pushed a few sheets of paper towards him.

'A list of all the people we interviewed,' he said, glancing darkly at Johnston on the word *we*, 'mostly at the Wooden O but as we know that Maguire was not killed there, it is already too narrow a list. That's one problem.'

McCabe pushed the list towards Salmon. Johnston looked at Benson, who said nothing, but tightened his lips. Salmon, feeling that she was being tested but not knowing what it was about, licked her lips and cleared her throat. She felt panic and was afraid to catch anyone's eye. If she failed this test, whatever it was, she would lose any chance of impressing her new despotes. She heard Benson clear his throat impatiently. Salmon breathed in slowly. She could hear her mother's voice in her head: *Concentrate.*

The paper seemed to give out a low, dark yellow glow. Salmon felt the fibres ripple and pulse, and she relaxed her hands. The words began to change to images, flickering and momentary, the letters and the pictures tumbling together. After a few seconds, during which she did not hear Benson clear his throat again or see Johnston peering at her, Salmon had in her mind every name on the page, and to every name she now had a link – to images, to places, to other people. She put down the paper, touching the tips of her fingers against the thick, uneven surface. She recognised the handwriting; Benson had a distinctive script – very firm, slightly flourished letters. The navy-blue ink that he used was thick and shiny in some places and thin and scratchy in others. Salmon smoothed her hand over it and saw Benson at his desk, flourishing his pen. But further than that she could not see. She pushed the page back to McCabe.

'Anything interesting occur to you, apprentice?' McCabe said casually.

'Two of the names that Second Deputy Benson has marked as being away from home were attending the scholarship reception at the library,' she said. 'I saw them there.'

'But they have not been home yet,' Benson said quickly. 'The reception did not continue until this morning.'

'Willow Brosnan goes to see his aunt in the Outland every week and will have gone there from the reception, and Marble O'Flynn will have gone over to Tubberderry race-course early. There's another thing, though.' She looked at McCabe, hoping to see what he thought. 'There was someone else near the Wooden O.'

'Who?' McCabe said sharply. 'How do you know?'

'I don't know who it was,' Salmon said. 'But when I went into the woods with Fallinish, he picked up two scents one after the other.'

'Why didn't you say so?' Benson pounced, and the yellow in his aura pulsed. 'One thing that you will have to learn is the importance of speed – you must tell us as soon as you notice something; straightaway or it will be too late and the chance to take advantage of the information will be lost for ever.'

'I didn't exactly notice anything,' Salmon said, feeling a bit hounded. 'It's just that when Fallinish picked up a second scent, he went after the very strong one and I went after the weaker one. I –'

'You followed a *scent*,' Benson said, almost laughing, glancing at McCabe and then at Johnston. 'How on earth do you think *you* could follow a scent?'

Salmon looked at him and, without really meaning to, she did what her foster-brother called *that freaky thing* with her eyes. The bands of colours in the iris began to glow very softly and to separate from each other as the pupil dilated so widely that Benson dropped his knife and Johnston put down his spoon, looking from Salmon to McCabe and back again. In the dark space of her eyes, they could see lights, swirling dust, glowing orbs. It lasted only a few seconds.

Then Salmon looked away and said, 'It wasn't as difficult as you might think. It is like seeing an aura, but very faint. But I didn't find anything, and I don't know who it was. The scent did not come up to the Wooden O but went towards the motte. Then when I went through to where the wood thins out, I saw that someone must have been working on the allotments at night. The last allotment just before the bridge – someone had been there during the night. There were all new cloches put down.'

'The frost was unexpected,' Johnston said, wiping his mouth. 'People were rushing to protect their darling plants with cloches and sawdust. Which allotment was it?'

'Right before the bridge. It belongs to Amethyst Corcoran but she's away.'

'Who looks after her allotment in her absence?' McCabe asked.

'I do.'

The three grown-ups and the apprentice looked up and Fallinish came out from under the table. Hunter Sessaire politely gave a shallow bow and patted Fallinish's gleaming neck. As he was not working that day, Hunter was not in uniform and instead was dressed in dark hiking clothes. He was a keen walker and often spent entire days on the Tubbercolm or the Black Bog or a whole weekend on the Wolftrap Mountain.

'We will be pleased to receive any information you might have,' McCabe said. 'As I expect that is why you are here. Get yourself a chair.'

'I didn't think that your people had much sense of public duty,' Benson said, and McCabe darted an unfriendly glance at his deputy.

'What you don't know about my people would very probably fill a book,' Hunter said agreeably, opening his brown eyes very wide. 'Especially if you added it as a chapter in a book about everything else that you don't know.'

He put his hat on his knees as he sat and smiled briefly at Salmon. Salmon quailed. She worried about Hunter when he antagonised people like Benson. Sombrists were already unpopular, with people thinking they were at best weird and at worse Up To Something. Nefertiti, who had been friends with Hunter for a long time, told Salmon that she had once said the same thing to him. Hunter had merely looked surprised and remarked that if people disliked him for circumstantial reasons, that was their lookout.

'There is no call to pass personal remarks, gentlemen,' McCabe said mildly. 'Apprentice Sessaire, please tell us what it is that you wanted to tell us.'

'There is not very much to tell, I'm afraid. On the night of the murder, I had been working late in the Early History Archives. My despotes wanted me to prepare some manuscripts for Dr Hughes.'

'Has he not wrung every drop of history out of that Book of the Orchard yet?' Benson, who saw no point to history, grumbled.

'He didn't request that. He was looking for some early medieval maps. In any case, I went home at about eight, dined with my family and was in bed by ten. But I didn't sleep well and at about two in the morning, I went down to the allotment. I thought if I did a little work there it would help me sleep.' He took a breath and crossed his legs. 'I was inside the shed, doing bits and pieces, and after about fifteen minutes I went outside with sawdust to keep the frost off the bulbs. The moon was still up. When I came out, two cloches had been left outside my gate, with this on it. I went up to the aornis and into the trees but I saw nothing strange.'

He reached into the crumpled paper bag he was carrying and took out a sodden woollen glove.

'A glove might not seem something to make a fuss about,' he said. 'But it was very obviously left for me to see. Then this morning I heard that there was some crime committed last night near the Wooden O. It occurred to me that there might be a connection. I thought it better to come to you, given how suspicious people often are of what you thoughtfully call *my people*, than wait for you to come to me.'

'There is something else, isn't there?' said Johnston unexpectedly, and Benson stared at him. 'Something else that makes this strange. Something that made you go up to the motte.'

Hunter got up.

'Indeed. As I was leaving the allotment, I noticed that there were prints over my plot and several other plots too. They came from the road to Cassidy's Bridge, and went towards Chlovis Woods.'

'Prints?' asked McCabe. 'Prints of what? Man? Woman?'

Hunter smiled and put on his hat. 'Mr McCabe,' he said, 'they were the footprints of a gigantic hound!'

'Why does he have to be so dramatic?' complained Benson when Hunter had left, and McCabe told him to read more detective novels.[27]

They had settled back to their food when the howling started. Miles away, in the Civic Coven's archives, Winter Sackville heard it also and opened the window, the better to hear. She could not understand everything that the werewolves were saying to each other, but she understood the important part. They had found a rogue werewolf.

A private house, near Roanoake Cross

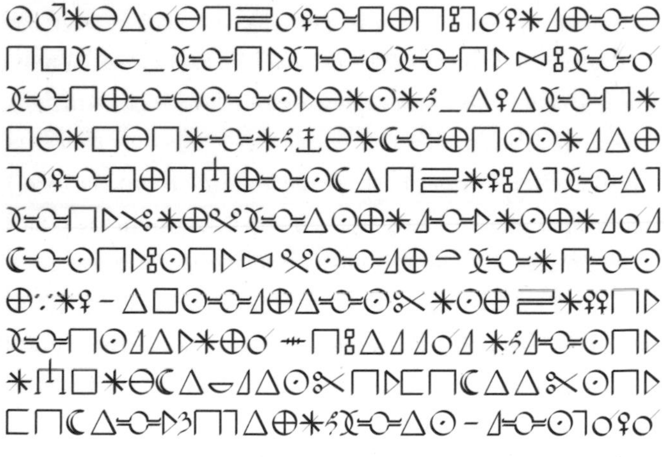

[27] And if you don't know what we were talking about, you need a bigger library. Mr Sherlock Holmes is a very great man indeed.

⚹ [coded symbol text — untranslatable] [28]

Objectively, I had guessed that it could go either way but I realised that in fact I had expected to sleep heavily as soon as I returned home. I subconsciously expected the surge of energy to be followed by an irresistible desire to sleep for hours, days. Hours of suppressed excitement, the sort of tension that is always associated for me with having to dissemble, then the tedium of waiting, the horror of realising that one has to live through each second, each multiple of seconds until the appointed hour, then the event itself, over immediately. Soundlessly, which surprised me. I did not realise how anxious I really was – what if she makes a noise? What if she runs away? What if there is some unforeseen possibility that, once the first movement is made, will suddenly loom from nowhere and take over, refuse to be managed? How would I cope with that feeling of terror at realising

---

[28] We have realised that you are not likely to be able to read the code, so we have translated it for you. Obviously, for the person who wrote this bit, the whole point was that the code was incomprehensible, but that's no way to tell a story. Anyway, that was then. This is now. In a manner of speaking.

that I forgot the vital safety-belt and it is too late now, with the rollercoaster plummeting, to try and clip it shut? What if it is only partially successful, so it cannot be concealed and will instead have to be explained? But none of these things happened. I walked away over the hard, trackless ground, bided my time until everything was finally still, then made my way home, unseen, by the canal-bank. The rush of endorphins that got me through the act itself, and the bracing cold of the walk home would, I thought, dissipate the moment the door shut behind me, and I would be limp as a rag. But no. I stowed my acquisition in the cellar and was still wide awake, making notes and laying out what I needed. I slept very little that night, but all of today I was just as normal, just as I usually am, hardly even felt tired. I will go to the gairm – I do not want to, because these things are pointless and make me laugh, but my absence would be noticed. Reed Cutler and those ridiculous birds. He cultivates that sullen, silent look, I am sure. No one could naturally look so much of a stereotype of a Thanatos. These people are ridiculous, at least as ridiculous as the Outlanders whom they so despise. They are as superstitious, as misled, as incapable of analysis, as incapable of seeing nature as it really is, as any Outlander. But I am, for the next blessedly few months, one of them, and as with any other hunter, my survival depends on being unobserved and fast. So I will just have time to finish what I need to do, and I will go to the ceremony.

The Goldsmith family's home in Marvaan

Conall was waiting in the porch when Salmon reached her foster-family's house and, as was his wont, sniffed her all over while she took off her outdoor shoes and pulled on the soft-soled slippers she wore for training. She ruffled his ears, and he made low, cooing noises, rolling his dark-red eyes back in his head. When she was ready to go in, he bounded ahead, cracking her across the knees with his tail.[29]

Inside, the Goldsmiths' house was a riot of steps, stairs, galleries, hallways, cubicles, cellars and attic-rooms. Some rooms were big enough to play bowls in and had vast fireplaces with hobs that could seat several children and a dog, some rooms so small that entrance into them was achieved by imitating a caterpillar. The kitchen was dominated by a cast-iron cooker, a magnificent beast festooned with dials and levers and wheels which, properly manipulated, could either heat the entire house or cook a single soufflé. There was a pantry filled with shelves, dressers and presses; there were studies, rooms perfect for snuggling down and reading (there were two libraries) or listening to the radio; rooms best used for vigorous noisy games; workrooms, bedrooms and an office. On the outside, the house was shaped like an E with the middle stroke missing, and had a great many windows and chimneys. Originally it had been a farmhouse and even though most of the land had been sold, the Goldsmiths had kept the farm buildings, so there was room for the horses, for bicycles and old furniture and bits of broken equipment that, some time or another, Archer would get around to fixing.

Salmon's foster-mother, Berry, was emerging from the loom-room with a bolt of new cloth, looking as fresh and relaxed after a day's weaving as if she had just had a week's holiday.

---

[29] Sorry – did we not mention that Conall was a dog? Our mistake. A Pharaoh hound, to be exact.

She put down the cloth and hugged Salmon. Berry's skin was pale and unwrinkled, and her abundant hair was dark and kept tidy by what looked like an elaborate arrangement of twists, coils and brass pins. Always, since she had first met her foster-family when she arrived, distressed and wretchedly tired, in Muinbeo, Salmon remembered two characteristics of Berry's – the faint scent of grass and clean laundry, and the silence. Berry spoke very infrequently, her orange-flecked aura shifted rhythmically and she almost carried silence about with her, as another woman might carry a watch or a book.

'You are in luck tonight, Salmon,' Berry said. 'Archer is cooking.'

Salmon picked up the bolt of blue cloth and carried it into Berry's store-room.

Following her into the store-room, Berry filled in a small label, tied it to the cloth and lifted the bolt of cloth onto a shelf.

Then Salmon said, 'Why do I have no second language?'

Berry didn't move or reply for a few seconds. Then she gave the bolt one last shove and turned around.

'What suddenly brings that to mind?' she said, smiling.

'The Witch Sackville. She was talking about the demonstration.'

Berry smiled again and relaxed.

'Routines have their places,' she remarked. Then she said, 'Salmon, I don't know the way it came about that you do not speak a second language. I can't tell you why.'

She patted Salmon's shoulder, and they went into the kitchen, Conall bounding ahead. While Salmon lifted the lid on a dish of what she knew would be roast duck meat, Berry crossed the freezing courtyard between the house and her work-room. As she arrived back, her breath billowing frostily, she met with Marigold, back from an afternoon run, and Rainbow came hurrying down from the study with the three other dogs leading the charge.

'I suppose the dogs will go out,' Marigold said, holding the door open.

The four dogs gave her a look that clearly said, *You must be kidding*, and hurried into the next room, to claim their places on the settee, toasting at the fire and listening to a radio play.

Marigold resembled her mother only in the length and abundance of her dark-red hair. In almost every other aspect, she looked like her father, Archer.

'How are you doing, Goldie?' Salmon said, as Marigold shut the door.

'Fine,' she said. 'Busy.'

'You're always busy,' Rainbow said. 'I thought the Guild of Bookbinders *invited* you to be an apprentice.'

'I still have to do thirteen exams.' Marigold laughed. 'It is a very competitive guild.'

'Don't work too hard,' her mother said, patting her shoulder. 'Come on, you three, help me to set the table.'

'What about you, little brother?' Marigold asked, as she and her siblings gathered together cutlery, glasses and carafes. 'How was school?'

Rainbow rolled his eyes. 'Oh, school was the exciting carnival of thrills and challenges that school always is.'

His mother tutted as she passed him, but more at the fact that he and Salmon were sneaking some meat out of the dish than at Rainbow's oft-repeated boredom at school life.

'This is delicious,' Marigold said, making a dive for the dish, but her father, blown in on an icy blast, caught her arm.

'I'll turn you upside-down and shake all the brains out of your head,' he scolded. 'And who will clean up that size of a mess?'

Marigold, almost as tall as her father, laughed at him. They had the same long face and high cheekbones. Archer had enormously bushy eyebrows and an abundant beard complete with moustache. His weather-tanned face and the profusion of wiry black-and-grey hair made his blue eyes look like two robin's eggs caught in a blackthorn.

'Is the dinner ready?' Rainbow asked.

'It nearly is,' his father answered. 'It's duck,' he added, unnecessarily.[30] He put the lid back on and turned down the heat. 'Now,' he said, 'a round of exercise will be just long enough for the cherries to be finished.'

The children groaned, as they always did, grumbling routinely at his ensuring they did at least ten minutes of ghost-fencing, a type of martial art that they all learned.

'It was perfected thousands of years ago,' Archer would tell them, 'by the leaders of the Fianna.'

'Just as well,' Salmon sighed, failing once again to manage to kick a target located at ear-level. 'It is certainly not being perfected here.'

'Not to worry,' Archer said encouragingly, 'it will make sense some day.'

---

[30] Archer could cook four meals. In spring it was duck soup, in summer duck salad, in autumn duck stewed with black olives and shallots, in winter he made shredded roast meat served with toast, mushrooms and sour cherries. His family loved his cooking. The ducks were less keen.

As Archer dished out the food, the family chattered about how their day had been. Archer was a cardmaker[31] and had spent most of his day at the office of the Guild of Cardmakers, Berry had been weaving cloth and Marigold had spent the day drowning parchment[32] in dirty water so that, in a few months' time, when they dug it back out of the ground, she and her fellow bookbinder apprentices could learn to clean and rescue the manuscripts. Rainbow complained good-naturedly about school but got little sympathy from his parents since he would have to stay in school until he knew where he wanted to be apprenticed.

'I could stay at home and help you,' he said, often and hopefully, but Archer and Berry merely smiled. Rainbow was so easily distracted that every attempt to help his parents ended in something that needed to be redone, or in disaster narrowly averted.

'Go on, then,' Rainbow said resignedly to Salmon, 'what is it like having a vampire as a despotes? Has the unbeatable team of Farsade and McCabe solved the mysterious murder yet?'

'I suppose a vampire is much the same as anyone who doesn't like strong sunlight,' Salmon said, loading up a forkful of food. 'But we don't know who did the murder.'

---

[31] The Guild of Cardmakers made any kind of picture cards that had meaning – playing cards, fortune-telling cards, picture cards you use so that everyone tells a story based on the hand they have been dealt, cards for solving murder mysteries, for playing word games, for reading horoscopes, for visiting cities … the list goes on.

[32] Animal skin – people used to write on it. Books on parchment have lasted for centuries, millennia, even; they are basically tough as old boots. (Apparently, if times got hard, you could use them as boots too.)

'I suppose we may never know,' Archer said and Salmon and Rainbow looked at him in horror.

'We can't have it unsolved!' Salmon exclaimed and Archer laughed.

'It is not entirely up to you,' he said. 'It wouldn't be the first unresolved mystery that we have had in Muinbeo.'

'What mysteries?' Rainbow asked and Salmon said, 'Deaths? Murders?'

'This is unsuitable talk for the dinner-table,' Berry said. 'You have classes tomorrow, Salmon. You need to think about schoolwork instead of clues.'

Salmon concentrated on her food, her mind stubbornly still fixed on the thought of not being able to unpick the secrets that had led to the death of Fen Maguire. Whatever Archer said, whatever even Dr O'Buachalla said about it not being possible to say exactly what happened, there would be some way of cracking open what had happened in Cluancorr. There was a challenge in the apparent neatness of the killing – the body taken from the place of death, meaning that if there were any clues, they were not attached to each other or to the murder. It was a blank wall, in which the moving bricks had to be found by careful searching.

'Detective Inspector McCabe said he was going to see Madam Porphyrogenitus this evening,' she said, her mind running along its own track.

'She's kind of scary,' Marigold said through a mouthful of vegetable.

Rainbow snorted. 'She's not scary, she's very funny, and full of information.'

'How do you know?' Berry said suddenly, eyeing her son sternly.

Rainbow was intrigued by people, and would plague with questions anyone who caught his attention. He always nodded dutifully when his parents, by stern ordering, reasoned explanation or playful cajoling, encouraged him to find some conversational alternatives. But when it came to it, if someone was interesting, then collaring and interrogating them always seemed to work.

Rainbow went pink under his mother's glinting eye and hurried on to say, 'She only seems scary because she's about a million years old and she teaches you. Old teaching people are always scary. And she's aristocracy. Well, she was when there were kings.'

'Isn't she related to Salmon's family?' Marigold said, her fork half-way to her mouth. 'Wasn't she some relation of the Kinnores?'

Berry and Archer looked briefly at each other. Archer got up to replenish the plate of potatoes.

Berry said, 'Distantly, yes. Salmon, have some more duck. Goldie, don't even think about talking with your mouth full. Rainbow, get your elbows off the table.'

The talk of murder and of Heron Porphyrogenitus passed and Salmon thought no more of the Lirs or the Kinnores.

Home of Heron Porphyrogenitus, Templeglass

By the time McCabe was ready to leave the Senate Chambers offices, it was already dark and he was glad of the chance to walk home in fresh air, instead of making his way underground through the town. He pulled on his hat, bundled his scarves and collars up around his neck and eased his fingers into fleece-lined leather gloves. He would call on Heron Porphyrogenitus on his way home.

McCabe still lived in his family's home in Templeglass, about five miles from Ballinpooka, and he set off now at a brisk pace across the canal bridge and southwards up the hill to the town walls. The wind shook the barley-pale lamps of the gate guardians who, bundled in coats and cowls, now walked slowly up and down, waiting for the senate bells to ring to tell them to close the gates for the night. As McCabe strode along, the bells rang out, as high and clear as struck crystal, and, rather than hurry for the gate that was now ponderously swinging shut, he merely rearranged his constituent elements and walked through the wall. Being a vampire, his constituent elements could also be rearranged to allow him to step through time and space[33] and be at his own front door in a matter of seconds but he preferred to walk, stopping to admire the view from the top of the hill that marked the southern boundary of Ballinpooka.

The Forum faced the film-house across the street and with square grey cottages huddled on either side. The town walls rose glimmering and black behind him. Beyond the Ballinpooka walls, the way was lit with the glow of phosphorescent plants planted at the order of the senate, mostly low-growing mosses and succulents, and crossroads were marked by shining

_____

[33] If you're interested in the details, it is the talarios gene (which incidentally is the same gene that means vampires can't stand sunlight) which gives some vampires the ability to step about in time, space and matter. They can't go backwards in time, of course, only forwards, and they can leave one place and reappear in another in just over a heartbeat.

guardian trees. McCabe headed west, by Great Grebe Castle. The top of the estate's boundary wall was fitted with lantern-bearing gargoyles to keep the traveller safe, and lights from the castle twinkled fitfully between groves of beech and oak trees. Past the castle, hawthorn trees cluttered the fields, and McCabe could see a glint of heavy frost where the turlough[34] caused by the rains of late winter had not quite subsided. As he passed, McCabe was bleated at by a herd of long-legged Killchryso Ridgeback goats grazing on the castle's common land. McCabe walked quickly and met no one, though he heard voices from Rafferty's shebeen that died down briefly as he passed and some low drumming and crackling from the Neanderthal settlement at McNaspy Cross. Once he was on the Templeglass Road, it was busier, with the farmers getting the last of their animals in, reluctant dogs being taken for walks.

A very small person, who McCabe at first thought was an infant, then a very small adult, then an infant again, was driving a herd of swine. The swine were sturdy and white and round, running evenly with the small dark figure keeping pace easily, holding a stick to the side of the leading boar. There was no sound

---

[34] We are certain that the turlough McCabe is walking past is just a turlough (a lake that dries up in dry weather and reappears at other times) and has nothing to do with what one Peregrine Hooke – a daredevil, brigand and murderer – buried there after his second-last voyage centuries ago. Admittedly, Peregrine never returned from his last trip, and the smarter dogs in Muinbeo have agreed amongst themselves that little puppies should not see the turlough at night. But we are sure there is nothing for you to worry about.

from them as they passed McCabe, and when he looked behind him, the road was empty. For the next few hundred yards there were only lamps and candles in windows to guide him to the house of Heron Porphyrogenitus, across the road from his own.

When McCabe first lived in the house, the Templeglass Road was a cattle track through high grass. Nothing had kept an inquisitive infant from exploring the fields and woods beyond, and making himself at home in every corner of what became Kinturk Farm. Centuries later, these twenty acres of working farm were given to Heron Porphyrogenitus by her father. Even older than McCabe, Heron had been the second of three exquisite daughters, and one of six children. Her father's family originally had been Outlanders and later rose to great heights in the Byzantine Empire, and on her mother's side she was part of the aristocratic clan of Lir. She was given Kinturk in the faint hope that it might keep her so busy that she had no time to engage her father's friends in strongly worded debates and that therefore she might not alienate all of her potential suitors. It was not her vampirism that made Golden Porphyrogenitus negatively assess his daughter's chances of matrimony[35] but her tendency to call a spade a spade. Indeed, as he remarked after

---

[35] Heron's father worked for many years as a telepath and a diplomat among the royalty of the Outland. Sweet man though he was, all the bickering and lies and the constant danger of having your head chopped off made him very inflexible in his views about how life should be lived. Conservative to the point of delusional, he firmly believed that women were unable to do any job other than being married. This, despite his own mother being the Deputy Khipu-Camayacos at the time, and his second cousin Daisy being one of the engineers working on the Ballybolivia Lighthouse.

Heron had swept from the room after a disagreement, 'she can hardly be persuaded not to call it a fecking shovel'. It was perhaps as well all around that Heron became a judge.

McCabe rang Heron's doorbell and stepped instantly into her sitting-room. Heron was sitting neatly by her fire, a glass of brandy and a history book on a small table beside her. Her room was very pale and elegant, and a perfect setting for Heron herself, who had a taste for clothing with strongly coloured geometric designs, and whose rust-red hair had not yet acquired grey. She was as tall as he, with a bronze sheen to her eyes. She favoured her mother's side of her family and had inherited the same firm nose and pronounced cheekbones that had distinguished mother and grandmother alike.

Her brooches twinkled in the dimmed light as she got up to greet McCabe with a hug, and the brandy gurgled softly into a glass for him. Heron and he had been neighbours since she had taken up residence on her own farm, and their friendship had been cemented by the shared and unsharable perspective of immortality.

McCabe was always oddly comforted by Heron. He liked the way she modernised by subtle alterations to herself and to her house, making everything look both fresh and alive and yet fully lived in. Not for her the ceaseless replacement with everything that was new, nor the dogged clinging to everything that was original. Her house was full of things of immense age, inherited by her, left there by passing relatives and friends, borrowed and not yet returned; the harp left to her by her uncle was the model for the harp in the Muinbeo County Arms; the original Book of the Dragon had a home in her library; her portrait by de Lempicka hung in her bedroom.

These things were not on display. They were part of the way she lived, but so too were the clockwork games which she designed as a hobby and the two avatars she had to help her around the house. Heron made aging gracefully seem easy, which, over so many centuries, was a talent.

Heron had received an iris from Winter Sackville, to tell her that McCabe would need to talk about Sand Butler's conviction for fraud, and so she had asked her Forum scribe to get the files back for her from the Registry.[36]

'It was quite a straightforward case,' she said finally, putting the sheets down onto her vine-green lap, 'but between you, me and the wind, I was surprised at the time. Sand had no previous history of stealing so much as a paper-clip. Once she had seen all the accounts together, Fen would have had little difficulty in seeing what was going on. He was stealing from the senate. Small amounts – though I know that that is not the point. And it was clever – he had a scheme to over-charge people on one of their levies, and he took the difference.'

---

[36] The Forum scribe is an underpaid dogsbody who does all the jobs that none of the lawyers or judges want to do. The benefit is supposed to be that the experts, free from all the demands of everyday life, can talk to the scribe about the cases they worked on, how they made their decisions and how they persuaded a jury. The unlucky scribes got landed with lawyers who wanted nothing more than an easy life and predictable cases and who could not string a sentence together even if they were given some string and a sentence-stringing guide with pictures. Heron's scribe – whom she called Young Wolf, as he was a descendant of an earlier scribe, Cynewulf – was lucky that Heron not only loved a good, juicy, complicated case that she could get her fangs into, but could talk for Ireland.

'And for small enough an amount that no one complained?'

'It was well judged. He never asked for so much that people would really have difficulty paying. Also he targeted certain types of people. He never tried it with anyone who had a lot of time on their hands, or who was careful about money. He went for people with jobs where you work odd hours, or people who paid their dues irregularly, who would be less likely to be very certain of what they owed.'

'Clever. Did it take long to prove?'

Heron shook her head and the tiger's-eye[37] clasp in her plait glimmered.

'He admitted it immediately. That was one of the things that puzzled me. He had never done anything like this before, and as soon as he was asked about it, he admitted to everything. He said he had run up a debt that he had not known how to pay back and he had discovered this ruse accidentally, having genuinely undercharged someone, and, when they sent a second cheque to make up the difference, he lodged the cheque as his own, distracted as he was by his personal worries.'

'What happened to him?' McCabe asked.

'Nothing much. The senate investigated, of course, but because he admitted it straightaway, and it was out of character, and his defence was that he acted irrationally due to over-work and stress, he kept his job. He paid it all back, and he was given a second chance.'

'What was the other thing that puzzled you?'

---

[37] Not actually a *tiger's* eye. But Heron did like to know what was going on behind her back.

'I never knew what he did with the money.' Heron set down her glass. 'Between you and me,' she said, 'I think he was being blackmailed. Fen thought so too.'

McCabe poured the last of his brandy into his mouth, held it there for a moment until the pungent aroma made his eyes water and swallowed. 'Did she know who?'

Heron shook her head. 'She helped Sand during the court case and she was a character witness for him. They were friendly afterwards. Fen thought someone was blackmailing Sand because, not only did he never seem to have any extra money, he stopped stealing just after his father died.'

McCabe put down the glass and rubbed his eyes. He did not think that there was a fish on the end of that line, but he would get Benson to check it out.

'I hear you have young Farsade as an apprentice,' Heron said, as a question.

'She was Bassett's,' he said with a sigh. 'With Bassett now joining our hairy brethren howling in the moonlight, Salmon needed a new despotes or the coven would take charge of her. When was the last time that we had a rogue werewolf in Muinbeo? Dunne could not have been more unlucky.'

'The coven never wanted Salmon to live on her own, did they?' Heron said, ignoring the question of Dunne's luck. 'They are never keen on the young ones living independently, though there's some adults shouldn't be left in charge of a knife and fork, never mind their own lives. Winter Sackville was very against young Farsade particularly not being placed with a coven.'

McCabe said nothing.

Heron, who could not read auras but who was very astute,

said, 'Was there something more to that? Does the Witch Sackville suspect something?'

McCabe said nothing but tipped his glass at Heron.

'Though Salmon's not actually on her own, is she?' Heron went on. 'She goes to tutoring like the other apprentices, so she has O'Buachalla, she's still in school, so there's the head-teacher – who is that these days? It'll come back to me – and the other staff. And she has the Goldsmiths as a foster-family. She's bright, isn't she?'

McCabe said, 'She's smart as paint. She's better off being apprenticed. And in any case, she has not only all the humans, she has Maccarrill.' He tipped his glass again at Heron.

Heron looked at him and her eyebrows crept slowly up towards her hair.

Knotty Down House, Rupert's Corner

Salmon never thought of Maccarrill as being her pet. He had been in her family for as long as she could recall, observing and advising in his acerbic way, doing exactly as he wished whenever and wherever he wished. He had a cage of sorts, a great polished tangle of wood and brocade cloth, which he decorated himself with bits and pieces of stones or paper or ribbons that took his fancy, and in which he usually ate and sometimes slept. When she came home from visiting her foster-family, while McCabe was playing board games with Heron and the two avatars, Salmon found Maccarrill asleep on the back of the settee. He had put on an audio-book to listen to, but his beak was already sunk down among his feathers even though the rich, plummy voice of the reader was still delivering a story of fog, frost and ghosts. Salmon tiptoed over to the book-speaker and took the pin out. The blue glow died away. The fluted brass horn folded itself neatly up and tucked itself between the dial – currently pointing to 'The Haunting of the Bridge' – and the slowly turning gears, and the whole gadget shut itself together like a book. Salmon slid the pin into the sprocket and put the reader on her bookshelf. She sat on the settee beside Maccarrill, leaning back against the big cushions and pulling the heavy throw over her knees.

Maccarrill opened one eye and inched over to perch by her shoulder. He was heavy, but ever since childhood, Salmon loved to fall asleep against his feathers, reassured by the steady beating of his tiny heart.

'How are you?' he said sleepily.

'Full as a duck,' she said happily, patting her stomach.

'Archer was cooking, then?' Maccarrill said and Salmon smiled.

'Maccarrill,' she said after a few moments, 'you know the way vampires don't have a reflection in the mirror? Well, McCabe and I were passing a mirror in Sparrow Maguire's house today. And when he was walking past, he had about six reflections. Why?'

Maccarrill said nothing for a few minutes but Salmon could hear the snap of his crest.[38]

---

[38] What? Well, yes, we *know* that African grey parrots do not, as a rule, have crests. As a rule, they don't sustain complicated conversations outside their own species, write verse and drink whiskey, either. Was the crest really the only thing that you noticed that suggested Maccarrill is not an ordinary parrot, if such a thing exists? Honestly.

Then he said, 'Have you ever seen McCabe's house?'

Salmon nodded without opening her eyes. 'It's that place near Templederry Woods, the cream brick one with all the gables and the orchard. I've never seen inside it, though.'

'Oh,' said Maccarrill and rustled his feathers. 'Then I am not sure that I can explain his reflection to you.'

Salmon opened her eyes and raised her head to look at him.

'Go back to sleep,' he said. 'When you understand more about yourself you will understand McCabe's reflection. In the meantime, get yourself to bed. You have to be up early for school tomorrow. Go on.'

Grumbling, Salmon went. A few hours later, Maccarrill flew up the stairs and perched on the end of her bed, watching. Salmon slept soundly, without moving, her moon-pale hair and her hand visible on the pillow, the rest of her buried under the blankets, invisible in the shadows. When he was certain that she was asleep, Maccarrill flew up into the attic, where Salmon kept her model of the network of portals that linked different points across Muinbeo.

Salmon had built the landscape on the suggestion of her foster-mother, starting it almost as soon as she arrived in Muinbeo. Berry had thought long and hard about how to occupy Salmon, to keep her from thinking only about her parents' death and the peculiarities of life in the Outland. Knowing that her foster-family were being kind to her, Salmon dutifully went along with the proposal but quickly found that Berry's idea, as with most of Berry's ideas, was flawless. She met innumerable people, when she was out walking, when she was in the model shop explaining what she was working on, when she went to the Registry to ask for aerial photographs. She got to know her foster-siblings, and the place where she lived. The landscape was laid out on a big table taken from one of Berry's workrooms, and Archer and Marigold helped make it, mainly from plaster and resin. Bow was good at art and he and she became friends over the paint pots. Adding the network of portals was Salmon's idea. Maccarrill helped her with that.

The portals themselves were signified by small metal funnels, about the size of golf tees. With Salmon asleep downstairs, and the moon still rising, Maccarrill walked over the map. After some thought, he grasped one of the funnels in his foot and pulled it out of the wood. The funnel rippled, as if it had just swallowed something very large. With a flash of pearl-grey light the parrot shrank, the gleaming mouth of the funnel gaped and, with a small starburst of ruby light, they both disappeared.

Chapter 3: Saturday

Third day of the full moon

Derrydrake School, the Doathain

Salmon was at her foster-house early the next morning, as Archer usually drove her to school, but this morning it was Berry who met her and asked her if she would mind going by horse instead.

'Archer's gone to town to get food and cat-litter and the like,' Berry explained. 'There is no one to take in poor Fen's pet cats and they need a home. You can take Tom here.'

Tom Mix was a small young grey horse with a white tail and a bristly grey and white mane. He stood patiently while Salmon scrambled and Berry heaved and, when Salmon was in the saddle, Tom looked behind him and then set off at a brisk trot towards Ballinpooka.

Five miles north of the town were the few square miles of Derrydrake Forest and near the western edge, where the ancient oaks and ash straggled into younger[39] beech and chestnut trees, was the Doathain. If you could see the Derrydrake forest from above – if, for example, you had been with Maccarrill as he flew over during the night to make sure that the school and its surroundings were still safe before Salmon arrived – you

---

[39] Relatively.

would see a long scar, where, centuries ago, something had ripped open the earth from the southern edge of the hill right up to the school itself. No one quite knew what had happened there, but it was known that whatever it was had shattered the original school to smithereens.

Consequently, the school had had to be rebuilt and this was done in the fashion of the day, with the main square building fronted with columns and flanked by long rectangular halls decorated with arches that glittered with many windows. The square building, topped with a dome, was where all the offices were, and where those teachers who lived in the Doathain had their rooms. The halls on either side held the teaching rooms, the laboratories and the eating-rooms, and each wing of the school finished in a tall, wide tower filled from cellar to widow's walk with books.

The people of the Doathain had carefully uprooted and replanted hundreds of trees to make room for the new school, and their own houses and workshops and barns, mostly undamaged by the – er – *accident*, were in a horse-shoe around three sides of the school. After some years the trees grew up again, shielding but not obscuring the buildings from sight.

Tom Mix trotted easily to the top of the Doathain hill, and turned in off the bridle-path that ran alongside the road, to the clearing where the high iron gates marked the boundary between Ballinpooka and the Doathain. The long narrow avenue was lined with rowan trees, winter-bare, and the pale yellow of the soft brick in which the school had been built was a faint, blurred glow through the morning fog. Salmon reached over and grasped a rung of the gate, burning cold on her bare hand, and it swung open. Tom Mix's hooves were nearly silent on the peaty path, and his breath made pearly billows as he trotted. The fog was too dense for Salmon to see much but she trusted Tom Mix's instincts, so when he slowed down and snorted Salmon dismounted and held the reins. Tom had sensed someone's presence. The fog seemed momentarily thicker. Salmon batted it away but it swirled, trailing opalescent colours and points of grey darkening like eyes. Tom Mix snorted again and tugged at the rein. He trampled the peat uneasily. The sudden rush of wings startled Salmon and she yelped in alarm but the figure that emerged, bundled up in brick-pink tweed and striped wool, was one of her fellow apprentices.

'This fog's mad, isn't it?' Velvet Corbuse said cheerily, her aura flickering canary-yellow. 'I can hardly see the end of my – nose. I didn't scare you, did I?'

'It's all right – the fog spooked Tom Mix, and that spooked me,' Salmon said.

The horse, placid again, trotted easily beside them as they walked to the school, Velvet and Salmon chatting idly.

The school had been rebuilt inside with marble and pale wood and a great many columns, to let in as much sunlight as one might hope to get in Muinbeo. The arches that lined the long corridors and all the large square schoolrooms were full of glass cases, guarded at a distance by imps and *luchrupán*s handy at throwing small thunderbolts, and displaying the remnants of thousands of years of life in Muinbeo. The side door to the school opened under the stairway which led from the public reception hall to the second gallery, where classes for the apprentices were held. As they reached the gallery floor, Velvet and Salmon stopped, as they always stopped, to look down at the array of history beneath.

The showcases with their pearly lights were ranged across the hall and along the walls were stands and plinths, all arrayed with treasures and gifts that were like family portraits from Muinbeo's past. There were chess sets and handbells, tiaras and tiny dragons in alabaster or horn. There were extravagant gifts from Merovingian kings and thoughtful ones from Carolingian monasteries. There were decorated satchels in leather from the Fir Bolg, a replica in bog-oak of the Derrydrake Boundary Stone, an artificial steel hand from the Fermorian kings. There was armour from Tír na nÓg, so thin that it wrinkled at the touch but protected the wearer from every weapon,[40] dishes and teapots from China that were so delicate it was said you could put one unnoticed on the back of a wren. On stands and in wall-niches were a fraction of the objects yielded up by the bogs of Muinbeo, lost or discarded by its inhabitants: bee bread and bog butter, damaged boats and dropped manuscripts, stolen silver and shattered canopic jars, a leather sickle, shopping lists and broken shoes, rings angrily flung away or sadly dropped, sacrificial bodies.

Like the old style of painting that tried to show everything in one picture, the entrance hall of the school contained some reminder of all times past, randomly packed together, without story or consequence. The hall, Hunter said, was an unfinished list of things that could be remembered about Muinbeo. All over the school the fragments of Muinbeo's past were collected, or replicated in stone and wood, in glass, in precious gems, in cloth – all shielded from air and sunlight and

---

[40] Except for Cuchullain's spear, naturally. Even the *sidh* have their limits.

damage by their cases and their protectors. But the thing that dominated the reception hall was not in a case at all, nor had it any imps or *luchrupán*s or thunder-bolts nor any protection at all. The Book of the Yew rested on a wooden lectern, the air around it thick and full of thread-like iridescent streams that eddied slowly. It was never possible to look quite directly at the Book of the Yew.

Even Velvet and Salmon, who were accustomed to looking at the blurs and fractures that surrounded the book, were soon dizzy. They turned away from the gallery railing and followed the sound of voices to the classroom.

All the classrooms and laboratories were built to the same design: small bright squares with high ceilings and a great many windows, a lectern in the middle and a semi-circle of chairs and writing desks around it. Bookshelves always lined at least one wall, and the other walls were free for whatever might be needed for the lesson – the molecules of the wall could simply be rearranged to create a screen, a painting-canvas, a telescope or a recreation of a submerged village.

Dr O'Buachalla had just begun the lesson as Salmon and Velvet hurried to the remaining seats.

'Sorry, ma'am,' Velvet said to O'Buachalla, 'we were looking at the museum.'

'That's what it's there for,' O'Buachalla said agreeably. 'Let's get started. Today's history lesson is about the history of history. Rainbow, take your head out of your hands, like a good lad. It's not going to hurt.'

Conger helped her to create a table out of the wall while Nefertiti and Bracken de Courcy brought some large boxes from the Library. O'Buachalla lifted off the lid off one while the dozen or so apprentices clustered around, leaning on their elbows and speculating as to what was inside. O'Buachalla lifted out a thick manuscript, bound between wooden covers.

'Listen to this story,' she said, 'and tell me what it says.'

The fog had thinned by the time the apprentices finished their lessons and went their separate ways. Conger was going skating with his brother Shadow, who was waiting for him in the clearing behind the bicycle-shed. They were alike enough to be taken for twins.

'Where are you going?' Bracken asked. 'Down to Greenmill Lake?'

Bracken was small and slight, but very robust, and even now, in the biting, frosty fog, he wore no coat over his jeans and jumper, just a hat and a scarf. He had coppery-brown skin and his hair, squashed down by the thick felt of his hat, curled tightly.

Conger shook his head. 'Shadow was down by Aber Bridge yesterday. It's perfect for skating, frozen all the way down towards Frenchman's Lot – we'll nearly be home that way.'

'Good luck to you,' Bracken said. 'Too energetic a way for me to spend a free morning.'

Shadow laughed and said, 'If half of what Conger tells me is true, you spend all your free time thinking up mischief.'

Bracken faked outrage. 'What has Conger been telling you? Every word a lie, no doubt.'

'He tells me you are a veritable Puck,' Shadow said.

Bracken laughed and nodded. 'Can't deny it.'

Conger and Shadow disappeared amongst the trees.

Marigold had brought her running clothes with her, counting on her brother to take her books home for her on the bus, but Rainbow, uncharacteristically enthusiastic after the history lesson, wanted to go to the library. Marigold was torn between wanting to encourage her brother's only known sign of enthusiasm for learning and wanting to be able to take a run. She was most relieved when Salmon received an iris from McCabe.

'Since I have to go to Dr Gentileschi's office now,' Salmon said to Rainbow, 'why don't you take Tom Mix? You can easily carry your own books and Marigold's, and you can stable him behind the library while you study.'

'I'll be back later than you then,' Rainbow warned Marigold, 'so don't be getting mad at me because you have to wait for your books.'

'That's all right,' Marigold said, jogging from foot to foot. 'If I'm back first I'll be there to revive Mammy when she passes out from the shock of hearing that you went to the library without being dragged there by the ear.'

'Well, it was an interesting class,' Rainbow protested, taking his sister's bag.

'Thank you for that assessment,' Dr O'Buachalla said, unexpectedly behind him, so that they jumped. 'Not the most blinding compliment of my career but I suppose an improvement on your usual expression of bewilderment and despair at being in a schoolroom.'

'Bewil …? I don't look bewildered and despairing,' Rainbow said, with an effort at dignity. 'I find all your classes interesting.'

'Isn't he a lovely little liar?' Dr O'Buachalla said to Hunter and Nefertiti beside her.

Nefertiti looked sympathetically at Rainbow. She herself

was endlessly inquisitive and found everything fascinating, even the most routine of classes.

'You have far too expressive a face to get away with it,' Nefertiti said to Rainbow. 'I hope you weren't thinking of becoming a poker player. Or a spy.'

She said it so kindly that even Rainbow laughed.

'Hunter, are you joining us in the archives this afternoon?' Dr O'Buachalla asked, but Hunter shook his head.

'Not today. Apprentice Fenton is working this afternoon I have to go to a lecture.'

'Oh, of course,' said Dr O'Buachalla. 'The Komnenos is visiting today, isn't that right? I'm afraid I'd forgotten you were a sombrist.'

Hunter, astonished but not displeased that anyone had forgotten he was a member of that small and unpopular group, nodded.

'I was invited to visit some years ago,' Dr O'Buachalla went on, 'when the Komnenos – the previous one – was giving a lecture on law. Of course, Heron Porphyrogenitus was there too – very interesting views on the medieval legal system.'

Hunter nodded, trying to look as though he thought that could be interesting.

'Though landscape is more your bag, isn't it?' O'Buachalla said. 'It is fortunate for Silvanus Hughes that your archives have such an extensive collection of maps.'

Marigold jogged off into the mist, Bracken had teaching practice, Rainbow saddled up Tom Mix, and Nefertiti and Dr O'Buachalla set off for the Killchryso Early History Archives, where Hunter worked. Hunter asked if he could join Salmon and Velvet on their way towards the town.

'I am obliged to pick up a cake from Battista's Bakery for the Komnenos's visit,' he said. 'And that is just beside the book-shop. What a happy coincidence!'

Nefertiti patted his arm sympathetically. The sombrists were very strict about reading material and approved only of a very few books. Hunter, who was a voracious reader, had to find excuses to spend time in libraries and bookshops. It was less his love of nature that made Hunter acquire an allotment and more the number of books he could hide in the shed that came with it.

Hunter, Salmon and Velvet set off, taking a shortcut through the edge of the woods.

'I suppose you can't really talk about Fen's murder,' Velvet said abruptly. 'I just wondered if there was any hint of who did it.'

'Not much,' Salmon said. 'There are odd little things that don't quite make sense but there's no telling yet – well, not by me at any rate – whether they will just have a simple explanation. She was your despotes?'

'Yes. Is it true that Detective McCabe would be coming around to see me this afternoon?' she asked anxiously. 'I don't know anything about what happened.'

'That's not the only reason for talking to people, though,' Salmon said. 'You knew Fen – she might have said something to you.'

'You mean about someone who might hate her enough to kill her?'

'Not exactly,' Salmon said, unsure of how she would explain what she meant. When Bassett Dunne explained things to her, they had always sounded convincing and complete, but crumbled away to vagueness when she tried to explain them to someone else.

'Whoever killed Fen might not have hated her but she might have known something that they were frightened she would tell. Say she said something to you, about, I don't know, someone she saw going to a meeting with a senator. That might only tell you that Senator X had a meeting with Mr Y. But if McCabe already knows something about Mr Y – so, say Mr Y told McCabe that he had never met Senator X at all, then you have *actually* told us something different to what you thought you told us. You've told us that they met, and that Mr Y did not want us to know it.'

Salmon stopped before she confused them both. It had sounded much better when Dunne explained it.

But Velvet's face brightened when Hunter said, 'It's like what Dr O'Buachalla was saying this morning. *What you say is not just what you say, it is also what is heard.*'

'So if you have pieces of a different jigsaw, then what I tell you makes a different picture. Isn't it gas how keen Rainbow was on the class today?'

Salmon was accustomed to the way Velvet tended to hop from subject to subject, like a bird in pursuit of seeds.

'He is very keen on journalism,' she said thoughtfully. 'I remember he was asking Berry about it after he read – you know that magazine that Cotton Donovan writes? That does the undercover investigations and mocks the senators?'

'*Pluck's Notebook*? I know it,' Velvet said. 'Fen used to read it so I saw it around the office. We had to hide it from Senator Woudes, though. She said that Donovan was taking huge risks by criticising the Pharaoh.'

'I don't think Ma thought Rainbow ought to be reading it either,' Salmon said, 'but *he* thought it was the cat's pyjamas.'

They had by this time reached the stile that separated the edge of the Doathain from the main road, and they clambered over, turning south towards the hospital.

Velvet's older brother Night was waiting for her at the side gate to the hospital, to give her a lift to their home in his steam-carriage. He was sitting on the wall reading a newspaper which he folded neatly into a square and tucked into his jacket when he jumped down to greet them. Night was taller than his sister, and though they looked quite alike, Night seemed more polished. His dark hair, tied back in a pony-tail, was sleeker, his nose more aquiline than beaky, and he was always immaculately turned out. Even in winter he had a light tan. It had faded from its hazelnut shades of summer and the scar on his lip, from a childhood encounter with the opposition in a hurling match, was less obvious. He was still in the uniform of the emergency response unit where he worked and from a pocket he fished out the keys to his steam-carriage. The carriage was second-hand and the clockwork in the fuel tank ran a little fast, despite the hours he had spent rebuilding it, so Night always insisted that his sister wore a helmet in case she fell out. Velvet was too fond of her brother to remark on his apparent belief that his own skull was immune to damage; she would not admit he had even so minor a fault as a little vanity.

As Night revved the engine and the gleaming silver flanks of the clockwork pony began to tense, Velvet took her big globe of a helmet off again and said to Salmon, 'There was just one thing I wanted to ask about Fen.'

Ballinpooka Hospital consisted of many thick stone buildings scattered over a wide area on the north side of the canal. The wards and recovery rooms were in the centre and had been added to over the centuries with glass and trees and stairwells so that people coming to see their family and friends would be cheered by the light and space, the mellow stone and the scent of flowers. The coroner's office, on the other hand, being where many of the cadavers were being examined, was kept discreetly to the side, behind some laurel trees. The fog was now entirely vanished but the glossy leaves of the laurels were still wet, and water trickled down Salmon's neck as she brushed past them, making her way around some delivery vans parked near the entrance.

The coroner's offices were two large rooms that faced onto the road. The mortuary discreetly took up most of the back half of the building's lower level, and the offices were populated by brisk medics, efficient administrators and druids or Page Coven witches who, having a dull moment up on the top floor of the warehouse, had wandered down for a coffee and a chat.

Ishka Gentileschi perched on her desk while McCabe and the quaestor stood a little apart, conferring, and she winked at Salmon. The coroner had a much more cheerful air than you might expect of someone who cut up bodies for a living. She had a Scottish accent and Italian forebears and looked – apart from having shortish hair – like a heroine from a pre-Raphaelite painting. This amused McCabe. Gentileschi was probably the least fragile and emotional human he had ever met, and he knew that the long muslin tunics she wore were for practical, if messy purposes in the dissection room.

The office was full of anatomy – happily, all of it made from plaster and wood and wire. Every available surface had reconstructions of bodies and faces. Everywhere there were small, serious-faced imps working diligently at building up bodies just to take them apart to show the effects of careless driving or the foolish use of a carving knife. Inside gleaming glass domes, other sprites worked on large models of tiny vessels and cells, wielding tools that glittered and sparkled and sent out vanishing beads of light, to show the effect of disease.

When the quaestor and the guardian saw that Salmon had arrived, they stopped their talk.

'Well, poor Fen Maguire, then,' Gentileschi said. 'The cause of death is clear. She was stabbed, once, right through the chest.' She pulled forward a tall glass case, in which a model of Fen, a perfect replica, revolved slowly. The model stared glassily ahead as she turned. The imps had made replicas of her clothes, and in an overcoat, scarf, hat and gloves, replica-Fen looked as though she was about to step out into a winter's night. 'She was struck here.' Gentileschi pointed and the model's chest turned green and transparent, allowing them to see the passage of the weapon, and damaged internal organs. 'She was facing whoever killed her.'

Finney peered at the green lights. He drew a breath and Gentileschi, who felt that you were never too young to know about disease but who never felt happy about showing violent injury to apprentices, winked at Salmon again, adding, as the quaestor moved closer to the model, 'I don't know exactly what kind of weapon, but it was long and smooth and it tapered. It was also flat.'

'Not a knife, though?' Finney said. 'Otherwise you would have said so.'

'We found some – organic matter,' Gentileschi said, with a quick glance at Salmon. 'We're analysing it now. Whatever was used, it grew, it wasn't made.'

'Did she die immediately?' Salmon said.

Gentileschi shook her head slowly. 'Not immediately. Her hands and knees and elbows all show signs that she dragged herself some small distance – cuts, bruises, gravel in the wounds, probably matching with the surface she crawled upon, and dirt and grass under the fingernails of the hand that had lost its glove. She had bruising on her left knee and a small bone was broken in her right hand. Looks like she tried to stand and fell.'

Gentileschi stopped and looked at Salmon sympathetically.

McCabe stared at the desk and tried not to think of Fen crawling in the dark, knowing she was dying. In some ways, he could barely conceive of death. He had no sense of natural demise. Hereditary vampires – those who inherited a vampire gene and were not created from being bitten – were not literally immortal, but they had had their origin in a world where time moved differently. Every second of their life lasted years, a decade of a human life. Even if they lived in the human world every fibre of their being was still part of that other world. In the same way as all humans seemed to him to be immeasurably young, even those who were now too old to walk or to talk, their lives seemed short as a gadfly's. For such a brief and flickering light to be snuffed out precociously was, he felt, a tragedy that should itself be mourned. He heard Salmon blow out a little breath.

'You know that the body was moved,' he said, and Gentileschi nodded.

'I guessed as much,' she said. 'The ground where she was found did not match the soil and debris we found on her body. Where was she actually killed? Somewhere out in the open?'

'On Casey's Lane – you know, through Cluancorr. Was she dead when she was moved? Would she have lived if she had been left alone?'

Gentileschi shook her head. 'No. Unless the Patriarch himself was on the spot instantly, given the damage to her heart and lung, the blood loss – she couldn't have lived.'

McCabe nodded, looking grim.

Salmon said, 'Sir? What about the paw prints?'

'Good point,' McCabe said, as though he had forgotten it, 'good point. Dr Gentileschi, paw prints were found in the vicinity of where we think the murder actually happened, near the allotments.'

'So what are you thinking? Erubian hound? Werewolf?'

'Salmon? What are we thinking?'

They all turned to look at her.

After a moment, to McCabe's intense relief, Salmon said, 'Well, sir – an Erubian hound does not use a weapon, other than teeth. And though werewolves will use a weapon that comes to paw, there are no known cases of them seeking someone out to harm them. If the paw prints had anything to do with it, I think we are looking for a dimorph.'

Gentileschi opened her eyes wide. 'Oh, dear,' she said. 'As if their reputation is not bad enough.'

The quaestor stayed in the office to talk to the coroner about arrangements for the funeral, while McCabe and Salmon went outside.

As soon as the door shut, Salmon said, 'Sir, we didn't find any parcels or packages on the body. I was talking this morning with Velvet Corbuse. She works – *worked* – with Fen. She said that Fen mentioned that she had to go and collect something that was being delivered for her.'

'Did she? Well, now,' McCabe said, stopping to ponder. He could see the body in his mind's eye, empty hands, empty pockets. He recalled no basket, no bag, nothing that had been carried away.

'She didn't know what it was. We were just on our way back from school so I couldn't ask many questions.'

'Not to worry,' McCabe said. 'We can ask her when we interview her. Come on. We will take a tunnel back to the offices. I want you and Benson to go to the Maguires' house to see what you can see.'

There was a network of tunnels under Ballinpooka as well as the portals that were all across Muinbeo, so that vampires and others who did not like strong lights could move about during the day. The tunnels were large enough that no one would feel cramped and lamps and light-giving plants kept away the gloom. None the less they were not entirely pleasant, and had about them always a faint scent of earth and dampness, and there was a metallic taste to the air.

'Sir?' Salmon said hesitantly, as she trotted along to keep up with McCabe. 'Sir – do you know where Deputy Dunne is?'

McCabe eyed her, uncertain of how best to answer.

'It's just – I sent him an iris this morning, and it came back to me saying he wasn't in the hospital any more. And Hunter

Sessaire said that they had had some witches and werewolves in to the archives, trying to find out more about rogue werewolves because one was seen – well, heard, howling, on the Gallagrene Bog. So – you know – I was just wondering …'

'You think Dunne might be the rogue?'

'Well,' Salmon said rather unhappily, as she was fond of Dunne, 'he has never been a werewolf before. He might not know what he is supposed to do.'

'Try not to worry about him,' McCabe said. 'Everything that can be done for him will be done.'

'I did try not to worry but it isn't as simple as that,' Salmon said, and she went pink when McCabe looked surprised at her tone. 'Sorry, sir, I mean, but he was my teacher. I can't just not know.'

McCabe was quiet for a moment. As they reached the stairs from the tunnel into the entrance of the guardian station, he stopped and said, 'All right. I was not supposed to tell you, but he escaped from the hospital. You have heard about the unidentified werewolf on the Gallagrene Bog. There was also an attack by a rogue werewolf, in the same area, beyond Hawkswood.'

'What does "rogue" mean? I thought werewolves were just werewolves.'

McCabe rarely answered questions immediately. Salmon waited as McCabe slowly climbed two steps of the stairs, and then he stopped.

'What do we hope to have done by the end of this murder investigation?'

'Catch the murderer.'

'Why?'

Salmon suddenly feared that McCabe was having some sort of ethical crisis where he stood.

'People can't just go around murdering each other,' she said.

'Because it's illegal?'

'Because it's wrong!'

McCabe nodded slowly.

'Exactly. Everyone – humans, elephants, vampires, werewolves, we all know what we mean by *wrong* or *unfair* or *outrageous*. A rogue decides that they are above all that. They only know what they want. Werewolves are *able* to be violent, to attack, to bite and kill, but they don't. Rogues can and they do.'

'So there is a werewolf roaming about,' Salmon said, 'with a violent nature and no inclination to restrain itself. And Dunne is all of a sudden a werewolf but we don't know *where* he is. We know that there is a werewolf near Hawkswood but we don't know *who* it is. So Dunne might be the rogue.' After a pause Salmon added, unconvinced, 'Are there really likely to be two unknown werewolves?'

'Well, now,' McCabe said, 'to my mind, that begs the question of who it was attacked Dunne in the first place, during the last full moon, a month ago. It has to have been a werewolf.'

Salmon did not like to say that she saw no connection between the two questions at all. Instead she said, 'Sir? What would happen if a person who was a dimorph committed murder but they did it while they were in animal form?'

McCabe looked at her. 'You have a convoluted mind, apprentice,' he said.

'But what *would* happen?' she persisted. 'Could they say that they were not guilty because they were an animal at the time?'

McCabe sighed. 'You'd need to talk to one of the Aristotle Coven for a real answer,' he said.

'Why Aristotle?'

'Ethics, girl, ethics,' said McCabe impatiently. 'Anyway, most of us find everyday ethics hard enough without indulging in speculation.'

Salmon was quiet. She was not sure if he was annoyed at the question. But her natural inquisitiveness got the better of her. 'Have we many dimorphs in Ballinpooka?' she said, carefully closing the trapdoor. 'As far as you know?'

McCabe shook his head, because he did not know how best to answer. They were in the anteroom to the reception hall of the senate buildings, where the Registry of Records, the senate and the guardians all worked. He watched citizens of Muinbeo waiting, talking, asking questions of the receptionists. He watched hands roll up papers and slip them into the overhead baskets to be sent to the filing room, the long fingers of the filing sprites tap reference numbers onto glimmering buttons, and he watched the baskets scoot along the filing wires, swaying gently. Just inside the door, the postal pipe, attached to the underground pneumatic postal service, pulsed gently with an almost endless stream of letters and telegrams. The whole world, visible and invisible, sending messages and signals, dropping hints. He did not like to tell other people what to think.

Dimorphs appeared to be human but they could turn into another animal at will, and that ability to metamorphose was an outrage to the minds of most people in Muinbeo. It was thought to be a perversion of the acceptable divides between species, a warped evolutionary cul-de-sac. McCabe did not see the truth of this himself, but he was old enough, and had worked in the Outland often enough, to know that a great many sentient species everywhere had some apparently random trigger that made them unable to think.[41] He had seen it many times and had long since ceased trying to work out the pattern. Over centuries he had seen perfectly normal people suddenly up on their hind legs announcing that this or that sort of person – vampires, for example – was going to cause the end of civilisation and not noticing that civilisations rose and fell on a regular basis for altogether different reasons. *Sentient my backside*, McCabe had thought, many times, but an apprentice's master, he felt, should teach the apprentice, not what to know, but how to think; not what was true and what was false, but how to figure out the difference.

'Over the years, of course, yes, we have had dimorphs in Ballinpooka,' he said, 'and in Cronna and Linnenshee and all over Muinbeo. At any given time you can't tell how many, or where they are.'

'Is it really true that you can tell if a person is a dimorph, just by looking? That they don't really look just like us?'

McCabe was amused. Salmon Farsade saying *just like us.* 'Salmon, all I can say is that even in all my lifetime I have never known by looking – I only knew if I was told, or I saw a person change. The question is not so much *Can you tell?* as *Do you care?*' Then he said, '*Do* you care?'

---

[41] Make long angry speeches and occasionally set fire to people, yes. Think, no.

Salmon shrugged. 'I don't know. I can't say I've thought much about it. But people at home sometimes rowed about them. It wasn't really to do with whether it was right or wrong to change species, though. It – well, people thought that the dimorphs were caused by experiment.'

McCabe looked at her thoughtfully. 'That old chestnut,' he said. 'What did you hear?'

Salmon scratched her head. There had been so many arguments, so much talking, about so many different things, with so many people talking all the time, at the same time. On the one hand, she felt that since she had heard and read so much – miles of details, mountains of examples – she ought to understand everything about everything in the Outland. On the other hand, all the details, and all the answers to questions, did not seem to equal any understanding at all, any more than counting grains of sand is a map of a desert.

'Some people said that the Pharaoh had taken prisoners and did experiments on them, to make them turn into animals. They said that it was so he could have a different kind of army, one that no one knew how to fight. And people said that the dimorphs – the people who became dimorphs – had offered to have the experiments done, because they secretly supported the Pharaoh. And maybe if people here believe that, they think that the dimorphs will lead the Pharaoh's army to Muinbeo.'

McCabe nodded slowly, thinking about the versions he had heard of the same tales; much more subtle, much more complex and much more frightening.

He said, 'It will take more than a couple of part-time horses or hounds to let the Pharaoh and his army into Muinbeo.

I think that you are right but I think that there must be something else behind the way that people hate dimorphs. Dimorphs are a sign of something people do not want to see.'

They began to walk up the back stairs, out of the sunlight. There was no trace of the morning fog now, and the sun was warm and full, though they knew the breeze was still icy.

'People accept werewolves,' he said.

'Yes,' Salmon said thoughtfully. 'But that's not the same. They are always werewolf. They are just more wolf than person at the full moon. The rest of the time they are more person than wolf. But it's always there.'

'But we are still talking about changing form. A werewolf changes from a person into a wolf. A dimorph changes from a person into an animal. What really is the difference?'

'A werewolf is not really a person? They don't move the same way as humans do, they don't speak the same. You couldn't mistake a werewolf for a human, even at the new moon, unless you have never seen a wolf. Like vampires. It isn't always full display and fangs all around but – er – um. Yes.'

She trailed off, suddenly remembering that McCabe was a vampire and she was not sure of his sense of humour.

'Yes, well,' McCabe said, amused, 'I see your point. 'But we are still talking about changing form. One coin, two sides. Why is a werewolf acceptable and a dimorph an outcast?'

Salmon cast about in her mind to think of an analogy. She failed.

'I haven't the faintest idea.'

'Well, tuck the question behind your ear for later. The ethics class is over. Benson – good. You've saved us a flight of stairs.'

Benson emerged from the main guardian office on the

third floor, straightened his tie and tucked in his shirt and began a slow jog down.

'Got your iris, sir,' he said, stepping behind Salmon to get to the coat stand. 'Where's next?'

'I want you and Salmon to go to Fen's house now and see what you can see. Take a carriage, it's quicker.'

Benson finished putting on his sleek camel-hair coat and took down his gloves. McCabe told him what the coroner had said as they began to descend back to the anteroom.

'Dimorphs, is it?' he said, when McCabe told him they were sure that the prints seen by Hunter Sessaire were not a usual animal. 'Hmph. That just completely complicates an already extremely confused case.'

'Maybe a dimorph killed her when they were in animal form?'

'A single stab through the chest, sir? We're looking for what then – a crazed unicorn? Sir, at best this means we have a witness we can't question. I don't think it helps otherwise. I'll note it, though.'

He held up the trapdoor lid so that McCabe could take a tunnel back to Cluancorr.

'Sir?' he said. 'Sir, I wouldn't mention the dimorphs to Johnston. I mean – well, sir, I know a factotum is not a high-grade job but it's pretty powerful, unofficially. And we don't want anyone stirring people up against dimorphs, saying they'll all murder us in our beds.'

'Finney trusts him,' McCabe said evasively. The yellowish mottle on Benson's aura dimmed and he made a twisted face that could have meant anything from 'You're the superior officer' to 'Then he's an idiot.'

'I know Johnston's views on dimorphs,' McCabe said. 'We will keep it to ourselves.'

McCabe disappeared into the dark.

Benson and Salmon went out the service door and around to the guardian stables where they could get a mechanical carriage. Salmon had been shocked to find that it was Johnston, easygoing, peaceable and quick-witted, who shared the popular disdain of dimorphs. To her real astonishment, it was the usually intolerant and confrontational Benson who said that if anyone could transform into an animal it was their business, not his, and if he could do it, it would be his favourite party trick. Salmon climbed into the carriage and Benson typed the address into the key-pad in the neck of the mechanical horse – Night Corbuse would have been jealous, Salmon thought – and he frowned silently over his notes as they travelled.

The Mirror House

The Mirror House was a curious house. It was a plain two-storey building built of pinkish brick, with black timbers supporting a white-plastered upper floor, as was the fashion in the sixteenth century. It was built in the shape of a T, with a door and chimney at each end, and a large garden all around, crammed with herbaceous borders, knot gardens and hazelnut trees. Built at McNaspy's Cross, the house had been a country retreat for a mirror-maker – an Outlander – and a glove-maker who set up home together. They quarrelled so bitterly, for reasons that no one now knew, that the one declared they could not bear to see even the other's reflection, and the quarrel lasted until they died.

A mulberry hedge sheltered the garden from the traffic going west towards Athenaeum or south towards Shanmullan and the porch was flanked by two bay trees. Benson rang the doorbell, and, as arranged, Sugar Henry opened it.

'Sugar,' Benson said, flicking open his identification, although he and Sugar knew each other quite well, 'this is Apprentice Salmon Farsade.'

A physicist at the Possible Institute, Sugar was a square-faced, round-headed man with black-and-white hair and fair, pock-marked skin. He was wearing a dark grey woollen suit and to the shoulder he had pinned mourning ribbons of dark violet. He shook hands with Salmon as though he was afraid he would break her and smiled kindly.

The hallway of Fen Maguire's house was light and spacious. The floor was tiled in red and green, a narrow stairs curled up against the wall and onto the upstairs landing, newspaper protected the carpet from dirt on the soles of the shoes and boots on the shoe-rack tucked into the corner on the left. Light from the porch's large square windows fell onto the pale pine of the banisters and on the light-coloured walls, showing up no dirt except a little dust gathered in the cloth petals of flowers in a floor-vase at the foot of the stairs. There was a small shelf with a little brass owl on it in a high corner by the stairs.

Sugar shut the door behind them and Benson opened the door on the left. It was a large sitting room, with a settee, armchairs, a table and some bookshelves. Fen had not had adventurous taste in books but evidently she read a great deal, and much of what they found was in Old Greek, her second language; Benson saw that she had translations into

Old Greek of many popular mystery stories from Muinbeo.[42]
Besides books and newspapers there was a very modern music
centre, mahogany and brass all polished to a high sheen and
closed over with pearl pins, folded neatly away in a corner.
There was an open fire and a wide hearth and a few paintings.
A dresser in light wood stood against the wall opposite the
door, and on the top of the cabinet underneath was a carving
of an owl taking flight, made of polished bog oak, with some
candles on a strip of brown velvet around it. The room looked
lived-in but well kept. Furniture, fittings and possessions were
worn, but nothing was broken or neglected.

Sugar led them down the hall, through the passageway that
joined the two sides of the house, and into the kitchen, which
took up the entire rear ground floor. The kitchen was well
stocked. There were some home-made meals in the freezer,
dishes washed and on the draining board, the whole area
clean but a little untidy. Honey Brown was at the big white
butler's sink, washing some pieces of crockery. Honey was an
amanuensis, which was how she knew Fen, and worked for the
Academy of Scientific Committees, which was how she knew
Sugar. She was small and wiry and buck-toothed, with untidy
light brown hair and her front teeth overlapped each other,

---

[42] Even Salmon, who did not know that *Hē Atopos Gephyra* was *The Weird
Bridge*, or that *To Chlōron Prasinon* was *The Green Shroud*, recognised the
familiar Art Deco style illustrations familiar to fans (such as Salmon)
of that well-known author.

Oh. Evidently not that well known. All right then, the author is
called Daisy Caius.

making her lisp slightly. Fen's three cats, two grey Burmese and a soot-faced, blue-eyed Siamese tom, were sidling and mewling around Honey's legs.

'I haven't touched anything apart from the dishes,' she said to Benson. 'We just fed the cats, and made sure that everything was switched off, the pipes hadn't frozen or anything.'

'I'm sorry about this,' Benson said. 'You must have known Fen well.'

Honey nodded and tears rolled down her face, but she didn't seem to notice.

'We trained together,' she said. 'We've been friends since then. It's been years now. I can't believe this. A hideous thing to happen.'

'You can't think of anyone who might want to harm Fen?' Benson said gently. 'She didn't mention anyone – anyone unusual, anything strange?'

Honey was shaking her head.

Behind them, Sugar said, 'She mentioned Senator Woudes was being more difficult than usual, but it was just work stuff.'

'She didn't say there was anything wrong – she wasn't worried?' asked Benson.

'No,' Honey answered, 'just busy. You know how it gets before an election – they all start looking for attention, making it look like they are doing lots of work.'

'You have a low opinion of our senators?'

Honey shrugged. 'Not especially. But there is too much room for people like Woudes. She's lazy and people only voted for her because they remember when her grandmother was a senator and they think that the family will all be as good. I only know Woudes a little, but she is on the Agricultural

Development Committee, and they often have meetings with different scientific committees.'

'We won't take too long to look around the house,' Benson said. 'Salmon, go upstairs and start going through each of the rooms. Don't touch anything unless you have to, and tell me immediately if you see anything at all that makes you think twice.'

Salmon obediently left, touching her pocket to make sure she had brought her notebook, her pencil and a thumb-sized camera. Halfway up the stairs she stopped and peered down into the kitchen. Benson was perched on the edge of a chair at the table, notebook open in front of him, and Honey and Sugar were sitting opposite. Sugar had one of the Burmese in his lap, the other was sitting pointedly on Benson's notebook and the Siamese tom was cleaning itself.

Out of sight, Salmon stared at the floor, concentrating, her mind focusing on anything in the house that sounded out of tune, anything that she could see in her mind's eye that stood out, had a dark line around it, had an aura that did not arise from the house. This was how her mother had taught her to listen to inanimate things, how her father taught her to sense every separate presence in a place. She moved silently, without hearing, from room to room, questions resolving themselves when she was close enough to see objects more clearly. She followed the scent-images under beds, among scattered clothes and shoes, fallen down behind furniture, until finally she found one thing that remained unexplained. She picked it up and looked at it, and found more questions, not fewer.

'Who is it from?' Benson said when she showed him what she had found.

'Well, that's just it, sir,' she said. 'Look. The message has been sent from the Gallagrene Group to Senator Albright, and then it was sent on again to Fen. But it wasn't sent to Fen from Senator Albright. The space for the sender's name is blank.'

Benson shot her a look and took the iris slough from her hand. He had never heard of such a thing.

'This is insane. This goes to the Deputy Khipu-Camayacos,' he said. 'If she doesn't know the answer Dr Boru will certainly want to know that there is a question. Honey, what is the Gallagrene Group? Do you know it? Did Fen mention it?'

Honey was shaking her head. 'No,' she said. 'Since the Gallagrene Bog is sacrosanct to many people, the Ghillies of Demeter look after it. I know that they have different sections to take care of different parts of the bog – the flora and fauna, the waterways, the pathways, so on, so forth – but that's all.'

'Maybe that friend of Fen's might know,' Sugar said. 'You know, the chap she used to call the Green Man?'

'That's a thought,' Honey said. 'Shear Amberson. He's a ghillie – he should know. And he was a good friend of Fen's, I'm sure he'd love to be able to help.'

Main guardian rooms, Senate Chambers

Benson went to talk to McCabe as soon as they got back to the guardian station, while Salmon took everything that they had removed from Fen's house to the evidence room so that the registrar could list it. There wasn't much, she thought sadly. She had hoped that the key to Fen's death would somehow be there, and be obvious. But there was just the iris slough, a recipe that had been lying out by the cooker and a small calendar in which Fen had written some notes and phone numbers.

McCabe's first action was to bring the iris slough to Copper Boru and ask her how it had managed to be sent without a sender. His second was to ask Salmon to tell him which was the most important ingredient in Fen's recipe.

The room of the Deputy Khipu-Camayacos, Senate Chambers

Copper Boru was the Deputy Khipu-Camayacos[43] and every dot of information in Muinbeo, one way or another, went through her office and very probably through her hands. She was a polyglot, thorough down to the last letter, and relentless in pursuing any question that had not been answered to her satisfaction. Dr Boru possessed not only a beady glare but a steely exterior which Salmon was quite certain did not conceal a kindly soul or heart of gold. Her feeling about this was reinforced by Boru's aura which, unusually, flickered with iridescence. The sight of her angular handwriting filled the hearts of her colleagues with either relief or trepidation, depending on whether the Registry had found what they were seeking or was sending officers to pursue the miscreant who had lost it. Dr Boru wore her auburn hair brushed sleekly back from her face and secured

---

[43] The use of the term 'deputy' might suggest that the *actual* Khipu-Camayacos was more influential than the deputy. In theory this is true. In practice ... well. The Khipu-Camayacos really is a bit of a mystery. It certainly exists, but that is all that we can say for certain about it. No one knows anything more. Apart from Copper Boru, of course. You can ask her if you like. You still won't know.

in the nape of her neck in a bun, in which glinted the decorated tips of the hairpins. She had smooth pale-gold skin, a narrow nose, and the corners of her dark brows curved up while the corners of her mouth turned down, giving her the overall air of someone who has just heard the most outrageous lie and wasn't born yesterday, thank you very much. She had a habit also of unexpectedly opening her large eyes very widely, and people who found themselves looking up into the dark green depths often were overcome with the impulse to confess to crimes and misdemeanours of which they were entirely innocent.

McCabe had known Boru too long to be unnerved by her, though he was sure that not even he knew the full truth about the Khipu-Camayacos or the Medon, spinning slowly above their heads. Boru wore a peat-brown velvet dress and a large sun motif pendant along with, characteristically, a patterned shawl, as the office was often chilly.

'There are not many things I have never seen before, McCabe,' she said grimly after examining the iris slough. 'An intriguing enigma indeed.'

Dr Boru's office was on the top floor of the senate buildings, and McCabe sometimes wondered if it was really there or if, like the spare room that Sparrow Maguire kept in her attic, the office existed in several different places. It never seemed to look quite the same any time he saw it. Today, Dr Boru's walnut wood desk was near one of the two east-facing windows and thin winter sunlight fell across it and onto the gleaming keys of the Rosetta Stone, the typewriter that could produce any language by a rearrangement of the keys. One wall of the office was entirely covered by the glass-fronted iris exchange, where the multicoloured lights of the irises flashed while they waited their turn to speed away into the ether with a message. The opposite wall was covered by bookshelves, and, in spaces among the books, there were small plants, a few heads carved in marble and one or two large and intricately painted vases. Near the door was an elegant bow-legged table with a porcelain tea service on it, from which Boru and Velvet Corbuse had been having tea while going through the mound of paperwork required to transfer Velvet's apprenticeship from Fen Maguire to Dr Boru. Behind them was a coat stand, draped with cloaks and shawls and scarves. In the middle of the room, in the centre of the rug that covered almost the entire floor, stood the only thing that suggested 'registry' to Salmon – a cabinet of drawers. It reached almost to the ceiling and housed innumerable index cards.

Dr Boru had no chairs, and her desk was tall and slanted so that she could write and read standing up. She rested her elbow on the lip of the desk for a moment, tapping the iris slough thoughtfully. Then she moved away and stood beside McCabe, frowning down at Salmon, raising her eyebrows as though wondering what exactly Salmon was. Salmon could not resist the impulse to straighten her waistcoat. Dr Boru merely looked away and went over to the iris exchange and plucked a glowing bead from a slot. It unfurled itself into a roll of silk paper and handed to Boru a stylus full of dew ink.

'I have some points of reference,' Boru said, 'some co-ordinates to plot out deductions as to who might be the sender. But I would rather have some facts. What was the name of –?'

'Sugar Henry, Dr Boru.'

Boru looked again at Salmon and then at McCabe. Out of Salmon's sight, McCabe raised one eyebrow.

'Indeed,' said Boru, writing swiftly. 'Well, a physicist at the Possible Institute is more likely to be able to say how this …' Dr Boru stopped speaking, looking unseeingly into the corner of her office. Then, dismissing the thought, she continued, 'How this – *miracle* was achieved.'

She finished writing, the iris rolled itself up, unfurled its wings, and its rear end glowed crimson as it sped away.

'The other question on the horizon,' Boru said, coming back to stand beside McCabe and eyeing Salmon carefully, 'is what exactly – or even roughly – is the Gallagrene Group. I have never heard of it, I've never seen records from it, I don't know who is the amanuensis. How can we know what it is?'

'That's not a good sign,' McCabe said.

Boru nodded. 'I'm glad you appreciate that fact,' she said. 'I don't know the nature of this particular storm cloud but I know it is not good.'

Her tone of voice suggested it would not be too good either for whoever was discovered to be keeping secrets from the Deputy Khipu-Camayacos.

'Thank you for putting it on my radar,' Boru said. 'Is there anything else?'

'No, not for the moment,' McCabe said. 'We are in pursuit of a fish. Good day, Dr Boru.'

After McCabe and Salmon had left, Velvet finished scribbling the notes she was making of Boru's instructions and her new despotes was moving quietly and swiftly through the office, clearing the surfaces and closing the doors.

Velvet said, 'Dr Boru? What exactly is the Khipu-Camayacos?'

Boru pulled the leather cover back from a glass-topped display case, slipped one of the small manuscripts into the case and closed the lid. As she replaced the cover, she said, 'That is a good question, Velvet. Not *who*, but *what*.'

Velvet put down her pen. Her heart was thumping. She had not realised how strongly she wanted to understand.

'To understand ...' Boru started and then stopped. 'It is important to understand perspective,' she said instead, 'to understand the landscape you stand in, to understand the changes you will see.'

Boru rubbed her eyes and with her other hand she made a pinching movement, as though she was plucking something from the air. Which indeed she was, and she set down the little egg cup on a table that suddenly appeared. The table apparently came with its own chalice, into which a medium-sized boxer dog could have comfortably settled.

'You are a clever person, Velvet,' Boru said, 'and this is you compared to me,' and she put the egg cup in front of the chalice.

'Really? Wow!' Velvet said, faintly offended.

Boru ignored her tone. 'And this ...' – she picked up the enormous chalice – 'is me compared to the Khipu-Camayacos.' The table seemed also to come with its own universe: it unfolded itself endlessly, plane after plane, layer after layer, of darkness, of stars and planets, of galaxies, of the motionless depths of oceans, feverishly pulsing corpuscles and synapses, of single, almost-familiar images flashing past. Velvet put her hand over her eyes. She felt shaken and sick.

Boru said, 'You have not even seen the Khipu – you have seen a picture of my idea of the Khipu. And that is the effect that it has on you. What do you think being in the Khipu's presence would do? That is why it will be some long time before that happens. I am not keeping things to myself because I want to know secrets. It is not for pride, or power or status. It is because it is necessary.'

Velvet opened her eyes again. The sun had disappeared below the horizon and Boru had switched on some small lamps that gave a gentle, buttery glow.

'To answer your original question,' Boru said, sitting down beside Velvet, 'is beyond my powers. I do not know what the Khipu is, where she came from, or how.'

'She?' Velvet said, grateful for a recognisable fact.

But Boru shrugged. 'I think so, but what do I know? Insofar as she appears human, she appears female. The Patriarch may know more but these are not the kind of questions that get answered. I cannot describe her, nor explain her nature to you.'

Velvet was feeling better. Her ears no longer hummed and she was a normal temperature, rather than shivering and sweating at the same time.

Almost on impulse, she said, 'Does it have anything to do with the Doathain? That huge crack in the earth?'

Dr Boru said nothing for a few moments. Then she looked at Velvet and said, 'What makes you say that?'

'I'm not sure. I think I am just putting two mysteries together.'

'Unfortunately, two mysteries put together give, not an answer, but a single great mystery. Yes, certainly there is a theory that there is a connection. But when did that rent happen? Did something come to the earth or come out of the earth? What was it? Why was it? What will happen when we find out? Is that a rock we should even turn over? Welcome to your new job, apprentice.'

The butcher's shop, Mayflower Market, Butchers' Square, Ballinpooka

Cedar Cullen's shop[44] had been in Butchers' Square for many centuries, in what was now a covered courtyard full of market-stalls, restaurants, barbers, tailors and repair shops. The underground passage emerged just outside the entrance to the butcher's shop and, while Salmon went into the shop to tell Cullen that they needed to talk to him, McCabe took refuge from the last few drops of dim sunlight, by slipping through the wall in the small room between the shop and the butcher's home.

The back of the shop faced the canal. It had its own mooring wharf for the boats that brought carcases and fish and exotica for sale. The windows of Cullen's residence opened out over the canal at the back, and over the glossy plants and bright statues of the courtyard. The room was ordinary but very pleasant and had a screen to pull over the windows to keep out the sunlight. McCabe was sitting down reading through his notes when Salmon came back.

'It's busy in the shop,' she said, 'because he's closing on Monday on account of he's going to the hurling match in Cronna. He'll be a few minutes.'

'Who's playing?' McCabe asked.

---

44   Though not Cedar Cullen.

'Beltane Wanderers against Danaan Athletic.'

'I thought Athletic won two weeks ago?'

'They did,' Salmon said, as Cedar arrived, 'but it was found that one of Athletic's supporters had raised a plague of boils so the Wanderers couldn't train.'

'What can I do for you?' Cedar said, wiping his hands on his apron and sitting uneasily on the edge of his seat.

Cedar Cullen was almost six foot six in height but it did not seem to McCabe that it was either his height or his large hands and feet that made him clumsy. Usually Cedar had a vigorous grace in action, like an athlete. But it appeared that he sometimes simply forgot how to do some perfectly familiar action, like buttering bread or wrapping greaseproof paper around a cut of meat, and he fumbled and stammered it, until the physical memory came back to him and he could move once more in tune. He had a very open face, unlined and friendly, with amber-brown eyes, untidy brown hair, a neat beard and a tendency to breathe heavily through his mouth.

The conversation was stilted at first, Cedar clearly wishing to be helpful but unsure how. But Cedar had learned to know people by the meat and fish they ate, and Salmon noticed that his words began to flow as soon as McCabe asked about the fish. She also noticed the change in tone being recorded faithfully by McCabe's spiky pen.

'I felt really bad about it,' Cedar said as he came to the end of his account. 'She had placed her order in good time. It was my fault that I wasn't able to get what she wanted – I should have sent the order straightaway but ... ah, you know how it is. I got distracted. But she just said frozen would do as well as fresh and she could pick it up if I got it delivered to the canal stop. But she had to be there not a second later than six, because the delivery boat had a tight schedule.'

'What exactly was it that Fen had ordered from you?'

The guardian rooms, Senate Chambers

The guardian offices were part of the Senate Chambers, and, as they climbed up the stairs to the third floor, Salmon and McCabe could hear that there was some disturbance. Doors being wrenched open and shut very firmly, voices raised, hurrying footsteps. As they reached the landing, three imps and five *luchrupán*s hurried past, carrying trays of papers and of the quartz pyramids in which captured threads of time were stored until the typing pool had created the records of meetings and interviews. One of the *luchrupán*s caught Salmon's eye and made a save-us-all sort of face. The air buzzed and tingled with gossip.

Salmon was somehow unsurprised to see Dr Boru striding down the corridor. She carried a leather-bound notebook in one hand and a copper pen in the other. Velvet Corbuse was trotting rapidly behind her, taking her own notes from Dr Boru's uninterrupted flow of speech and trying to keep control of the files and volumes already under her arm. As she passed Salmon, Velvet said a hasty greeting to McCabe and then winked at Salmon. She looked incredibly excited. McCabe merely raised his eyebrows.

'Well, now,' he said, when they reached his office, 'come in and help me remember.'

The windows in McCabe's office had been blocked up and instead the room was lighted by bonsai phosphorescent plants

that had been cultivated to produce different kinds of light –
cool, pale, warm, honey-coloured, strong or fading. A screen
shielded off the back of the room, and behind this, Salmon
knew, was where he kept his notes and ideas about the case he
was currently working on.

'Sit down, sit down,' he said, waving his hand towards a chair.

'Yes, sir. Sir, where would you like me to put this?'

Salmon held up the object that had been occupying the only
available chair. McCabe glanced at it as he reached for the
screen.

'Oh – that. Yes, well, if Boru is on the warpath, you had
better send it back to filing when we've finished.'

'Yes, sir,' said Salmon obediently and balanced the glass
case on a cluttered surface. She had no idea what the rules
were about returning a mummified raccoon to the Registry.

McCabe's entire office was filled with curiosities. Every
surface, every shelf and every press gave a home to bits of
mosaics, strigils, pomanders and other scraps of evidence from
long-solved cases, with medical models, divination devices,
trees made of gems, hand-drawn maps of the Silk Route,
unfamiliar musical instruments, oddly shaped bottles with
elegant labels reading *Snake oil* or *Hydra scales*, a small notebook
containing instructions on how to create a fake pre-historic
man. The only concession to modernity that she could see was
a delivery pipe from the pneumatic postal system that serviced
all of Muinbeo, curved up from the floor like a periscope.
A little pile of unattended post lay accusingly beneath it but
McCabe was immune to the accusations of inanimate objects.

'Apprentice,' said McCabe warningly as Salmon pulled up
the lid on a small chest, and she closed it again upon the dull

glint of objects carved from basalt and marble. McCabe had pulled back the screen. Salmon drew the chair forward and sat down.

Seeing as how they live such a long time, vampires have prodigious memories, and from the time that McCabe was very young he had cultivated his memory to be better than most. At first, he had copied the techniques of ancient poets, who left prompts littered through their poems as reminders of the sequence when reciting narratives that could go on for hours. When the first of the symbiotic races came to live in Muinbeo, McCabe learned to mimic the way that, when they learned something, symbiotics placed the information carefully in a particular part of their brains, so that they could locate it again easily. After a few centuries, though, he had so many mental files that he found he needed some place to put the excess memories and he hit upon the idea of recreating in three-dimensional space a sort of combination of the two techniques. The result of this was that McCabe used model settings for his memory. For every complicated case he worked on, he[45] created a landscape, the theatre in which the crime and the investigation took place. It was populated by oval-faced wooden puppets, dressed like their human equivalents, able

---

[45] McCabe gets all the credit for his theatre of memory, even though all sorts of fairies and sprites and *luchrupán*s were involved in building the smooth-jointed puppets, the tiny clockwork mechanisms upon which everything ran, and for providing him with silk paper and dew ink with which he could write hundreds, sometimes thousands, of notes to himself about evidence. We're just saying.

to quickly change their appearance. Attached to the puppets and to all the buildings in the landscape there were notes, as faintly visible as breath on a frosty day. Everything was linked to everything else, everything referred to everything else. As McCabe spoke aloud, talking through what might have happened, what evidence they had found and what questions were left, scrolls of thin parchment descended from the ceiling and his words appeared.

'You see now, apprentice,' he said when he had finished adding in questions about the paw prints Hunter Sessaire had reported and what Cedar Cullen had told them a few hours ago. 'You see how it is useful to stand back from what you have been told and look at the whole shape it is taking? We started off looking closely at Fen – who she knew, what she said, where she was – because she was the corpse, and everyone was focused on her as the most important thing. But now – now we have the question of the minutes of the Gallagrene Group. Which is a sign of a much different kettle of fish.'

'Sir, are we absolutely sure about the Gallagrene Group? That someone in the senate has to be involved?'

'There is no possibility that I can see for the alternative. Fen was sent a copy of an iris that had come from the senate building and had been addressed to at least one senator – Coast Albright. The iris mentions a group, and it says that the chairman signed the minutes. Where there are minutes, that tells us there must have been a meeting, otherwise there is nothing for the secretary to write down. What else is it a sign of? What should we look for?'

'The name of the secretary, traces of meetings,' Salmon said, thinking about how people arranged meetings. 'There should be orders sent to the security elves that there will be visitors, it should be in someone's diary. There should be requests for tea and coffee and biscuits.'

'Yes. Yes. The Gallagrene Group,' said McCabe, 'should be a name that Velvet or any senate amanuenses or any of their apprentices should have heard of somewhere. And yet, nothing. It exists and there is no sign of it. That is very suspect.'

'Getting back to Fen,' said Salmon, 'are we any closer to finding out who – or even what – actually killed her? I mean, Cedar Cullen's evidence adds more questions, not more answers.'

McCabe sat down and closed his eyes, his long fingers forming a steeple in front of his face, his forefingers wedged on either side of his nose.

'Tell me again. Why is it complicated?'

'Well, sir, we know from Immo Harper that a group of people who had been friends in school were going to have dinner together and that Fen was one of them and she had said she would help with the cooking. We found a recipe for baked fish lying out on her kitchen counter, as though she was planning to use it. Cedar Cullen tells us that she ordered a fish from him, and that the fishmonger he ordered from couldn't supply it. He asked Hopper Brycc, who has the refrigerated delivery-ship, to pick up a frozen fish for Fen and to deliver it to the canal stop near Cluancorr, where Fen will pick it up.'

'That sounds clear to me.'

'Yes, sir, but there she had no fish with her when she died. Where did it go? And, sir, Cedar said Hopper Bryce was doing them both a favour, because stopping at Cluancorr was out of his way on his trip. Cedar said he had made Fen promise she wouldn't be a minute late. But look at the time Velvet Corbuse said that Fen actually left – it was already half past six, and it would take her twenty minutes to get to Cluancorr.'

'What do you think?'

'I wondered if she asked someone else, maybe someone who lived around there, to meet Hopper Bryce for her. But Hopper is away, he went out on a Newfoundland trawler and isn't back yet.'

'Do you know, Salmon, I wonder if perhaps we are one step closer at least. I think we know what the weapon was. And I think we know what happened to it.'

Salmon looked at him blankly. McCabe shot to his feet, making her jump violently, and beckoned her to the theatre.

'Cullen sold her a frozen fish,' he said, 'but it wasn't just any old fish, was it?'

Salmon was bewildered but she said, 'No, sir, it was a Mercurian cutlass. But she was stabbed, sir, not clubbed with a – oh!'

'Exactly, apprentice.'

Salmon tapped the elbow of the Cedar puppet, and thin scrolls of silk paper unfurled, noting what the butcher had told them and providing a picture of the Mercurian cutlass. It is an uncommon fish, found in the lakes in the northern part of Muinbeo where it feeds on a type of underwater grass which gives the fish violet flesh. The Mercurian cutlass grew to be about the size of a large salmon, and had once been part of the food chain for a small predatory dinosaur, which was, biologists thought, the reason that the cutlass fish had developed its most distinctive feature – a long, broad, sharp weapon growing from its nose, like a marlin. Salmon recalled the coroner saying, *We found traces of organic matter in the wound.*

'And if we think that the murder weapon was Fen's own fish,' said McCabe, watching Salmon covertly, 'where do we think the weapon is now? Why have we not found it?'

Salmon looked at him, and the logic of the evidence – the dinner, the recipe, the fish – seemed to come together.

'We think,' she said, 'that the killer took it home and cooked it.'

'Bright girl wanted to light dark hallway,' said McCabe.

Chapter 4: Sunday

Waning moon, Great Banb sinking

A private house, near Roanoake Cross

⊓⊕✱▷⋉⛢⊖⊓✱⊙⊕⋈⋊⌿△⊙△⊕△⊓⛢⊖△⊓
△○△⊙✱⊂⊖⊓⊕✱▷✱⊓✱⊙⊕⋈✱⊓✱⊖⊓⊕⊖⊖
⊓⊖⊕⛢⊖△⊓⌿⊕○□⊕⊓⊕✱⋊△○⊔△⊖⛢⊖✱
⊒⊖⁇○⊖✱⊓□△⊺⊖⊖⊖⌿△⊙△▷⋊∴⊙⊖⊖○⋈
⛢⊖⊓⊕⊖⊖⋈○⊺△⊕⋈○⊏⊏△⊂△⊓⊖–⋊✱⊕
✱⊙⊕△⊺△⊙⊂△⊓⊖⊒△⊺⛢⊖⊓⊖⊓△⊙✱○⊙
⊙✱⊺⛢⊖⊖⊺△⊕⁇⊓⊔△⊁⊖⁇⊙⊓⋇⊒✱⌿✱⊔△
⊙⊕⊖⊖▷⋈⊒✱△△_△⊕⊖⊺△⊙▷△⌿⊂□⁇△⊕⊓
⊒⊖⁇⊖□⊕⊓⊕⁇△△_△⊕⊓⊕⋊∴⊓⁇△⊔✱⊖⊙
□✱⊖⊙⊓✱⁇△⊔⊖⊙⚊⊂⊖⊓⊔○⊖⊖⊖⊔⊕⊓⊕
⊓△⊙△△⊙✱⊖▷_△⊕⊒✱⁇△⊔⊖⊙⋉⊙⊖▷
⊖⊖⊕⊏⊖⛨⊓⋔⊓⊓✱⛢⊖○⊒⊖⁇⊖□⊕⊓⊕△○
△□⊖⊓▷△_△⊕⋈⊂○⊖⊙△⊕⋈△□⊖⊖⌿⊺✱
△△⊖⊖✱□✱⊖△⊓⊕△⊺✱⊔△⊕△⊓⋊✗⊂○△⊙✱⊺
▷⊓△○✱⊒✱⊖○⊒△⊕○⊺△⊕⊙⛢⊖△⊺▷○⁇⁇⊓
△✱△△⊕✱⛨□✱△○△⊖✱□✱⊖✱⚊△✱⊖⊓△⊖⊓
⊺○⁇○✱○⊙⊓□✱⊖⊓✱⊙⊕△⊓⛢⁇⌿⊖✱⊓⊕⊖△

I know that Marl is lying. His brother is a werewolf, yes, but when he turned up for the meal I wondered why it was that the brother needed to change in the flat. Logic led me to the next question, was Marl even entitled to let his brother change form at home? *I knew it was a risk, since that annoying witch Boru can tell if anyone has been reading her precious records, but it was a small risk. Any building where werewolves take on their true form has to be secure, walls and doors reinforced, windows barred. I see why this is needed but it is a sadness of the world nonetheless; ideally, everyone else would just take their chances while the werewolves expressed their reality freely. In any case, no sign of Marl's house as a registered premises, inspected by the Wolf Lodge. Why would he let his brother change at home, illegally? The safest place in the county and he would be with his fellows. Marl is lying, I am sure of it. But why would he be so determined to attend a small dinner party? The Teacher must be right – Marl suspects something about the Institute and he will ruin everything. I must do as I am asked. It is too late to turn back because the Master has prepared, from his stock of mysterious little bottles, a clear chemical that he says will not be traced. But I must take care of everything. I am sure that I would anyway, because the Institute is more important, but of course, now I know that I was seen, the night of Fen's death. But there is no room for hesitation. That will be the night. A tiger will kill her own cub if she knows it is the right thing to do. It will have to be that night.*

The butcher's shop, Mayflower Market, Butchers' Square, Ballinpooka – and beyond

The afternoon before the gairm Thanatos was gloomy, with heavy mist and low cloud. Cedar went home from his shop, and got ready to go to Cluancorr. First he ate a substantial dinner, as he always did before he reckoned his territory – enough to keep his hunter self from being distracted by hunger but not so much that his luxury-loving self, far preferring to stretch its hairy paws before the fire, would win out. He ate in his scullery, gobbling a steak and kidney pudding while he watched the town go by, through the gaps in the buildings. He could glimpse the street lights being lit early, and the lights from the boats reflected on the unruffled surface of the canal. Dark figures hurried about, hunched against the cold, silhouetted momentarily in a bright doorway. Cedar liked to watch lives passing by on Canal Road. He felt at one with it, reassured and comforted and fundamentally separated.

Before he left, his mouth tingling with heat, Cedar damped down the fire in the scullery and dimmed the lights. The stove in the kitchen was low, so the house would stay warm. He switched on the radio, waited while the batteries warmed up, adjusted the reception until it was clear, and then turned down the sound. When he transformed it always took him a short time to adjust to his hound self with the smells and the sounds suddenly being so overpowering. Equally when he turned back into a man he took a little time to adjust and the music and low light were, so far, the best way he had found to ease the change. He closed up his overcoat and tucked the folds of it neatly about him as he lifted up the trapdoor in his scullery.

A few minutes later, a large wolfhound trotted out of the tunnel that ran from Canal Road to the top of Ardgellan Hill, near the town walls. Standing just at the top of Cassidy's Bridge, near where he had first seen Fen's body, Cedar breathed the smoky air slowly. From where he stood he could distantly see the low belt of urban lights of Ballinpooka town through the iron grey mist. He could see, though no longer recognise, the pearly glow from the Tubbercolm Pan near the edge of the bog, and the blocky, densely black silhouette of the Great Cernunos statue on the top of Aonghus's Hill. He was about to run down to the gate, but he stopped, listening. His ears twitched. He could hear odd noises from south of the Pan. He could not understand them. They seemed sometimes to come from different places, even behind him, as the low wails bounced against the mist. Cedar licked his snout and listened intently, but he could make no sense of any of it. After a few minutes, during which he shifted about uncomfortably, moving across the bridge and back again, the sighs and the whimpering stopped. Cedar ran across the road and through Cluancorr.

Fen's scent was almost gone. The blood had soaked decently into the ground so that only a trace, a metallic taste on the tongue, remained. Cedar tried to recall the other scent he had encountered – the harsh smell that had startled him, perfumed sweat when he had been disturbed. The smell of blood. The smell of the land itself. A faint whisper of a smell, disconcertingly familiar, that he could not place; it was reassuring, like the smell of yeast, but disturbing because it was out of place. Something so familiar should not be near death.

Cedar heard and scented Velvet Corbuse long before he saw her come through the belt of dark trees between Cluancorr and the Wooden O. He backed into the yew grove so that he would not disturb her, watching Velvet stride out to the silvery ice, her head cocked to one side, her movements brisk but curiously without rhythm. She moved in wide arcs, back and forth, stretching her long fingers as though to ease them of pain or stiffness. She was closing in on a particular tree. He gave a couple of warning barks, and, realising that she was not intending to change form, he changed back into a man[46] and joined her.

'I think we need to speak to Hunter again,' she whispered.

The field was empty but the night was so quiet, even a whisper seemed quite loud. She held up her hand and unfurled her fingers – or, rather, feathers – to reveal a scrap of cloth, torn from some red woollen garment by a blackthorn tree.

Cluancorr: the ceremony of the gairm Thanatos

There was a big turn-out on Sunday evening at the gairm Thanatos[47] for Fen, about two hundred people, all told. Evening had drawn in by the time the first mourners arrived; the moon was rising beyond the crown of trees that surrounded

---

[46] Just in case you were wondering, dimorphism works by (to put it very simply) dismantling all the elements that make up the person at the time of the change, and putting the elements back together again in a different shape. That includes the clothes that they were wearing. Once or twice, a dimorph has changed absentmindedly, and so has incorporated the book that they were reading, the orange they were eating and, on one really fun occasion, the basket of snakes they had on their head. That, incidentally, is the explanation of the look on the Medusa's face.

[47] This is a very solemn ceremony that happens before the funeral, because only close family and invited guests attend a funeral. The gairm Thanatos, which means something like *greeting death*, has a great deal of music, and orations, and very complicated rules about what to wear and how to dress your hair should you have any; people in Muinbeo like to show that they really do take death seriously.

the motte, and the Great Banb star, trailing her constellation, was overhead. The core of the crowd was beginning to settle down, arranging themselves in neat, dense lines, grouped by mourning clothes – everyone in white came together, everyone in black, everyone in violet. The druids, congregating together, made a large clot of shimmering, pale iridescence amid the bare, night-black apple trees. The lamplighters had lowered the flames of the street lamps along Ballinpooka Road so the procession of chief mourners who walked from Killchryso Temple to the gairm were sombrely lit on their way.

Sparrow led the procession into the clearing. She and her family, all dressed in identical violet tunics and trousers, and holding chaplets of silver beads, stood a little in front of the rest of the mourners, a few feet away from where the body would be placed. Reed Cutler, the Thanatos, approached with the two Thanatos birds.

High above them and out of sight, half-way up the motte in Chlovis Woods, Salmon could hear the muffled drums beating. Maccarrill was with her, perched in the darkness of the overhead branches. Salmon had been a little surprised that McCabe had allowed her to investigate the motte, and not at all surprised that Benson had been against it. She knew that Benson did not quite believe that she had been able to follow a scent, and he did not like any part of an investigation happening without McCabe or preferably himself being present. But McCabe had been firm, and Salmon had been dispatched to see what she could discover. So far, that had been very little.

The sun had set in a blaze of red, and by five, when the gairm started, the shadows and the inky air still seemed to have a crimson stain. The temperature dropped as the sun set and Salmon's breath was white and smoky. She was climbing up the motte from the northern side, which faced the Wooden O, and she had barely caught any trace at all of the scent she and Fallinish had followed the morning of Fen's death. Maccarrill could not help her. He seemed uneasy and distracted, snapping his crest and fluttering from tree to tree.

Salmon continued slowly up the motte, trying, impossibly, to find something without knowing what it might be. She could distantly hear the voices from the assembled people, the chanting and now and then a little harp music, carried on the breeze. The path was steep now and she paused for breath. Below, she could see the Thanatos arrive and move through the crowd.

That Reed Cutler was large and black-haired and of grave and saturnine aspect made it seem fitting, to some people, that he had inherited the role of Thanatos. He wore a long charcoal robe with black ribbons and the crowd parted easily at the baleful glare of the two great ravens perched on his arms. When he reached the bier on which Fen's body lay, the ravens began to caw hoarsely, their voices fading as they flew away.[48] Salmon turned away and looked up, straight up the overgrown path that led to the peak of the motte.

'Well, now,' she said to herself, unconsciously imitating McCabe. 'Well, now.'

---

[48] Ravens are battle birds and do not hang about if they find a body that had met a violent end – to them, violence means battle and battle means they have work to do.

The light she saw flicker and pulsate seemed to come from a foot or two above the earth, around a narrow, mossy cave mouth. Puzzled, Salmon turned off onto the higher path and began to climb. The motte did not have caves or caverns.

She saw Maccarrill's pale feathers glide between the trees. She narrowed her eyes, squinting into the darkness around the distant ring of light. Without warning, a body suddenly exploded from the trees beside her and sent her sprawling backwards. The breath knocked from her by the collision, bruised and momentarily stunned, Salmon scrambled to her feet. A dark, bulky figure sped away amongst the trees, down the south face of the motte. Ignoring Maccarrill's shrieks, Salmon gave chase, leaping over fallen trunks and ducking or rolling under low branches, skidding down slopes and crashing through thorns and bushes.

She was not quite fast enough. The figure disappeared and only the faintest sounds of snapping wood and the crashing of feet told of its progress. Maccarrill flew on, but was soon back, peering anxiously into her face and trying to test her for concussion.

'Come on,' he said finally, 'let's go down to the gairm. At least you have proved that there is something worth following up here.'

Brushing herself down as best she could, but still looking like the Muinbeo Mud Monster,[49] Salmon set off, Maccarrill keeping close watch until he thought she was safe. During the

---

[49] What do you mean, what is the Muinbeo Mud Monster? Do they teach nothing in schools these days?

pause in the proceedings when the Thanatos had joined the drummers, the ravens had returned, and, to the astonished murmurs of the gathered mourners, four strapping figures carried out the *cathedra*, the chair in which the Patriarch sat during public attendance; immense and heavily decorated, the weight of the *cathedra* suggested it had been made from an entire copper yew tree. As the *cathedra* was being carefully placed on the east side of the clearing, Salmon arrived and stood on tip-toe to try to locate McCabe.

She saw the gleam and glint of Fallinish trotting determinedly through the crowd. The little pouch, housed in what had been Fallinish's spleen, into which McCabe had put the fragments of cloth given to him by Hunter, was glowing very slightly, and Salmon could follow Fallinish's path through the crowd until he came to a stop behind McCabe. He sat, triumphantly, upon the feet of Dr Silvanus Hughes. McCabe recognised Hughes instantly, though it took Salmon a little longer to remember seeing that narrow, thin-lipped face at the Swanhill Library, the night of the scholarship awards. As Salmon joined them, McCabe was smiling at Silvanus – the charming effect spoiled by a glint of fang to the side – and Silvanus was smiling in ghastly fashion back.

'Do you want to come with me,' McCabe said softly, 'now, before the Patriarch arrives, and tell me all about why you thought it was a shiny-bright idea to move a murdered corpse?'

From behind him, Dr O'Buachalla said, 'Hal, if you come to the Early History Archives, I can show you why he did it.'

Silvanus Hughes glared at her.

McCabe took Silvanus's elbow.

'You come with us,' he said. 'Salmon – Salmon, you appear to be wearing most of the motte – get one of the carriages ready to take us to the archives. We will collect Apprentice Sessaire on the way.'

He had Silvanus bustled out of the crowd almost before anyone noticed. Salmon, stricken with the unfairness of fate that meant she would now have to miss the Patriarch's speech, hurried away.

The Patriarch stood up.

The staff room, Early History Archives, Kilchryso

While the mourners at the gairm Thanatos were recovering from the Patriarch's words, Silvanus Hughes was sitting in the staff room at the Early History Archives, looking both terrified and defiant. Salmon was making tea for three.

'Thank you for coming along,' McCabe said smoothly, and Silvanus gave a noisy bark that might have been a laugh, a cough or a cynical 'Ha!' McCabe was not certain. From the reading room they could hear Dr O'Buachalla and Hunter Sessaire opening drawers and moving about.

'Where were you on the night that Fen Maguire was murdered?'

The colour drained from Silvanus's face and McCabe could sense the historian's mouth drying out. Against his will, McCabe felt a creeping sensation that Silvanus might not be their murderer. Still young, Silvanus was a narrow but oddly soft-looking man, with a chin evidently so shy it ran almost immediately into his neck. He had inherited his brown eyes from his mother, but the dark red hair, the freckles and the easy blushing had descended on the spear side of the Hughes family.

'I was ...' Silvanus's voice came out like a mouse rustling in sand, and he cleared his throat, reaching gratefully for his mug of tea the moment Salmon placed it on the table. 'I was at the Swanhill Library, for the presentations by the candidates for the Peterson Scholarship. Dozens of people saw me.'

'Did you leave this gathering at any point?' Salmon asked.

'No. That is – no.'

McCabe sighed and took some tea.

'The thing is, Mr Hughes,' he said, 'that we've found some evidence. And evidence is a thing that always needs to be examined with great care, as I am sure you, being an historian, will agree.'

Having alarmed Silvanus by mentioning evidence, McCabe changed the subject. To reach the same point by a variety of different routes was usually more successful in winkling the truth out of evasive people. Silvanus was still clutching his mug of tea, and was slumped in his chair. He was beginning to sweat a little.

'Do you not think,' McCabe said, 'that it was a bit of a strange time to be cavorting around Cluancorr with a few drinks under your bib?'

'I was not cavorting, Detective Inspector McCabe,' Silvanus snapped with a credible attempt at dignity, 'I was visiting.'

'A scrub field in the middle of the night in the middle of winter, and you want to visit? Who were you with?'

Silvanus was acquiring a look that was familiar to McCabe – a shifty, desperate look, the look of a juvenile who will be forced to admit to mischief and whose fear of telling the truth is now outweighed by the hope of relief from the strain of lying, and of forgiveness. He saw this look creep over the historian's face and his own heart sank. It meant, almost certainly, that Silvanus Hughes was guilty of nothing worse than mistaking a drunken impulse for a good idea. McCabe had been around long enough to remember other people's inebriated risks that over several centuries had begun to turn into folktales of high-spirited or even dashing adventures. He did not think that moving a murdered corpse to improve an academic career was one of them. He laid the scrap of red cloth on the table.

'What was so important that you had to leave the ceremony as soon as you finished your speech? And who was so important that you only had one chance to talk to them? And why did you have to walk through the trees by the Bast, where you could have fragments torn from your academic gown?'

Silvanus looked quite blankly at McCabe, and then suddenly sagged.

'It was so stupid of me,' he said, 'I know. But I didn't kill her.'

Having once admitted it, Silvanus kept on speaking, rubbing his hands over his face, staring past McCabe as though he were watching himself, helpless to stop himself in his lunatic actions.

'Almost every night since then I wake up in a cold sweat. Every night now in my dreams I'm dragging poor Fen's corpse all over Ballinpooka. Last night I dreamed my aunt Woodie caught me trying to hide the body in her rhubarb patch. I'm taking tablets to try to get a night's sleep. I cannot believe I did what I did. I can't believe I *could* do it. Poor Fen. A dead body. But I swear to Apollo I didn't kill her. She was dead when I got there.'

'And if she hadn't been you would have been up to your oxters in trouble,' McCabe growled at him, 'if there had been the slightest chance that she could have lived if you hadn't moved her.'

Silvanus was shaking his head vigorously.

'I might have been drunk as a lord but she was dead as a sparrow,' he said. 'I checked everything, everything. There wasn't a spark.'

'And if we never discover who did this,' McCabe pounced, sternly, 'it may be your fault. You moved the body, who knows what evidence you have destroyed.'

As Silvanus hung his head, McCabe added, 'The least you could do is tell me who was with you. Don't look at me like that, I don't care who it is, who it shouldn't have been, or what you were up to. It matters only because you might be able to help us.'

Silvanus huddled back into his chair, defeated.

'It wasn't really sinister, you know,' he said, somewhat bleatingly. 'Everything would eventually be revealed.'

Dr O'Buachalla put her head around the door.[50]

'The maps are out, Inspector McCabe,' she said.

Hunter had unlocked the reading room, switched on the lights and found what Dr O'Buachalla had asked for in less time than it took the Patriarch to finish speaking; Salmon was

---

[50] We mean only that O'Buachalla leaned in to look around the door, not that she sent her head in by itself. That was McCabe's trick. One of them, at least. Vampires have a very elastic relationship with the physical world.

impressed. She had stood out of Hunter's way while he laid out the map and put small leather pouches filled with sand on each corner to keep the parchment from rolling up again. She stood beside him now to read it, and Maccarrill perched on the brass lamp rail above the desk and read it upside down. The map was badly stained, but had been expertly cleaned and restored so that the writing, the different colours on the plots of land, and the tiny drawings of trees and pigs and cottages were perfectly clear. She and Hunter stood back when Dr O'Buachalla arrived, and then everyone, including Maccarrill, leaned over the map.

'See?' said O'Buachalla. 'Here – this is now Cassidy's Bridge. There's Cluancorr. There's the motte, and there's the site of the Wooden O. Can you read that writing? That tells us everything about why Hughes was in Cluancorr.'

'Demeter's Handkerchief,' Salmon spelled out slowly. 'There are a lot of names written one on top of the other.'

The adults all looked at each other. Into the profound silence, O'Buachalla said, 'Actually, this map is very early medieval.'

'In that case,' McCabe said, 'it must say "Fiachra's Corner".'

'How do you know?' Hughes demanded. 'Since when do you read medieval Irish?'

McCabe looked at Silvanus Hughes with one eyebrow raised and Silvanus suddenly snorted, slapping his hands on his knees, which McCabe thought people only did on cinema screens.

'Apollo's teeth! You didn't need to read it, you remember it!'

'Remember what?' Salmon exclaimed. 'Remember what? Will one of you tell me what's so special about Cluancorr before I blow apart with the curiosity!'

'It's a lost garden,' McCabe said to Salmon. 'The whole field of Cluancorr, from the canal to the river. People grew medicines and food and rare plants there since very ancient times. It has had lots of names – Demeter's Handkerchief, then St Fiachra's Corner – and eventually it was left untended and disappeared. Historians and archaeologists have been searching for it for hundreds of years. The only trace left was in the manuscripts and books and in folktales.'

'That's right,' Dr O'Buachalla said. 'It was described in many manuscripts – a perfect and mysterious garden, laid out in an astrological pattern and so fertile and of such medical potency that it was said that it had been designed by the Dagda himself. But nobody knew where it was. Even you, McCabe, didn't know the location.'

'But how could there be a mystery,' Salmon said, confused, 'when there was a map?'

'The map depicts the garden,' Hunter said. 'It doesn't show where in Muinbco the garden is placed, merely where everything is placed in the garden. The garden was thought to lie further south, on the bend of the River Livia, where the old forge used to be.'

'But the soil is all wrong there,' Hughes said. 'It only struck me – I don't know – a month ago? two? – that there was another candidate for the location. And when I visited again, I knew I was right. I knew it. I was terrified someone else would realise the same thing.'

'How did you think you were going to stop them just by coming to Cluancorr in the middle of the night?' Salmon asked. 'Did you know Fen had been killed, and you were afraid that an investigation would draw a lot of attention to it? Lots of talk about this history, lots of pictures – maybe some other historian would realise the same thing?'

'That, apprentice,' said McCabe, 'is quite a good deduction. And nearly right. He moved the body to delay the investigation rather than stop it. He needed to be able to show off Cluancorr without any distraction. It was his only chance. Who did you bring with you the night Fen died, Hughes?'

Hughes looked at O'Buachalla, then at McCabe and back again. He was less willing to make this admission than even the admission that he had moved Fen's body to Bast Bridge. O'Buachalla scared him more than did McCabe.

'I had to,' he said at last, beseechingly, to O'Buachalla, 'I had to. It was my only chance. I knew he would award the scholarship to me if he knew I had cracked this mystery.'

'Who?' Salmon repeated. 'Who did you bring?'

'His trump card,' said McCabe, and Hunter explained: 'Geoffrey Ballantyne Logan.'

'He knew that Logan had the last word about awarding this Peterson Scholarship,' O'Buachalla said, leaning over the map again. 'Fame and a small fortune. He also knew that our Mr Logan is not above persuasion. Not exactly bribery, but the more publicity and fame he can wring out of any situation, the better he likes it.'

'Anyone who did actually find the garden after all these centuries,' Hughes said, touching the map affectionately, 'would have their academic name made. I could easily persuade him. I got in touch with him about a month ago – he was going to be in Muinbeo on business, but we never managed to find a time. I knew he would be here for the scholarship event and I just took the plunge, asked him to come with me after I had given my paper. I arrived at Cluancorr first, he insisted on travelling in his own carriage. While he was parking his horse, I went into the field. I panicked. If he saw Fen's body, my only chance was gone. He would never risk the bad publicity of being at a crime scene.'

'Classy, Dr Hughes,' said O'Buachalla sourly, 'very classy. The Swanhill University is lucky to have you.'

'Trying to cheat to win an academic award isn't a crime,' McCabe warned, 'however unattractive you might think it is.'

'I suppose,' said O'Buachalla reluctantly, 'I was hoping for a suspended sentence for Hughes. Suspended by his thumbs for six months. Still, it was lucky that someone did find it – the land was very nearly sold a few years ago to the senate.'

'I remember,' said McCabe. 'Some development group wanted to buy it. They were going to do some kind of agricultural research.'

'But the allotment-holders protested. I've never heard of them since,' O'Buachalla said thoughtfully. 'The Cluancorr Group. Maybe they didn't get any more money for research.'

McCabe looked at her, then looked at Salmon. His aura sparkled.

Salmon said, 'Two senate groups that mysteriously appear and disappear?'

'Apprentice, please put the map away,' O'Buachalla said to Hunter. 'And well done. Hal tells me that it was you who found the cloth ripped from Hughes's gown that allowed Fallinish to find the scent. Fortunate that you found it today. Otherwise we might have missed our chance.'

Hunter smiled and looked awkward. Salmon looked at him.

'Come on, Dr Hughes,' McCabe said. 'Further questioning at the station. We will collect GB Logan on the way.'

O'Buachalla escorted McCabe and Hughes out and Hunter busied himself lifting up the weights from the parchment and arranging the map back under the glass.

Salmon said, 'How did you manage to be in Cluancorr finding shreds of cloth torn from academic gowns at the same time that you were attending the Komnenos's lectures with your parents?'

Hunter didn't look up.

The relief at having revealed his part in confusing the investigation of Fen Maguire's murder made Hughes chatty and light-hearted on the journey to Ballinpooka. He travelled with McCabe, with Fallinish dozing on the the floor of the carriage, and Hughes talked non-stop on every random topic that popped into his head. McCabe was not at all sure, when he and Fallinish got out of the carriage at the hotel to collect GB Logan, that Hughes did not simply continue chattering to the empty seats.

Logan, in reluctant response to McCabe's iris, was waiting for them in the foyer of the hotel. He was impeccably turned out as always but he badly needed a shave and his eyes were heavy, almost sullen, with sleep. Fallinish, unusually, trotted forward briskly and began sniffing.

'Mr Logan,' McCabe said, and stopped. Fallinish and Logan were pacing, and as Fallinish came forward for a closer sniff, Logan stepped back with what was unmistakeably a low growl.

'Mr Logan,' McCabe said again, taken aback, 'I hope you don't mind Fallinish. We have a carriage outside.'

Chapter 5: Monday

The day after the gairm Thanatos

Derrydrake School, the Doathain

While the extra classes and the classes for apprentices took place in the upper rooms of Derrydrake School, the regular classes were held in the lower rooms. As all the rooms had doors on each side, as well as trapdoors in the floors and descending ladders in the ceilings, it was much easier to get everyone into whichever laboratory, glasshouse, kitchen, workroom or library that they needed to be in. Although apprentices had additional classes along with their practical work, they all attended regular classes for half the week.

The day after the gairm Thanatos, Salmon was itching to give classes a miss and spend the day working with McCabe, but he would have none of it.

'Look,' he said finally, 'leave aside the fact that the rules are not just there to annoy you. And leave aside the fact that if I say you can mitch school and come and work with me, I am going to be up to my eyeballs in trouble – with your foster-parents, Maccarrill, Professor Peterson, Dr O'Buachalla. Leave all –'

'I thought Professor Peterson was dead?' Salmon said.

McCabe looked at her and then nodded. 'Yes, of course,' he said, 'let's go with that. Anyway, the point is. You can't know what you might need to know in the future. So, all right, you *say* what use are maths and politics and all the rest of it? You *say*, if I am going to be a guardian, am I not better off actually being involved in detecting?'

He stopped and Salmon waited. If she had been older she would have recognised the expression on McCabe's face, the expression of one who has just reversed himself into a tight corner and realises that he is now immobile.

'But, you know – you never know who ... you know ... will give you ... em ... the tools you need – ah – in your life. Oh, look – if you want philosophy, go ask the Platonists. From me you get this: do as you're told and go to school.'

Which was not satisfactory but at least it was clear.

Dr Grattan was not a patient man, and he was prone to nervousness. He was an Outlander, a refugee from the Imperial Pharaonic wars, and had lived in Muinbeo for many years but never seemed to quite get used to it. So affected had he been by what he had seen during wartime that for some years after his arrival he had been unable to work, and instead lived in virtual seclusion in Uisneach University, doing research on history and politics, and learning how to keep bees. Now he taught politics and ethics at the school,[51] and he and the students had a kind of understanding. He learned that a bit of light-heartedness did not mean the road to chaos and ignorance, and they learned that Dr Grattan was a floorless

---

[51] He still keeps bees; they inspire him when working out difficult ethical problems. He also keeps a pig called Aristotle. You work with bees, but you can tell your troubles to a pig.

sea of information on all sorts of random topics, and not to take some of his sharper remarks personally.

He was a tall, well-built but rather stooped man, bald on the top of his head but with thin, untidy, mostly white hair on the sides and back of it. He was, he said himself, going south, baggy about the chin and sagging about the belly. He had large horse-like teeth, and a beautiful voice, compelling and melodious. All Outlanders were obliged to comply with very strict laws about clothing but with different places in the Empire having different local laws – so moving from one place to another often required not only a barrow-full of visas, licences and identification papers but a whole new wardrobe too.[52] Dr Grattan wore a dark green toga over a T-shirt and jeans, and though togas were not so uncommon in Muinbeo, his was in fact an act of rebellion.

They had very nearly come to the end of Dr Grattan's class, in which he had introduced his own special subject, which was demonstrating the link between money and power. The class had either been interested or had faked it convincingly, so the hour had gone smoothly without any of the sudden surges

---

[52] The Pharaoh had acquired, or more likely created, a 'very old manuscript' called 'Biblicula Mondum Panos', which the Pharaoh's Court said meant the Little Book of the Whole World. It is said to be a book containing the 'real truth' about the Outland and from this book the court derived a labyrinth of laws about how Outlanders are to live. At first everyone thought that it was a huge joke, and that it just showed you that the Pharaoh and his court were stupid as rabbits. But when a professor was executed for pointing out that 'Biblicula Mondum Panos' was neither dog-Latin nor bad Greek, it stopped being funny.

of irritation that sometimes were a memorable feature. To Salmon's dismay, just as the class was about to end, Rabbit-Nut Smith began to be objectionable. Or, as Nefertiti said, woke up.

'I don't think that money has anything to do with it,' she said, and Dr Grattan gave her a look that would have opened a grave.

'Indeed,' he said.

'I was in the Outland once,' she said, as though that settled everything, 'and everyone seemed to have enough money. They could buy anything.'

'That is not the point. The point is, where are they getting the money from? The point is, what is the exchange? Give them bread and circuses, they said in the ancient Outland, and so they will not have time to think about what we are really up to. What is the payback?'

Rabbit-Nut was remarkably pretty, with glossy brown hair, big blue eyes and dimples and she was small and neat and deft in her movements.

'I just think the whole war is stupid,' she said, and Dr Grattan snapped.

'Why didn't we think of that? I'll alert the Pharaoh.'

Salmon was watching the side of Dr Grattan's neck nervously. If the side of his neck started going purple, sarcasm and detention would follow. Rabbit was not stupid, she thought resignedly, but sometimes she was incredibly silly.

'Well, it can't affect us, anyway,' Rabbit-Nut said, 'so I don't see that it matters any more than it matters to us what happens on the planet Klio.'

'Muinbeo is not joined at the hip to the planet Klio, you goose,' her brother Hedge said, and Goose Tierney, offended, threw a notebook at him.

'You think it is happening "Long ago in a galaxy far, far away," do you?' Dr Grattan said, sarcastically. '"Once upon a time in a faraway land." Well, let me enlighten you, you bunch of rascals. In my country we used to think that we just had to sit out the storm. Let the Pharaoh have his war, we are not part of it, eventually it will just go away.' Dr Grattan started to tidy up his books. His hands were shaking slightly. After a few moments he spoke again, very calmly: 'If someone else commits a crime that starts an avalanche, your innocence will not protect you from being buried alive. And when you have to start picking bodies out of the wreckage of your quiet life, you have to remember that being neutral is not the same as being innocent.'

Hunter said suddenly, 'Outland politics are a bit like a murmuration of starlings. Only they know what direction they are going to go. They all move at once. But if you take one starling, it doesn't know where the group is going. It only knows when it is in the group.'

'Finally,' said Dr Grattan, 'one of you reprobates seems to have been paying attention.'

Seeing that Dr Darwin, the school's physicist, was at the door, Dr Grattan bade them good morning and strode out, nodding briefly to Dr Darwin as he left.

Dr Darwin's wardrobe was limited to heathery tweed skirts and turtle-necked jumpers, but with thick honey-coloured hair swept up into a beehive, eyes as blue as violets and a dazzling smile she was very nearly glamorous. She set her books down, and fanned them out on the desk like a magician with a pack of cards.

'Right,' she said, 'today we are doing the *Alice in Wonderland* class. Erratic portals – what they are, what causes them and how to recognise them.'

'And what happens if you go into one,' Goose Tierney, irrepressibly adventurous, said hopefully.

'Oh, that's easy,' Dr Darwin said reassuringly. 'You will die, and probably quite horribly. Now, page seventy-nine, how to see an erratic portal. We'll have a look at the Whedon lights first, and see what causes them to appear.'

Main guardian rooms, Senate Chambers

When Hopper Bryce came to the station neither Salmon nor McCabe was present so it was to Benson that Hopper recounted his unwitting meeting with the probable killer of Persephone-Fen Maguire. Hopper was the same age as Benson, though taller and stouter, and he was recently off his ship so that he brought with him the bracing smell of salt air, and the less bracing smell of fish, though his face and hands had the look of skin recently scrubbed.

'I came back as soon as I could,' Hopper said apologetically. 'We were off course a short time when another ship got into trouble. I got back on land about an hour ago.'

'We appreciate you coming to see us so promptly,' Benson said in a fair imitation of the way McCabe spoke.

'No trouble. I hear it's over the death of the poor Maguire girl,' Hopper said, shaking his head and running his hand through his black hair.

'It is,' Benson said. 'You did Cedar Cullen a favour by bringing your vessel to the stop at The Tapper pub near Cassidy's Bridge. And someone picked up a delivery that was meant for Fen.'

'That's it,' agreed Hopper. 'That's right.'

There was a pause.

Then Benson said, 'Well, could you tell me exactly what happened?'

'Oh – yes. Yes. Well, Cedar asked me to drop off a frozen cutlass fish, because he'd not been able to fill an order for a fresh one. It's not a usual order for him – though I know he's had to get shark before and marlin and stuff. But anyways, he arranged with Fen that I'd drop the fish at the stall stop near Cassidy's Bridge and she'd pick it up. I said I'd be at the stall stop at six and that she isn't to be late because it's a detour, like, for me and I need to be getting on. Cedar said he had pressed the point with her and she said that if she was running late she'd ask someone else to lift it. The fish, like.'

'OK,' Benson said encouragingly.

'Anyways, I got to the stall stop a few minutes early, and bang on time a lad comes running down the bank towards the boat.'

Hopper hesitated. The first part of his account came easily to him but he was aware that he was coming to the significant bit and was also aware that he did not really have anything to tell them. He felt an awful urge to make something up, something to have made it worth the guardians' effort in getting in touch with him. He rubbed his hands through his hair again to help him concentrate and he stared at the bland-coloured floor, picturing as clearly as he could in his mind the dark figure jogging towards him, briefly lit by the lamps along the side of the canal.

'So anyways,' Hopper said, 'he just runs down the bank and hops the little bit of fence and comes up to the stall.'

Hopper stopped again. The man had climbed up the few shallow steps from the bank into the stall stop, where there was a very simple counter, some shelves for display in case one of the big boats had received a lot of orders for food or books and then some shallow steps down to the boat on the water. Most of the stall stops were very small and dark, being in use only infrequently and then only for very swift transactions. The stall stop where Hopper had waited for Fen, which was opposite the small pub called The Tapper, had had lights missing and he himself had been in a hurry to get on and was too busy with relief that he would not be delayed to really pay attention to his customer.

'He said that Fen had been delayed at the office, so he was picking up the fish and he hoped he hadn't kept me waiting. And I said no, and I got the fish out of the freezer, and I gave it to him. He said thanks and I said no trouble and he left.'

'You didn't ask his name?'

'No,' Hopper said, apologetically, 'there was no need.'

'It was someone else's fish. You gave it to a stranger.'

'Well – yes, but, you know, it was a fish. It wasn't the Salmon of Knowledge, it was just a fish. Why would anyone want to steal a fish?'

'No reason,' Benson sighed. He had been hoping for more and had not yet learned the truth of McCabe's repeated warnings that investigators never get anything handed to them on a plate. They have to dig it out of the midden for themselves.

'What did he look like, this man?'

'I've been trying to remember anything I could about him.' Hopper sighed in his turn. 'But there was nothing I noticed. He was average tall – about the same height as me. He looked fairly well built but it's hard to say because it was a bitterly cold night, so he was all wrapped up, woolly hat on him, scarf up over his mouth, jacket with the collar pulled up. I mean he didn't look like he was hiding, it was just a freezing night. He had gloves on.'

'What colour were his clothes?'

'Dark. Just – all of them. Black hat, dark stripy scarf, like grey and black or navy and black or something. Dark jacket, dark britches, I didn't notice his shoes. Well – boots, I think they were. I remember thinking when he was running over to the stall that he looked like a lad that was used to running. You know. He looked like he spent a lot of time outdoors – his gear was all good gear, hiking boots, proper all-weather sort of jacket, fleecy gloves.'

'How far did he have to run?' Benson asked.

'Well, I'm not sure. I don't know where he came from. I was looking round, up and down, you know, along the canal. So I only saw him when he had come onto the canal bank from the Killyduff side. I took it that he'd come from one of the houses.'

Benson looked past Hopper, picturing the geography.

'But he might have come onto the bank either from the houses near the crossroads,' he said slowly, 'or he might have run up the bank not from the road, but from the houses further down. From where all those sombrists live.'

Hopper looked at him. 'He might have,' he agreed. 'He might have come from there.'

'Was he out of breath?'

'No, just enough that you knew he had been running. The minute he came up he was talking to me, saying he hoped he wasn't late. He must have been very fit.'

'But you couldn't see his face?'

'Not clearly, no. I mean I could see enough to know he had one, he was white-skinned, he didn't have on glasses or anything. I don't think he had a beard but I can't be sure, he had the scarf up on his face. Two of the lights were broke on the stall, so he was only lit up for a few seconds. I don't know what colour his eyes were. I could see he had a nose, but not if it was, you know, broken or hooky or pierced or anything.'

'I'd like you to take a look at some photos,' Benson said, pressing a button on the wall behind him. It took a moment or two to connect with the Registry of Records' identification list, then Benson selected the album Salmon had created of everyone that they knew had ever come into contact with Fen.

As Hopper moved closer to look at each picture that dropped from the ether into the elaborate picture frame, Benson turned at a knock on the door, and McCabe came in.

'I'm sorry to interrupt,' McCabe said, 'but I heard that Mr Bryce had come back and I was anxious to see how you were getting on.'

'I'm no use to you, I'm afraid,' Hopper said.

'Well, it's not that bad,' Benson said reassuringly. 'We at least know that we're not looking for some, you know, some unfit short chap, for example. It's a start. You're certain you don't know any of them? Him, maybe?'

The gliding photographs stopped at Sand Butler.

'It wasn't Sand,' Hopper said.

'You're sure?' McCabe asked, drawing up a chair.

'Sure I know Sand well,' Hopper said. 'I used to go out with one of his sisters when we were in school. This fella had his face sort of covered but if it was Sand he'd have to be wearing a winding-sheet for me not to recognise him.'

'Fair enough,' McCabe said, relieved. 'In any event, Sand was training that evening.'

Hopper gave McCabe a suddenly astute glance.

'You checked up on Sand?'

'It was another line of enquiry,' McCabe said smoothly.

Hopper went back to the photographs but when the list finally ended, he was still shaking his head.

On the way towards Roanoake Cross

Thanks Tower, the former keep of Fairblood Castle, stood at the northernmost border of Ballinpooka town land. It was six miles along the canal from the town walls and had been converted by Reed Cutler into two very comfortable flats for Night and Velvet after he had fostered them both. They lived happily separate, companionable lives with dinner together once a week. Velvet had travelled back from the gairm with Cedar, Night and Ishka Gentileschi in Cedar's carriage. She was curled up on the sofa reading now, and Night was cooking their dinner, when the iris arrived. Night made exasperated noises as he manoeuvred the potatoes into the colander, but Velvet knew as soon as he rolled up the message that she would be dining alone.

'But the moon is only just starting to wane,' she protested as he grabbed his medicine bag. 'What about the rogue werewolf?'

'I know, my dear, but what can I do?' Night squeezed her arm in passing. 'I can hardly refuse to attend, can I? The hospital is instructing over the phone but they need medication immediately – it's an allergy, it's a very bad reaction. As to the rogue – well, the Wolf Watch are out looking for it. And you don't think any of *them* will attack me.'

Velvet protested that she had a bad feeling about rogue werewolves but she knew Night would have to go. As he checked over his medical bag, he tried to comfort her.

'It isn't even that far,' he said. 'The man collapsed in Shearwater Amberson's house.'

'But the Ambersons live in Killyduff!'

'That's his brother, Mack, he lives there. Shear lives in the Old Mill Field – remember he built that log house there? And everyone thought the sombrists at Roanoake Cross would object and they didn't?'

'No, but Dr Grattan did,' Velvet remembered. 'He lives practically beside Shear. But it's still a long way if there's a rogue werewolf about.'

Night snapped his bag shut.

'The rogue was last heard of in Hawkswood,' he said firmly.

Velvet pounced on this. 'No – in Ballinpooka,' she said, 'and not in some isolated house either, but in the guardian station. The werewolf attacked – someone, I don't know who – and if it hadn't been for McCabe ....'

'None the less,' said Night. 'Come on, Velvet. You know I have to go.'

He patted her shoulder and went out to get his carriage. Velvet went disconsolately up the spiral staircase to her room. She opened her window.

Velvet still felt a thrill of rebellion just before she began to morph. Dimorph children were encouraged to have quiet, almost isolated lives because the change into their species animal could happen at any moment. They learned from a very early age how to control their ability to change, but the habit of a quiet life, of avoiding attention, was usually instilled by then. Adult dimorphs did not usually choose to change; they could go their whole lives without changing even in the privacy of their own home. Velvet had gone along with this without comment until her aunt, who hardly had words enough to express how much she despised dimorphs and aliens, said she was just glad there were so few, and they were best not mentioned. Velvet had a biddable mind, but also a logical one, and her aunt's remarks seemed to cancel each other out. How did everyone know there were so few if everyone was so busy covering it all up? Muinbeo could be hopping with shape-shifters and Martians and no one would ever know the difference. Look at Frost Paschalides. He was an alien, though his parents had lived undercover, as it were, even moved from Muinbeo when Frost was five and rumours about his parents not being from Earth first started. Frost had come stomping back in to his native world, took no care whatsoever to pretend that he was Earth-born and faced down anyone who rejected him. How many others were watching him in admiration, wishing they had the courage to do likewise? How many watched him in a sweat of fear, wishing he would just shut up about it before someone noticed that they, too, were only a skin-deep human? How did Aunt Ash know that there were not many dimorphs? You could not tell by looking. Dimorphs could look just like normal people, as Night sometimes said to make her laugh, to make her remember that not everyone spoke about her kind in hushed tones. Velvet was not yet ready to take on the world by declaring that she was a corvid in her spare time. But she continued her secret rebellion by perching on her tower window every now and again, hearing the world sound different, hearing the winds and the rustle of mice in the bracken become louder than the cars driving past her house. She watched the sky change its patterns and began to see the wind her world began to move abruptly from one state of being to another without her being conscious of the connections in-between; things were, then they were new once more. Velvet hopped forward, stretched and beat her wings vigorously and took flight.

Once her eyes adjusted to the monoscopic vision, Velvet spotted Night easily. There was not much traffic on the roads and any carriages or bicycles moved quickly to one side at the flashing blue light that Night had attached to the side of his carriage. Velvet flew fast to keep up with him, scanning the tangled ditches and glittering fields for any sign of rogue werewolves. Now that they knew there was a rogue somewhere in the area, the Wolf Lodge Watch had been out each of the nights of the full moon, hunting. The werewolves led the way, alert to the smallest change in the scent of the landscape with which they were so familiar; alert too to any sign of anxiety or disturbance amongst the wild wolves. The werewolves were unarmed – apart from inch-long claws, a bull-like strength and a bite that could splinter a small tree – but the civilians who helped them mostly brought cudgels or missiles[53] while the guardians were armed with tranquiliser guns. But the Watch were probably over near Hawkswood where the rogue had attacked a woman and her dog and

---

[53] No one liked to tell them that not even Setanta could get a hurling ball down the throat of a werewolf and that as for cudgels, a rogue werewolf can eat a cudgel for breakfast and still have room for pancakes.

that was too far away from the desolate couple of miles to Shearwater Amberson's house.

Night was almost at Roanoake Cross when a werewolf that had been hiding in a hazel copse leaped out and gave chase. Night heard the cry and, seeing his pursuer, increased his speed. Velvet dived down towards the leaping werewolf, jabbing her beak savagely at it. Startled and angered, the werewolf fell back, holding its heavy forearms over its face to protect its eyes from the raven's slashing beak and rigid claws. Velvet swooped away and circled, and the werewolf was confused. They always were by the scent of a dimorph. It shielded its eyes and suddenly it turned, crouched and sprang. As it did, the shadow of a huge owl fell across it.

Night was kneeling on the floor of Shearwater Amberson's dining room, breathless from the unsuccessful attempt to resuscitate Marl Fitzwilliam.

'Sit down, Shear,' Night said gently. 'I can hear the ambulance now.'

Shear did not stop pacing up and down. Night squinted at the chalky face, wondering if he should give Shear something, but decided against it as Shear went to a shelf and took down a bottle of whiskey. Night got to his feet and slipped into the kitchen to send a message to Velvet. He hurried to open the door to the ambulance crew and told them briskly that Marl was dead. The older medics dealt with the body while Night and the younger staff dealt with Shear, who didn't speak, and Shear's guests, most of whom were openly sobbing. The exception was an elegant woman of about Shear's age, whom Night vaguely recognised but couldn't name. She merely sat very still in the deep windowsill, not looking at anyone. Night thought that he saw a shadow in the kitchen, but when he went to look, he saw no one there. Meanwhile, the chief medic sent irises to the quaestor and the guardians and within a few minutes Night was able to pass the death along, and return home.

By the time Night arrived home, Velvet was back in human form, shaken and exhilarated. Velvet was usually a peaceable person and was shocked to realise she had found the fight thrilling. She had swooped easily out of the rogue's way when he leaped for her, and neither she nor the werewolf had expected another combatant. But, diving so silently that not even Velvet heard it, an eagle owl sank its claws into the werewolf's back. Between them, the raven and the eagle owl had kept the rogue werewolf away from Night and, of one accord, hounded the rogue away from the houses around Killyduff and drove it south towards Hawkswood. Just as the rogue emerged from the Blackwoods, two of the watch appeared, and the real hunt began.

Velvet had followed even when the eagle owl had disappeared, keeping pace with the werewolves' sure-footed progress over the uneven surface of the road into the Gallagrene Bog. The rogue was faster and more aggressive, more reckless, and the watch stopped twice, briefly, to howl and call the rest of their team to the bog, while the rogue raced on. The moon reflected dully in the frozen surface of the lake, and its light shimmered on the frosted reeds. The rogue bounded almost soundlessly off the main track onto the soft peat path towards Ciplacti's Ear and it was Velvet's astonished caw that alerted him to his danger. Skidding to a halt, the werewolf turned towards the scrubby field in which, past the stout shapes of a few robust goats still outdoors, the figure of a fourth werewolf came gliding out of the dark. The rogue steadied itself, shoulders hunched and bristling, and the new werewolf pounced. The fight was short: less than three minutes of vicious, inelegant scrapping while the watch galloped up, and the rogue tore himself away, fleeing eastwards. His attacker watched but did not pursue. When the rogue was gone from sight, the remaining werewolf bayed and howled, and then, as if certain that the rogue was gone, became as silent as the night, sniffing and circling peaceably, until he too padded off into the depths of the bog as the watch arrived.

Velvet flew home. She changed her form and settled down to wait for Night to return, staring sightlessly at her book while her mind turned over and over again the question: after all these years of transforming into a crow, why had she this night become a raven?

With the raven, the rogue and the eagle owl all gone from the scene there was no one but werewolves left on the bog when the lights began to glow and moaning sighs, at first so slight as to be mistaken for the wind through the branches of the bare trees, grew ever louder, until they could be heard for a mile over the still air. The eight members of the Wolf Lodge Night Watch looked at each other, and looked around, up into the sky. Silently communicating, as wolves do, they moved forward towards the source of the sound, and stood in a semi-circle near where the fourth werewolf had disappeared into the shadows of Ciplacti's Ear.

Chapter 6: Tuesday morning

The gibbous moon, Great Banb sinking

The Grand Hotel Abyss, Stoker Court, Ballinpooka

The Grand Hotel Abyss was opposite the senate buildings on the other side of the canal, and it was usual for the senators and the guardians alike to use the hotel for impromptu meetings or public announcements that did not quite warrant calling everyone to the Forum. On the morning after Marl Fitzwilliam's death, Quaestor Finney called a press conference. He sent his iris first to Cotton Donovan,[54] as the president of the Guild of Journalists, and then sent the same message to the editors of the four main newspapers in Muinbeo, inviting them to attend.

As the quaestor walked into the foyer of the hotel with Benson (smoothing his tie and rearranging his cuffs in an important manner), Salmon (looking pink and serious) and the coroner (who had been up most of the night and looked it), he checked the small crowd quickly, to make sure that

---

[54] Cotton was not Donovan's real name: it was Beech. In his younger days, he spent a lot of time in New York. He was so regular a visitor to the Cotton Club, with his jazz trumpet as a cover story, that by the time his investigation was finished, and he had to leave not only New York but the continent on which it is situated, his nickname had stuck.

McCabe and Donovan were both there. McCabe was lurking in the shadows away from the windows, and Donovan was keeping him company.

Donovan was very old. He dressed in a snappy, pristine fashion of many years ago: a broad-brimmed white hat and a champagne-coloured suit with faint green stripes and light-green shoes. His only concession to age was a walking stick, which his staff grumbled was used more to bang irritably on the floor than to assist him in getting about. Donovan had been apprenticed to Dingo Fleming, the legendary financial journalist from Ballybolivia, and Donovan had proved to be as astute and fearless in reporting politics as Fleming had been in turning over the stones of high finance to see what might crawl out.

As he joined the alabaster-skinned, black-cloaked McCabe in the corner, Donovan, black-skinned and pale-clad, laughed and said, 'If you were better-looking you could be my negative print.'

Quaestor Finney cleared his throat, and everyone went silent.

'Thank you, ladies and gentlemen of the press, for attending to us at such short notice,' Finney began, trotting up a few steps of the sweeping staircase so that everyone assembled could hear him. 'We felt it was necessary to let you know the unfortunate events of yesterday evening, and to seek your support in solving the crime.'

Finney glanced down at his notes, and McCabe watched the crowd.

'You are all aware, I am sure, of the shocking killing of Fen Maguire,' Finney said, 'and we must now tell you that there has been a second murder.'

McCabe saw the faintest flicker of movement at the corner of his eye. He turned, but there was no one to be seen. He looked away, convinced he could almost see something. He glanced over the crowd again.

'Yesterday evening,' Finney went on, 'emergency services were called to a private home, where Marl Fitzwilliam, a public relations officer in the senate, was taken ill. The paramedics did what they could, but Fitzwilliam was pronounced dead at the scene. He had suffered a fatal allergic reaction and died of anaphylactic shock.'

The journalists were silent. They knew the quaestor had not called a press conference over a tragic accidental death. The coroner yawned enormously. Rather to his surprise, McCabe saw a young boy move forward through the crowd. Why, he wondered, was a child there? He saw Salmon's eyebrows shoot up and he looked again, recognising Salmon's foster-brother, What's-his-name Goldsmith. Maybe he had just come to see his sister at work.

'However, as you know, where someone dies of a condition that they did not know they suffered from – and his friends are certain that Fitzwilliam had no idea he was allergic to any food – the coroner does additional examinations and tests, to see if there is something we could have done to prevent the death. I will let her explain. Coroner Gentileschi.'

'Anyone who wishes to read the full medical report can do so. Dr Boru will make the usual arrangements,' Gentileschi said. 'The nut at the centre is this – Fitzwilliam was allergic to a substance called histamine. Many of you already know that this is naturally produced in the body and that it mainly makes its presence felt by nasty doses of hay-fever. It is also found in some types of food. Many people are slightly allergic to histamine, but some are dangerously so and will go into medical shock if they consume it. People who know how allergic they are to histamine will carry medicine with them. Marl had no medicine. He may have been aware that he had a mild sensitivity to histamine, but he clearly did not think he could die from exposure to it. Now, histamine is also found in certain foods, some of which Marl had eaten – cherries, fish, avocado. But we found the level of histamine in his blood was so high, there is no natural way for it to have happened.'

Immediately, the journalists began to move, to write fast and to murmur to each other.

One of the journalists said, 'He was allergic to histamine and he ate food with histamine in it. Why is it not accidental?'

'He was only slightly allergic – at most, he should have felt his lips tingle, or his eyes would become itchy. He would not fall down dead. For that, he would have had to eat nothing except food containing a lot of histamine, and eat it for about three days. If the dinner had been tampered with, then all the guests would have been affected, and they were not. It is our belief that someone deliberately introduced histamine to Fitzwilliam's system in order to sensitise him, as it is called, that is, to make him have a fatal attack the next time he ate, for example, fish. We don't know how this was done, but it was with the intent to kill him.'

'Is there significance to the guests who were at the same dinner party last night?' Rainbow's voice shook a little, but he tried to sound confident.

Everyone turned and looked at him. Salmon put her hand over her eyes.

Benson stepped forward briskly and snapped, 'You are not a journalist – we could have you charged with disrupting the course of official duties.'

McCabe put his own hand over his eyes. Benson was right, of course, on both points. But he never seemed to learn that it didn't take a trip-hammer to crack a peanut shell.

However, Benson had reckoned without Cotton Donovan. Rainbow was about to speak again, but Donovan stepped forward, took his elbow and said smoothly, 'He is an apprentice. So freedom of the press applies.'

Donovan gave Benson a reptilian smile and Benson glowered.

While the journalists continued with their questions, Donovan, still holding Rainbow's elbow, drew him aside to where McCabe was standing.

'Sorry,' Rainbow said. 'Did you mean it about being an apprentice?'

'Depends,' Donovan said cautiously. 'I only did that because I can't stand the sight of Benson since he tried to have two of my journalists arrested for contempt of court.'

'They were in contempt,' McCabe pointed out mildly.

Donovan snapped, 'With a half-witted judge and the dumbest decision since Eris threw the apple on the table,[55] what sane person wouldn't be in contempt? Of course they were in contempt. If they had not been, I would have sacked

---

[55] She wasn't called the Goddess of Strife for nothing, admittedly, but really, it was just a petty argument. *And* she started it. But – well, the Trojan War was a bit more than we had anticipated.

them as idiots. Now, boy, what was all that about people at the dinner party? Who was there and why was it significant? What's your name?'

'Who was having the party?' McCabe asked.

'It wasn't a formal party, so I've heard,' Donovan answered McCabe. 'Just people getting together to watch the match. Over at Shearwater Amberson's house. Who was there, Rainbow?'

'And how do you know?' McCabe demanded.

'You know that Night Corbuse was attacked last night by the rogue werewolf? His sister Velvet's in my class, and so I went over to see if they were OK. And Night was just saying what happened – I mean, he thought it was just allergy, not foul play. And he mentioned people who were there. And they were all, one way or another, working for the senate, and all of them were to do with cither the environment or planning.'

Rainbow stopped, but Donovan just raised his eyebrows.

'Hardly a crime,' he said.

'No – no, it isn't, but you wrote an article in *Pluck's Notebook* about these rumours about, sort of, shady deals to do with some of the unused land around Ballinpooka, and then you said there were rumours about people in the senate being approached by, like, Outlanders to let them buy property in Muinbeo.'

'There are always rumours about that,' McCabe said. 'Have been for years. Doesn't mean they are true just because someone died.'

'Well, he must have been investigating something,' Rainbow said, uncomfortable at realising that what had seemed so convincing to him was failing to convince anyone else.

'Who must have been investigating something?' McCabe asked.

'Marl.'

'Marl?' Donovan repeated, looking at Rainbow as though he was beginning to regret speaking up for him. 'Why would Marl be investigating anyone? He was a public relations officer.'

Rainbow looked in astonishment at Donovan and Donovan looked blankly at Rainbow.

Rainbow said, 'You didn't recognise him?'

Rainbow was carrying the satchel he brought to school, and he fished out a newspaper. Donovan took it and looked at it. Then he looked back at Rainbow, and finally up at Salmon.

'Well, well, I must be getting old,' he said, astonished. 'The *pincín*[56] here is right.'

He handed the paper, an Outland paper from some years back, to McCabe. McCabe looked at the photograph of Marl Fitzwilliam, and read the name underneath: *Boll Mason, Investigative Journalist*. The article was about an investigation into hygiene standards in a chain of Outland restaurants.

'Well, now,' McCabe said, 'an undercover journalist. Aren't you a clever minnow, Rainbow?'

Donovan turned back to Rainbow. 'Well, on your head be it, minnow. I have not had an apprentice for many years so you're taking your own chances.'

Rainbow nodded casually, as though people of his age were

---

[56] A small fish, a minnow. Can also mean, as Donovan means it here, 'mouthy little squirt'. Pronounced pinkeen.

regularly taken on as apprentices by legendary journalists. *Wait till he gets home*, Salmon thought, pleased by how pleased she knew Rainbow would be. *He'll be unbearable.*

'Come down to the Forum with me,' Donovan said. 'We've a hearing today on a libel charge.'

'Who is being accused?' Rainbow asked excitedly.

'Me, of course,' snorted Donovan. 'For publishing that very article, about a conspiracy to let Outlanders into Muinbeo illegally. But it is all true. And finally, I found a witness. And if it all comes out in the wash, McCabe, it would be worth following up our little minnow's idea.'

He swung his stick and walked out of the hotel, Rainbow keeping pace with him and listening intently.

'What on earth brought that on?' McCabe asked Salmon. 'Since when was your foster-brother so keen on journalism?'

'I think,' she said, 'it might have been since our last class with Dr O'Buachalla.'

She walked with McCabe to the back entrance of the hotel, where the quaestor had arranged for a closed carriage to pick them up, there being no direct tunnels between the hotel and the senate building.

'Dr O'Buachalla told us a story, and as evidence she showed us this book – well, I mean not a book you'd get in a library, she called it a codex. And she asked us to say whether we believed it or not.'

McCabe let her into the carriage first, then pulled the door shut behind him and rapped his knuckles on the roof. The carriage set off and Salmon grabbed the door strap to keep her balance.

'What was the story?' McCabe asked.

'It was this bizarre yarn about a boy who starts playing football with his friends and one of them kicks the ball into next-door's garden. Then this woman in a green frock comes out and she throws him down a well. Anyway, before you know where you are, there's this king – she said it all happened a long time ago – and he gets very sick and his doctor says that the only thing that will cure him is eating the ashes of the ogre's feathers.'

McCabe was laughing so hard he had to hold on to the edge of the seat. 'And did you believe it?'

Salmon looked at him. 'It didn't make a marble of sense. I thought it had to be true, though, because she had the book there, and it was all written down, but then I thought, *An ogre? With feathers?* And once you ask one question, all of a sudden there's fifty others. Why would anyone suddenly throw a little boy down a well? And the well was about three hundred feet deep. Who has a well that deep? Was the lady digging to Australia in her green frock?'

'And the other apprentices?'

'Well, Marigold said the story could be true but the book wasn't the record of it if the story was the age that Dr O'Buachalla said it was, that kind of ink hadn't been invented and the pages wouldn't have been bound together like that. Hunter said he didn't believe the story because he'd seen other manuscripts about ogres and everything sounded what he called *suspiciously similar.* And then Rainbow – Rainbow doesn't usually have much to say in class, well not anything that's related to the class, he suddenly said he could believe anything but only if he knew where the story came from, because whoever wrote it down might have been up to something. And the only person more surprised at him than Dr O'Buachalla was Rainbow himself.'

McCabe wiped his eyes.

'Well, I am relieved to know that you can all recognise a pile of horse-pucky at fifty paces,' he said. 'O'Buachalla was showing you a book of fairy-tales and folk-songs, but she was telling it like it was a newspaper story, to see if you could tell the difference.'

Salmon thought for a moment. 'Maybe we should have thought about the name of the codex,' she said thoughtfully. 'It wasn't called the Book of the Shaggy Dog for nothing I suppose.'

A private house near Roanoake Cross

⅂ℴ𝍩ℴ⌷⊕⊓𝍩𝈐ℴ⊓⊳⋈ℴ⊳⊿⊿⊳⊏ℴ⊥⊿⊓⊿⊓
⊿⊿⊂⊕ℴℴ⊖✳⊷⊕ℴℴ⊷⊕ℴℴ⊖⊂ℴ⊳✳⊓⊕
✳⊕ℴℴ⊙⅂⊓⊷ℴℴ⊘⊖✳⊳ℴ𝍩ℴ⊿⊓ℴℴ⊿⊕⋈
ℴ⊳⊳ℴ𝍩ℴ⌷⊕⊓⊕⊿⊙⊙⊿⊕✳⊓⊷⊖⊂_
⊿𝍩⊿𝍩ℴ⊓⊕⊿⊿⊕𝍩𝍩ℴ⊖✳ ⌷⊟ℴ𝍩✳⊂⊓✳
⅂ℴ⊂⊿⊳⊙⊖⊖ℴ ⊟ℴ𝍩ℴ⊖✳ ⊿✳⊳ ⊏⊓⊂⊿⊳⊿⊂
⊕✳⊳𝍩ℴℴ✳⊙✳⊂⊓⊔ℴ⊖✳⊳ℴ𝍩𝍩✳⊿⊕ℴℴ⊕
⊿⌷⊙⊓⊳⊓ℴℴ⊕✳⊓ℴℴ⅂⊓ℴ𝍩ℴ_⊖ℴ⊟⊿⊕⊓⊕
𝍩⊓⊕𝍩ℴℴ⊿⊓𝍩 ⊿⊕⊿⊔ℴℴ⊙⊂✳⊿ ⌷⊓✳⌷✳⊖ℴ

That I did not kill Marl – Boll – whatever was his accursed name – because he had stumbled upon the secretive Gallagrene Group, I will not be believed. It is the honest truth, not a commodity with which I am that familiar. I did not know the little blight was a journalist until I was told. I believed him, that he was as

193

he appeared to be. The camouflage of other animals is always a risk but the risk I have taken is vast. It gets bigger each time I look upon it. I have not yet been asked. But the hare that has been started will race straight past my door with the vampire in hot pursuit. I must think this through. I had taken it as a given that if the fool Guardians could find no motive for me to have murdered Fen then they would never discover our motive for Marl. In fact, I did not have a motive at all – as he knew nothing of Fen, she had said nothing to him. The Guardians have not yet come to me, but they will.

Gallagrene Bog

Salmon and the quaestor's factotum, Johnston, walked with Fallinish from the road into the bog. Salmon buttoned her coat up to the chin, her scarf wrapped over it so that only her nose and eyes were visible under her hat. Johnston left his jacket open and bounced as he walked. Neither cold nor heat bothered Fallinish and he trotted companionably by Salmon's side, stopping now and then to sniff at the ground. He still had many of the impulses of the dog he had been and Salmon wondered whether sniffing was to Fallinish now as eating was to McCabe – something they did but that was unrewarding. She wondered if Fallinish missed the sensual world.

To the east lay the lakes, shrouded with mist and clotted with reeds and rushes and stunted hazelnut trees. Cattle were making short work of the rough grass and thistles by the fence, and a dun bullock ate steadily while his red companion eyed the visitors belligerently over the wire. Salmon loved the soft density of the black earth through the bog and wiry undernourished plants that sometimes made spectacular flares of colour – bright green, flame yellow and gleaming berry reds. The sky hung low and the clouds, briefly bright, gathered darkness quickly on the short days. Neither she nor Johnston spoke on their way to meet McCabe at the ghillies' hut, which was a mile or so into the Gallagrene Bog.

The hut had been set up by the ghillies so that visitors could sit and watch the wildlife go past. It had been in frequent use in recent months, as the ghillies were surveying the fauna of the area and both the ghillies themselves and volunteers spent hours in the hut waiting to catch sight of a grey partridge, or a hare, a whooper swan or a fritillary, depending on how good their eyesight might be.

The hut had a tunnel entrance, and the day was a dim one, so McCabe had no difficulty in spending a little time there, partly distracted by the glint of moisture on the neck-feather of a distant marsh-harrier. The day had struggled to start, being dark and heavy until late morning when the sun finally began to show through. At first it was just a stubborn sulphur spot in the wet sky but eventually the fog began sullenly to thin out and lighten to silver. The air was still so heavy with water that the bright drops hung from every damp-blackened twig, glistening like damp fur on every leaf and strung like pearls on the strands of every spider's web.

Inside the hut, McCabe's ears suddenly blocked, as though the air pressure had dropped, and he was horribly startled by the door crashing open as Frost Paschalides came stamping in with an armful of glass jars.

Frost saw the ends of McCabe's coat hanging down, and he looked up at the ceiling, to which McCabe was clinging.

Salmon, who had just arrived at the hut with Johnston, was holding on to the doorjamb, tears of silent laughter on her cheeks.

'Sorry, there,' Frost said, startled in his turn. 'I didn't mean to give you a fright.'

McCabe, feeling faintly foolish, let go his gecko-like hold on the ceiling and dropped to the floor. Frost was an alien, and though McCabe could scent a human almost half a mile away, he never could distinguish alien scent. Unfortunately for Frost, aliens were the other social group usually excluded from polite Muinbeo society; fortunately for him, he had a sense of justice a mile wide and a hide like an elephant's. The result of the combination was that he was one of very few aliens who did not hide their ancestry, and all but the most anti-social Muinbeons admitted a grudging respect for him.

'Hardly a good time of day to be observing?' Frost asked, bending over the table and carefully letting the jars settle before unlocking his fingers and uncircling his arms. One of the jars rocked and McCabe shot out a hand to steady it before it fell.

'Thanks,' said Frost and smiled.

Frost was tall and wiry, with long red hair bundled into such a hay-twist that McCabe was almost overcome with the desire to hold the man under his arm and shave his head for him. Having lived through so many centuries, McCabe was accustomed to men wearing all sorts of decorations in their hair but matted and ill-kempt was not, he felt, quite the same thing as the debonair queue that had been his own most extravagant hairstyle. Frost had heavily freckled skin and grey eyes, and was wrapped against the cold night in a large heavy overcoat and a striped scarf. He wore expensive-looking hiking boots and muddy gaiters, and his fingers looked raw and bony sticking out of fingerless gloves.

'Alas, we are not here to admire the Gallagrene wildlife,' McCabe said. 'We heard a report that the rogue werewolf attacked Night Corbuse and was last seen at full pelt through the bog. And yourself?' McCabe added. 'You look like you are settling in for a day's work here. Is there something needs to be investigated?'

Frost was the current secretary to the Ecological Assessment Committee, which over the years tried to keep the physical world of Muinbeo in the public mind, to ensure that the impact on the environment was included in the reckoning of the cost of any new enterprise.

'Not officially,' Frost said, taking out some gardening tools and industrial-sized bottles of liquid with chemical formulae for names, 'but a little bird told me that the environmental office has received an application from Senator Postmaa proposing to cut away this part of the bog, because it seems to be infected.'

He heaved as he spoke, and pulled out a large metal gadget, with a shallow dish, a clockwork mechanism and several glass bulbs, with thin antennae waving in all directions.

'I heard that there have been reports of weird noises,' Johnston said. 'The land smells bad, the animals are moving off.'

'Absolutely true,' Frost said. 'The Ghillies of Demeter are investigating that, along with the Wildlife and Landscape Committee.'

'So where exactly are they saying is damaged?' Johnston asked. 'I – eh – happened to see some irises between Postmaa and the others on the committee about some kind of infection somewhere.'

'Here.' Frost swept his hand towards the horizon. 'All around Ciplacti's Ear, and off to the south. They say it should be cut away and burned. And Postmaa is usually a reliable kind of a fellow, but he is a politician, he has no special knowledge of the bog or the environment.'

'So where is he getting his information?' Salmon asked suddenly, and Frost nodded at her.

'Your apprentice is on the ball,' he said to McCabe, and Salmon thought, *The credit really should go to Dr O'Buachalla.*

'He is getting his information from Senator Albright,' Frost said. 'They know each other – they used to work together in the Outland.'

McCabe raised his eyebrows and Frost shrugged.

'Just because Albright is not known for being as honest as the day is long, it does not mean that he is wrong. If there is damage or infection, it needs to be dealt with, sooner rather than later.'

'Cutting away the bog seems a bit extreme,' McCabe said. 'Why do it?'

'The bog has a lot of rare species,' Frost said, gesturing towards the window, 'and the balance between all the flora and fauna surviving or dying out is very fragile. One log, a fallen branch or something, is home to all sorts of beetles and bugs and frogs and butterflies. If one thing is infected, suddenly everything is in danger.'

'But Ciplacti's Ear,' Johnston said, 'I mean – that is the oldest part of the bog. There's no knowing … what is in there.'

Frost shook his head. 'I don't know about that,' he said. 'I don't have the same attachment to places that people from Earth have. Some people think that the land around the Ear is uncanny, sacred, that whether it is healthy or sick indicates some kind of moral state in Muinbeo. All I know is that if there is damage or disease, then we have to cut it away and lose some of the wildlife, because otherwise we put all the species at risk.'

'So you think Postmaa may have a point,' McCabe said, 'and yet here you are, doing some extra investigation.'

'The reason it smells like a dead mackerel at low tide,' Frost said, 'is that this very talkative little birdie that I mentioned also told me that Albright and a few other senators have been in touch with the planning office. They are concerned, apparently, about the lack of facilities for patients recovering from long-term illness. They should have fresh air and a healthy day-to-day environment, not months in the interior of a hospital.'

Johnston and McCabe stared at him. Of all senators likely to develop a sudden concern for their fellow-citizens, Albright would be last on anyone's list. He was a competent politician, and reasonably hard-working,[57] but he did not have enough polish to hide the fact that other people did not really interest him unless they were attractive, wealthy or able to further his career. Sick or poor people did not exist for him.

'So he wants – they want – to build a convalescent home,' Frost added.

'Where?' McCabe said, his eyebrows closer again to his top hat.

---

[57] Or, to put it a less charitable way, he was not unreasonably lazy.

'Here. Take up Ciplacti, cut away the bog and build on it.'

McCabe's eyebrows could go no further up, so they came right back down again. Johnston and Salmon looked at each other.

The Ear is about three miles square of a unique ecosystem, with plants and insects not found anywhere else in Muinbeo. It supports corncrake and grouse, mosses and grasses and is the only place where there was a colony of phoenix outside of Linnenshee. The Ear itself is unknown. No one knows what it was, where it had come from, why it was there or of what material it was made. The earliest reference to it in written records is a letter that mentioned that many people believed that the object was the ear of the sleeping earth dragon Ciplacti but there were many other beliefs as to its origin and meaning. Looking at it from the observation hut, it protrudes at an angle from a place in the bog where a water-filled dike bristled with black-stemmed reeds, and it is an uncharted feature. It looms twenty feet and more above the ground, and its tip is visible from every point on the bog. It is known to sink many feet into the bog but the exact measurements remain a mystery. In the same way that, each year, at least one potential Peterson scholar tried to explain the nature of Muinbeo's existence, so each year, new hopefuls arrive at the Possible Institute in the north, gleaming with plans to measure and account for Ciplacti's Ear. Whatever it is, it has a distant similarity to an Easter Island head, thrust sideways into the peat and covered with vivid lichens and tiny, gem-like flowers, which picked out random shapes and patterns, even through the remnants of snow. The material of the Ear itself is only partially visible, covered in flora as it is. In some places it is black and corrugated, like bog-oak, some places it is pale as mother-of-pearl, others it is grey and gleaming.

'Again, even at that,' Frost said, 'there might be a point to some development. You don't necessarily protect a thing by not going near it – I mean the cattle are encouraged to go onto the meadowlands[58] so there's the manure for insects, for pollination, and they turn up the ground, and all that sort of thing. So we do have to check it. It's just …'

'If it wasn't Senator Albright …?' said McCabe.

'Frankly, yes. If the Thanatos or the Patriarch or Green Man Amberson came and said, what we really need is people trampling through bog, we need to shoot more hen harriers, we need to catch frogs, we need to dig up the Ear, it'd be one thing. But Albright. And it isn't like his supporters in this are reassuring. Scarlet Woudes, for example.'

'Who is the chair of the Ecological Assessment Committee now?' McCabe asked. 'Bean Robbins finished his term, didn't he?'

'It's Kale Lake,' said Frost. 'She's very good. She's a microbiologist, trained in the Outland, and very sensitive to the way bogland works.'

'Can I go and look at the Ear?' Salmon said. 'I haven't been here in a while and it looks strange.'

Frost and Johnston went with her.

---

[58] A meadow, over the river from Killchryso Temple, that had been left to grow wild for several centuries, with only enough care from the Ghillies of Demeter to keep it healthy. And – all right, let's be honest – to keep Muinbeo safe. You never know what might grow in such a meadow.

'There is certainly something wrong,' Frost said, and Salmon exclaimed, 'The smell!'

Instead of the brackish tang of bog-water and peat, the air had a metallic, sulphurous taste. Years of people keeping a respectful distance from the Ear had led it to develop its own unique ecosystem in a sprawling ring through which visitors could pass one at a time, but even without getting closer, Salmon and Johnston could both see that it was deteriorating. Fallinish sniffed the reeds and the small pools of stagnant water and trotted around the Ear. Salmon was puzzled; the smell and the strange rippling colours on the reeds seemed familiar, but she knew she had never seen the Ear like this. She reached out and grasped a reed.

Now she could remember: standing with her father at the edge of a sea; he was speaking angrily about the pollution that the Pharaonic army had deliberately poured into the ocean. The shore-line reeked of dead fish and rotting sea-weed. Salmon remembered it clearly – the same burning, metallic smell, and the sand had that same rippling grey where it touched the water.

As she let go of the reed and stood back, Salmon, Johnston and Frost heard the peculiar sighing; she thought at first that it was the wind, but there was something both mechanical and mournful that made her nervous. Fallinish stopped in mid-trot, startled, and looked around. He sniffed, turned, seeking the cause of the noise. He came and stood by Johnston, whining.

'How very singular,' said Johnston.

Salmon shivered and the noise, a subdued, wailing breath, came again and, with it, the sour metallic taste in the air.

'What is the matter with it?' Johnston asked, and Frost shook his head.

'We're working on it,' he said. 'Kale and Hobbs and the rest of us. It isn't any of the obvious types of infection that we've had before.'

'You don't look convinced,' McCabe said to Salmon when she joined him, and she shook her head.

'I might be remembering wrong,' she said, 'but years ago I saw damage that looked very much the same, and it was deliberate. Someone had brought in a virus.'

Frost was struck by a thought. 'It isn't out of the question,' he said. 'Cotton Donovan thinks the same thing – that is why he is being sued for libel this time, because he named names when he wrote his article about a conspiracy to damage the bog.'

'I hear from Heron Porphyrogenitus they have had to postpone the hearing,' McCabe said as Frost was locking up the hut. 'Did Rainbow say why?'

'Poor Bow,' Salmon said. 'He was horribly disappointed. But he did say why – oddly enough, the witness Donovan found was that woman in Hawkswood who was attacked by the rogue werewolf we're looking for.'

To keep McCabe company, they all walked back through the tunnels to the edge of the bog, where Salmon, Frost and Johnston had left their horses.

As they walked and Salmon looked up at where roots pushed their way through the brick roof of the tunnel, McCabe said to her, 'Did you know that a bog is the embodiment of a boundary? Between earth and water, between one state and the next.'

'Between one world and the next,' Johnston said. 'That's what they used to believe. It is always in a state of becoming;

plants becoming peat, peat becoming coal. That is probably why people buried bodies in bogs.'

'Are there bodies in Gallagrene Bog?' Salmon asked, not entirely comfortable with the idea.

'Almost definitely,' said Frost.

'Certainly,' said McCabe. 'A bog is alive with meaning.'

Once they reached the steps up from the tunnel to the surface, Frost said, 'No sign of that rogue werewolf?'

McCabe shook his head.

'It was just a chance. I was looking for inspiration more than werewolves to be honest. Two murders are enough to occupy me.'

'Two – oh, Marl Fitzwilliam? Though I hear now that's not his name.'

'That's right. And there is some hint that perhaps he found something going on, hints that there had been secret meetings with Outlanders, that kind of thing – we went through his flat earlier and found notes, but no real detail yet. Inducing an allergy is a very tricky way to try and kill someone, but the coroner seems very sure.'

'Why should anyone want to kill Marl?'

'You don't think there's a motive?'

'There's a motive for getting rid of him,' Frost said, 'if it is true that he had found a story about someone's misbehaviour – but why kill him? Get rid of him, don't let him finish his investigation, even pay someone to rob him of what he had done so far. Remember the row over airspace?'

Unexpectedly struck, McCabe nodded slowly, while Frost told the story to Salmon. A scandal now almost forty years old, a senator in secret negotiations to allow the Pharaoh's medusas[59] to use Muinbeo's space-portals. An investigative journalist had joined the Ghillies of Demeter, posing as a photographer. Upon being discovered by the secretary to the senator, the journalist was told that his contract was ended, and before he left, his house was burgled and everything he had recorded had been stolen and was never seen again. But, as Frost pointed out, he had not been killed.

---

[59] Medusas are organic spy boats travelling in space; they have a large pulsing bell in which the pilot and crew travel with the ship's brain, and trailing behind for miles are the long, lethal tentacles that absorb information, dark matter and any living thing that they touch.

Chapter 7: Wednesday

Gibbous moon, Wild Boar constellation rising

An empty apartment in Cow Lane, Ballinpooka

Salmon wished she had an amanuensis. She was not by habit neat or tidy, and as she faced the desk in Marl Fitzwilliam's apartment, upon which Benson had piled every scrap of paper that could be found in the three rooms that had made up the journalist's abode, she quailed. Johnston had been dispatched to interview all those who had attended the dinner, McCabe was going, he said, to try to join some dots and Benson had to go and visit everyone whom Marl had known in Muinbeo. Evidently her dismay showed on her face, because Benson said, with that air of faintly outraged innocence that came over him whenever he had the chance to foist upon the reluctant an unwanted task, 'It's a routine part of a guardian's work. It isn't all visits to the coroner's office and *following scents* at a crime scene.'

Benson, Salmon decided, was impossible. He told you things that you already knew; if you went along with the unnecessary lesson he hinted at the end that he was surprised that you didn't already know. If you pointed out that he was, in fact, teaching a lamb how to bleat, he quizzed you mercilessly until he finally found something that you didn't know. And then he gave you a lecture about not over-estimating your abilities. She settled for pretending his voice was the buzzing of a large fly, and keeping a bland smile on her face until he went away. Then she walked disconsolately around the desk, wondering where to start and how best to give McCabe a coherent account of the contents. Making a list of everything was the easy bit – she fished in her pocket for her indexer, which was a hand-held device she had been given when she lived in the Outland. It looked like some strange form of marine life. It was made of brass and fitted over her thumb, with coils and antennae making themselves at home among her fingers. Attached to it was a small silk bag, and as she wiped the brass thumb over the pages, the bag gradually became bigger and brighter (and heavier). Once she plugged the device into one of the typewriters at work, all the information would come back out again, in the form of beautifully typed, perfectly in order index cards. When she had finished indexing, she brought the letter, or newspaper, or photograph or whatever it was over to the kitchen table, which she dragged into the study and pushed under the window, and laid it neatly out.

Then came the tricky part, that of reading everything and putting it together into a coherent whole to describe to McCabe. For the first hour and a half she thought she might explode with boredom. How did grown-ups get up in the morning, only to face such dull lives? Bills and shopping lists and odd little bits of sticky paper on which Marl had written some random instruction or reminder, reading lists from a book group to which he belonged, iris sloughs about planning a trip to the Outland or ordering a book, reviews of films. However, she thought as she dutifully ferried paper about, she was not there to make moral judgments on what other people thought made for an interesting life. She was there to find – something interesting.

Salmon slowly brought the list of names over to the window. Whistler. Albright. Smith. O'Meara. Hobbs. Currie. Ribiero. Logan. Woudes. There was nothing else on the piece of paper, no date, no indication of the relationship between the names. But because Benson was good at his job, he had carried all the heaps of paper as he found them, without mixing one with another, and without separating anything from its neighbours. The neighbour to the list that Salmon found was a small notebook with a pale green cover. The first page was blank, but on the second page there was a name – Pothinus – and a line was drawn between each side of the name with a circle on each end. It looked like the name Pothinus was lifting weights. Over one circle was written *Cluancorr? Six Years* and over the other circle, *Apeteh*.

Salmon put down the little notebook and sat down. Half an hour later, Maccarrill came tapping at the window with his claw. When she let him in, he instantly asked her what was the matter and when she did not answer immediately, Maccarrill settled on the back of her chair to read the little notebook over her shoulder.

'Look at that,' she said unnecessarily. 'Apeteh. And Pothinus. Do you think that might be –?'

'I expect so,' Maccarrill said curtly. He did not like surprises, and certainly not dangerous ones. He waited while Salmon sent an iris to McCabe. Almost instantly, the answer came back. Salmon was to book the feel-good room for that very afternoon and they would start talking to Marl's fellow dinner guests again.

With Salmon in Marl's flat and McCabe and Johnston arranging new interviews, there was only Benson left in the guardian offices when Mackerel Amberson came to speak to someone in relation to the murder of Marl Fitzwilliam. Mackerel Amberson made Benson rather uneasy – he made most people uneasy – and so Benson asked one of the junior officers to stay and take notes.

When Mack walked through the door, Benson was struck by how similar the glazier was to his brother Shear, and how strongly dissimilar too. Mack smiled rather tightly and stood until Benson, remembering that Mack was even more literal-minded than Apprentice Farsade, told him to sit down. He offered him refreshments, and Mack asked for tea. Mack was much smaller than his brother but they had the same nut-brown hair and greenish-blue eyes, and exactly the same kind of nose, long and straight with a flattened tip. Mack wore clean, faded jeans with a white and green striped shirt tucked and belted in. Over the shirt he wore a dark charcoal cardigan, buttoned up, and his black boots were tightly laced and vigorously polished.

'I wanted you to tell me whether or not it is possible that Marl Fitzwilliam died because the food he was eating was not properly defrosted?' Mack said.

He spoke clearly and quite slowly, with a deliberate air that disconcerted Benson. Mack spoke like a competent but not a natural actor. Whatever Benson had expected it was not this question.

'No, Mack,' he said, 'I don't think so. The coroner seemed quite clear that it was allergy, and a suspiciously high level of the stuff he was allergic to. Why did you think it might have been about defrosting?'

'My brother Shearwater called to see me on that day,' he said. 'He was out on duty in one of the forests near the Great River, and he wanted me to go to his house, take out a fish curry to defrost because he would not have time. I meant to go over straightaway to do it, but I got busy with something and I went later. I was afraid I had not left it enough time.'

'I don't think it could have mattered, Mack,' Benson said, 'even if Shear had forgotten to defrost the curry –'

The door squeaked as the cleaning imp held it open so that a tea trolley could come through. The imp and the *luchrupán* followed, brooms and dusters in hands, while the trolley unloaded itself and offered round the biscuits. 'He didn't forget,' Mack corrected Benson, 'but Marl had just invited himself and Shear told me that the chicken casserole he had prepared for his guests would not be enough with an extra person'.

Benson nodded slowly and made a note. Somewhere in the back of his mind he was fishing for a detail. Would there really have been such a difference having one more guest that Shear had had to entirely change his menu? Perhaps. Or perhaps not. Could Mack have added something to the curry when he was in Shear's house? No – the histamine was not in Marl's last meal, but given to him some other way. Where would Mack, or anyone, get large amounts of histamine? Johnston had spent the morning going through the medical registrar's files to see if any of the medics in Muinbeo had had medicine stolen from them, to no avail.

'Was Shear surprised that Marl wanted to join them for dinner?' Benson asked.

'I think so,' Mack said, mulling it over. 'I don't think he knew Marl that well. I know Marl worked in the senate but he was in media, or public relations or something like that. He didn't have anything to do with the landscape, and Shear's friends usually were involved in that kind of work.'

'The other Ghillies of Demeter, you mean?'

'Anyone who loved the landscape. That was why Shear got on so well with Valerian Hobbs. That was why he wanted to join Hobbs's Pachamama Institute.'

'The Pachamama Institute. That's Hobbs's Outland place, that does the career courses,' Benson said, and shut his notebook.

Even before Mack left, Benson's mind was running ahead on what answers he needed to find out about the institute – where it was, how much it cost, what it did, what connections it had to Muinbeo, who else was involved. He realised then that Mack was standing up.

'Well, thank you very much, Mack,' he said, standing up also and holding out his hand, which Mack shook while bowing slightly. 'Thanks for your help. Mack?' he added, as Mackerel walked towards the door. 'Did you know Marl?'

Benson had no real reason for asking his question. It just popped into his head and straight out of his mouth.

Mackerel turned slowly and said uneasily, 'Well, I knew him a little. Yes. Not very well. Just a little.'

Benson watched Mackerel's shifty, uncomfortable face for a moment, then smiled and nodded. Mackerel went out.

'I wonder,' said Benson to himself – and, being alone, he said it aloud – 'if we have caught a fish.'

Interviews with members of the public who were not suspects were held in what Benson derisively called the feel-good room. He preferred to roll up his sleeves and get down to a good, thorough quarrying of witnesses' minds, however uneasy it might make a person. But Johnston, cynical as he was about his fellow-beings, was a bit softer-hearted and saw that even someone who was entirely innocent might be uncomfortable recounting a crime that they had witnessed. Benson snorted and asked if Johnston really thought that making sure the room was south-facing, painting it in pastel shades and having lots of cushions would make everything all right. Johnston invited Benson to think of something better. So the feel-good room remained. The cleaners were still in the room when the interviews started, grumbling gently about not being given enough time to prepare everything, but they had in fact settled it nicely, even with some fresh flowers.

Shear Amberson, wearily turning up for a second interview, did not seem to notice the sun or the pastel colours, though he did fidget a lot with one of the cushions, pulling at the fringe, tossing it to and fro, bouncing it on his knee. He sat in one of the armchairs, while Benson sat sternly behind the desk, Salmon sat unobtrusively near the window with McCabe in the shadows behind her, and Johnston, just arrived back from Barrow Upper and slipping quietly in, leaned against the wall near the door.

'So in fact you had not invited Marl to your dinner get-together,' Benson said disbelievingly.

Shear shook his head. 'No. He asked me if he could come over and join us. He said his brother was a werewolf and wanted to be alone.'

'His brother should have been in the Wolf Lodge.'

Shear shrugged. 'That is not my business. His brother is probably embarrassed about being a werewolf.'

'Why would that be embarrassing?' Johnston asked, and Shear shrugged again.

'At his age, everything is embarrassing. Anyway, I had invited all of the others – it was no formal thing, just we were going to watch the match, you know, the replay, and thought we'd get together, have something to eat. That was it. Then Marl – Boll – whatever his name was, he asked if he could join us. I didn't mind. Then – well. He ate what we all ate, and collapsed.'

Shearwater looked tired and anxious, but even Benson recognised that a man whose friend has been murdered and whose dinner guest died horribly would be a suspicious character indeed if they had turned up looking refreshed and rejuvenated. Shear was wearing an odd mixture of clothing – a heavy jumper, but with a shirt and tie underneath, lightweight trousers and stout hiking boots; he looked less as though he had got dressed and more as though he had run with his eyes shut through his washing-line.

'And the people who joined you for dinner?' Benson asked.

'My brother-in-law Thorn Grace; Patience Flynn, another ghillie; and River O'Malley, her husband.'

'Kale Lake? Valerian Hobbs?'

Salmon saw the slightest flare of dark in Shear's aura.

'Kale Lake is, as you know, a member of the Ecological Assessment Committee. As I am a Ghillie of Demeter, I've worked with her quite often. That's how I know her. She asked if she could invite Valerian Hobbs, and I said yes. I know him slightly.'

'He's one of these back-to-nature types, isn't he?' Johnston asked.

'I suppose you could say that,' Shear said tightly. 'He's involved with various organisations that train people in how to live in a less – damaging sort of way, especially in the Outland. They are very successful,' he added defensively. 'People who do these courses are able to live more – naturally. And his organisations are affiliated with several philanthropic institutions in the Outland.'

They went through the detail of the meal again. What Shear had cooked, how everyone had eaten the same thing, how his kitchen opened into the sitting room where the screen was, so someone was with him at all times when he was cooking.

Eventually, Benson said, 'And you were a friend of Fen Maguire too, I believe.'

Shear's aura darkened again, a dusty shade of violet. He looked very sad. 'Fen was lovely,' he said. 'We had been friends for several years. I hadn't seen her so often lately. I mean, we were both busy, but I was very, very sorry that she died. I saw her that morning, you know. We had coffee together at the senate. That was the last time I saw her.'

Johnston asked more questions – had Shear bought his meat and fish from Cedar Cullen? Who knew that Marl was going to join them for dinner? Benson also asked more questions – when he had last seen Fen, what had she been like? Did she seem as usual, did she mention anyone? Shear answered wearily and in detail – what she had been wearing, what she had said, how she had seemed.

Finally Johnston said, 'Any questions, apprentice?'

'With which philanthropic institutions in the Outland is Valerian Hobbs associated?' Salmon said.

'Different ones for different activities,' Shear said, frowning slightly. 'Let me think. There's the Gold Leaf Company. That gives advice on managing forests. There's, let's see, there's the Liebowitz Academy, that's for literacy. And Apeteh, of course.'

If either Benson or Johnston was able to read auras, they would have seen Salmon's flicker and turn a very strange shade indeed.

While Salmon was turning up unexpected names in Marl's journals and watching Shear Amberson's aura, Dr Boru, Velvet and Waxie, one of the two senior apprentice amanuenses, had sought in vain a single record of a single meeting of the Gallagrene Group. Starting from different corners of Dr Boru's office, they searched every single iris slough and index card, each of which told them where to find one of the millions of pieces of information that had, over the years, passed through the office. Boru rifled through some card drawers that she forbade the apprentices to touch, and from which came some strange, strangled noises. To be on the safe side, she sent Velvet and Waxie away to get some sandwiches and drinks for lunch. While they were gone, the cleaners came in. The imp dusted the curtains and the *luchrupán* began plying his broom vigorously to the corners of the office.

After a few minutes Boru noticed that her sleeve was being tugged and she looked down. The *luchrupán* had left his broom to one side and, when he had Boru's attention, he pointed to her coat stand. Boru spoke the melodious language of the *sidh* very well, and obediently followed the *luchrupán*, who took from the coat rack a greenish-blue shawl that had hung there since the day after Fen Maguire's death.

'No,' she said, in answer to his question, 'it isn't mine.'

'No,' said the *luchrupán*. 'It was Madam Maguire's, wasn't it? I often saw it in her office when I was cleaning.'

Boru picked up the shawl.

'Yes,' said she. 'Fen thought that she had lost it. She was upset – it was a birthday gift from Shearwater Amberson. She was wearing it the day she died. But she dropped it somewhere at lunchtime, and when she went back it was gone. It wasn't handed in until the day after she died. I held onto it to give to Fen's mother.'

'Perhaps Madam Maguire borrowed a scarf from you for the evening?'

Boru was silent for a moment.

'She did. It was an icy day and Fen was a cold creature at the best of times. When she went looking for her own shawl, I lent her one of mine, a dark green and red one. I said she could keep it. Why, what on earth is the matter? You're not supposed to be grey.'

'In the coroner's office, they have a model of Fen, as she was when they found her. I saw it when I was cleaning there. The scarf they have on her was yours, then – a red and green one.'

'Here, sit down,' said Boru and, from nowhere, there was suddenly a chair. 'Why is this causing you distress?

'Because I'm after realising something. Someone who said that they last saw Madam Maguire in the morning of the day she died should have seen her wearing her own scarf, this sky-green one here that I have in my hand. But there is someone now who says that they saw her in the morning but they described her in detail. And the scarf she had on her then was yours. The green and red one she is wearing now that she is dead.'

'That she was wearing when she died,' Boru corrected him automatically and the *luchrupán* was surprised, but far too polite to say anything. 'Have you told McCabe?'

The *luchrupán* shook his head, and Boru, kneeling beside him, patted his hand. Velvet and Waxie came back into the office, carrying trays of food and only mildly surprised – having worked with the Deputy Khipu-Camayacos for some time – to see the *luchrupán* stand up and the chair vanish. They put the trays on the deepest windowsill and Waxie began setting out crockery.

Velvet picked up a file that she had balanced across the crockery. She brought it over to Boru.

'Dr Boru,' Velvet said, 'I meant to show this to you earlier. I found it when I was cleaning out Fen's desk. It wasn't a formal file, just bits and pieces. But I thought I should bring it to be registered since ... well, just in case. You never know.'

Dr Boru took the file and, reading the name, said, 'I can hardly believe Fen had a file called *Miscellaneous*.'

She could hardly bring herself to say the word which was absolutely forbidden as a name for any file. *If it is important enough to file*, she always said, *it is important enough to have a proper name. You can call your children and your pets anything you want, but name your records correctly*. Velvet blushed, as though it was she who had so outraged the rules.

Dr Boru opened the file and immediately saw why Fen had used the name. There were all sorts of random scraps in it – receipts for presents, in case they needed to be changed, old lottery tickets, addresses and phone numbers hastily scribbled down, an old letter from the institute in the Outland where Fen used to work, some shopping lists, ideas for presents. There was a wealth of information, but it was of use only to Fen. She closed the file, but then opened it again, flicking through the records once more.

'Do you want me to take it to the guardians' office, Dr Boru?' Velvet asked.

There was a slight pause as Boru reread a letter, and then she said casually, 'You can leave it here. I will register it myself, and then the guardians can take it.'

McCabe's rooms, Senate Chambers

McCabe knew that there would be no avoiding the unpleasant meetings with the senators who were mentioned in the mysterious iris that had been found in Fen's house, and especially those whose names also turned up in Marl's little green notebook. He wanted Quaestor Finney's view on the wider implications of the questions that had to be asked.

'It is not quite as much of a shock as you might think,' Finney said, when McCabe finished speaking. 'Albright's early life seems to have been spent dodging in and out of Muinbeo like a pinball. Every time he made a new part of the Outland too hot to hold him, he'd come running back here. He only went into politics about five years ago.'

'He's popular enough too,' McCabe said. 'He got elected on an environmental ticket, oddly enough, promises to put wasteland to good use, encouraging more imaginative ways of using land.'

'A diversion perhaps?' Finney suggested. 'Depending on how long a game he was playing. If everyone associates him with a push for being conscientious about the environment, who is going to think that the same man is selling it down the river? And it gives him every reason to be associating with the likes of Valerian Hobbs. If the Pachamama Institute is up to mischief in the Outland, then Valerian Hobbs may well have many reasons to want to keep an investigative journalist quiet, don't you think?'

'Yes, but I doubt that Albright had anything to do with the institute, or Fen's murder,' McCabe said. 'It's about the Gallagrene Bog we need to ask him. While Marl seemed to be chasing a story on Hobbs, Donovan's accusation of a conspiracy of senators and Outlanders looking to get control of Gallagrene for whatever reason seems to be holding water. Diplomacy is your wicket, Quaestor, but it seems to me that we will have to be prepared for a substantial hue and cry when this gets out. There have been some murmurings already.'

'It's been leaked?' Finney said sharply, looking at McCabe.

McCabe shook his head. 'No. But the defilement, however it was done, had started to damage the land beside Ciplacti's Ear. And there have been complaints of dreadful noise coming from the bog. I have no idea what causes that, but it does mean the bog has been getting more and more attention.'

'And no chance of it being accidental?'

'I have asked to have it examined. Frost Paschalides is taking care of it for me. He will arrange to have tests done. But – this is worth mentioning: Apprentice Farsade saw the damage on the bog and she says that she has seen that kind of infection before. Apparently in the Outland, one of the ways of waging war is to damage the earth so badly that your enemy can't survive on it. It used to be just burning the crops and the trees but now it is infecting the land, making it infertile.'

Finney raised his eyebrows.

'The bog is protected as environmentally important,' McCabe went on, 'but if it is infected and damaged it is not protected any longer. If that happens to Gallagrene, then the bog can be cut back. It can be built upon.'

'Indeed. It seems likely to me that someone has been playing a long game.'

McCabe fished out a sheet of paper from under a pile on his desk. 'Dr Boru tells us that six years ago first Berliner Richards and then Coast Albright used the Registry office to investigate who is entitled to claim or buy land that has changed its environmental status.'

'It isn't for open sale,' Finney said, thinking through the procedure. 'It can only be bought by a senator. Hence, we suspect, Albright's entry into politics.'

McCabe stood up and closed his notebook over the jottings he had made of Finney's advice. Just as Finney was leaving, the postal chute belched and McCabe received from Velvet Corbuse the information he had requested in the form of a list of anyone living in Muinbeo who had training in microbiology.

'Six years is a long time to plan an infection of the bog,' Finney said thoughtfully. 'Albright is not usually so full of foresight.'

'So it would make a person wonder,' McCabe said, reading through the list, 'whether it is just a coincidence that Valerian Hobbs set up his Pachamama Institute six years ago.'

'Why the bog?' Finney said. 'Are they up to something we have not noticed? Why would it be so important that they get the bog? You don't believe this business about a convalescent home and neither do I. But what on earth would they need from Gallagrene?'

Finney and McCabe both turned at a knock on the door. Finney's secretary came in, holding a pulsating red iris gingerly between finger and thumb.

'It's from the Deputy Khipu-Camayacos,' said the secretary. 'She says it's important.'

Chapter 8: Friday evening

A week after the first death; the planet Delphia
appears in the east as the Wolf Star

The Weavers' Guild House, Catte Hill, Pallas Road, Ballinpooka

Each year, at the end of the first week of the first school term
of the new year, one of the Muinbeo guilds hosted a meal for
the students, and this year it was the Guild of Weavers. The
Guild House was a tall stone building on the top of Catte Hill
near the northernmost of the town walls, with a long driveway
that curved up the hill and was densely lined with pine trees.
As was the custom, the guild sent out carriages to collect all
the guests. Salmon, Rainbow and Marigold travelled with
Hunter, Nefertiti, Conger and Bracken, all spilling out to join
the noisy crowd who were greeting their friends as though they
had not met in a year, speculating about food and exclaiming
over the weather, as though a heavy snowfall was the last thing
you could expect in winter.

Inside the Guild House was lit with fires and lamps. The
ceiling of the great hall had been decorated with thousands of
tiny coloured lights wound around the beams, twinkling in the
dimness. Every surface had some example of the weaver's art
on it: vast wall-hangings, some already centuries old, drapes
that mimicked the fall of the snow and the movement of the
trees, table-coverings and chair-cushions. The centrepiece,

over the stone flags, was a great stretch of carpet, into which had been woven the appearance of an unswept floor, with food and papers scattered upon it, dropped cutlery, mice, the shadow of a dog.[60]

The president of the guild stood up to make a short speech, thanking them for attending and exhorting them to enthusiasm for their schoolwork, but Salmon was distracted. With one part of her mind she was thinking that it was very odd to see Berry being president and looking at once both utterly familiar and utterly unfamiliar. With the other part of her mind, she was wondering how best to get Hunter to tell her why he was lying about having found the piece of cloth that had been ripped from Silvanus Hughes's gown.[61] She felt quite indignant about it – that is, she felt guilty that she could not tell McCabe without making Hunter a suspect, but being indignant with Hunter was easier than worrying about what would happen if McCabe found out she was withholding something he ought to know.

Cedar Cullen was at the same table as Salmon – he taught butchery and fish-mongering at Derrydrake School once a week – and he was chatting and laughing with Velvet. Salmon momentarily wondered if they were related, as they shared

---

[60] This was extremely old. The person who created it was an Outlander, who had created a mosaic of pretty much the same subject on the floor of a Roman villa. We think perhaps housework preyed on his mind for some reason.

[61] The rest of her mind, to be honest, was sorting out the order in which she intended to eat the food that was being set out on the tables as Berry spoke. But we thought you might have guessed that part.

some similarity she couldn't quite name, but then she recalled that Velvet only had one sibling, her brother Night. Salmon was sitting between Nef and Bracken, and the conversation catapulted from one topic to another like a pinball – what was the most rare type of meat Cedar had ever been asked to provide, did Velvet really, really not know what the Khipu-Camayacos looked like, did you hear the one about the duck that went into a pub, how many languages were there in the whole world?

'And I hear you've been apprenticed,' Bracken said to Rainbow, who beamed and nodded. 'To Cotton Donovan, no less. We'll soon be able to get all our gossip from you! Isn't your new despotes about to start his trial for slander – or is it libel? – the one that was delayed because the werewolf ate the witness out in Hawkswood?'

Rainbow looked momentarily disconcerted. He suddenly realised that people would look at him differently because of where he worked.

Then he laughed and said, 'Bracken, if there was a guild of gossip-mongers, you'd be president – it will be me coming to you for news!'

Everyone, including Bracken, laughed, and then Bracken lowered his voice. 'You must have heard, though, that they're investigating some of the senators. You know the Deputy Khipu was on the warpath over an iris that had been sent from some group that never registered any minutes.'

Velvet glanced at Salmon to roll her eyes sympathetically. But Salmon was frowning, looking very worried, as Bracken was talking. Bracken, not noticing, lowered his voice again and leaned further over the table.

'Well, I heard that there were some senators involved in a group to buy up that part of the bog that's become infected. You know, it was in the paper the other day – and that they will have to be removed from their jobs.'

'That isn't the first time that has happened, though, is it?' said Nefertiti. 'I seem to recall hearing something similar five or six years back. Not the bog, though.'

'Cluancorr,' said Hunter. 'Remember, Salmon? Dr O'Buachalla said Cluancorr was nearly sold to some group who wanted to develop it.'

'It might not have been the same group,' said Salmon.

'Still, though,' Hunter said thoughtfully. 'Two groups wanting to develop two under-used bits of land. But what on earth could the same people want with a nice fertile bit of land like Cluancorr that they could also do on the Gallagrene Bog?'

The question, despite echoing Quaestor Finney's question to McCabe, being unanswerable, the dessert having been served and the music having started up meant that the subject was dropped. But when the food was finished and the apprentices began to scatter from the table, Salmon spotted her chance to get an answer from Hunter. He had remained in his seat, smiling slightly, watching others dance and be foolish. There was no one else at the table. Salmon sat down and Hunter smiled at her.

'Why did you lie to us about finding the bit of cloth from Silvanus Hughes's gown?' she asked. *No point beating about the bush*, she thought, *when you can just walk right through it*.

Hunter's smile dropped like a sail in the doldrums.

'Ah,' he said, 'I rather feared you would not let that question go.'

Salmon didn't answer, just raised her eyebrows.

Hunter sighed and said, 'Wait here.'

He got up and went over to where Cedar was doing a very nifty foxtrot with one of his many nieces, and managed to catch the butcher's attention. The niece, unperturbed by the interruption, plunged back into the milling crowd while Cedar and Hunter spoke and nodded. Cedar and Hunter came back to the table, scooping up Velvet on the way.

'I lied not only about the scrap of cloth,' Hunter said amicably, 'but also about the glove I found. Well, that was less of a lie, but a lie it was. The reason was that in both cases, the clues were found by dimorphs.'

'I found the glove,' said Cedar.

'I found the cloth,' said Velvet.

'And they do not want people to know that they are dimorphs, so they came to me and asked me to pretend I had found them.'

'You already knew about them being dimorphs?' Salmon asked.

Hunter smiled. 'It is one of the advantages of being a sombrist,' he said. 'Being something of an outcast yourself can, with the right frame of mind, make you less judgemental about other outcasts. Especially if you do not believe, as I do not, that there is any truth in the rumours about dimorphs being the result of a Pharaonic genetic experiment.'

'Is that why people dislike dimorphs so much?' Salmon asked, with McCabe's question still tucked behind her ear.

Hunter looked from Velvet to Cedar but they shook their heads.

'Who knows?' Velvet said. 'More people hate us than think about the Pharaoh at all.'

'I think we frighten people,' Cedar said, looking sympath-etically at Velvet, who clearly did not want to discuss it. 'We're the opposite of too many things. People think that they are who they are and that the core of them never changes. That's important to them. And yet here we are, hopping from shape to shape, species to species like there was no tomorrow.'

'But people don't mind werewolves,' Salmon objected.

Velvet shrugged uneasily. 'A person who is born with pale skin isn't an outcast because they get a tan easily,' she said. 'It just means that they have a gene that makes their skin dark in sunlight. Werewolves have a gene that makes them more a wolf at the full moon and more a person the rest of the time. A dimorph changes everything about them, at will. Cedar's right. People will worry about what "a human being" means if the boundaries aren't nice and firm.'

Salmon looked at Velvet and Cedar and nodded rather awkwardly. She wasn't sure what to say.

'You're looking for logic,' Hunter said, almost kindly, 'for reason. This isn't logical. It's bigotry. There are no reasons, only impulses.'

There was a difficult, melancholy silence. Salmon said, 'I'm sorry.'

'For not being a dimorph?' said Cedar teasingly. 'For being all normal?' And Salmon laughed when the others laughed.

'I can dislocate my eyes,' she offered by way of exchanging weirdness, 'and I'm part-Outlander.'

'Do you think that's enough?' Hunter asked Velvet, pretending to consider it. 'Think we can let her into the Monsters' Club?'

'Oh, go on, please!' Salmon said and Velvet giggled.

'Well, all right then,' Cedar said, as though he was giving

in. 'But your first duty is to go and get us a jug of that blackberry punch. That niece of mine can dance like a dervish. I'm parched.'

When Salmon came back and poured out that purple-glistening drink, she said to Hunter, 'Why did you tell McCabe about seeing the paw prints?'

'He had to,' said Velvet. 'Think about it. If we tried to hide the prints, since it was where poor Fen actually died, we might have destroyed evidence that meant you could find who killed her. But if Hunter came to you and didn't mention that he'd seen great big paw prints the size of your head –'

'Hey,' said Cedar, 'I dance well for a big dog.'

'Well, you see what I mean. You would definitely have thought there was something suspicious about it all. The chances of you finding out who was the dimorph were tiny. So it was safer to draw attention to it.'

The rest of the evening they spent talking about the murder, about their respective despotes (Cedar kept in touch with his from years ago) and what it was really like to have a hound's sense of smell or a bird's vision.

In the middle of the night, Salmon woke up, and sat up. As clearly as if she was standing in front of it, she could see her portal landscape. She remembered the flickering lights she had seen on Chlovis Aornis, the night of the gairm Thanatos. She knew the answer to Hunter's question, and what it was a fertile piece of ground like Cluancorr had in common with bogland in Gallagrene. Tomorrow morning she would go to Cluancorr first and see if she was correct.

And the next day, Bracken's prediction of a scandal came true.

McCabe was in his office with Benson and Johnston late into the evening to update the memory theatre. After the interview with Amberson, Benson had spent yet more hours at the public library, hunting through the newspapers for any reference he could find to Pachamama and the other philanthropic institutions that Shear had mentioned.

In the offices of the *Muinbeo Times*, Cotton Donovan was laboriously typing telegrams to journalists he knew in the Outland, while Rainbow scoured the *Times* correspondence files and sent the telegrams. Johnston, in his element with gossip and conspiracy theories, had been helping them, and came to McCabe's office just as Benson finished arranging copies of newspaper articles across McCabe's desk.

'A right little nest of vipers we have,' Johnston reported cheerfully, 'and every single one of them claiming a level of altruism not seen since Prometheus stole fire.'

He looked over Benson's shoulder at the articles.

'Apeteh is the most important one,' he said. 'Been there since Methuselah was a boy. All the others – your Gold Leaf, your Liebowitz Academy and all the rest of them – are Johnny-come-latelys compared to Apeteh.'

He sat down, and McCabe, pulling the newspapers closer, gestured to him to continue.

'So this seems to be the way of it,' Johnston said. 'The important thing to remember is that all of these corporations are connected in some way or another with the Pharaoh's court, so that should give you a hint about the level of deviousness we're talking about, and the amount of skill there is for sleight-of-hand. Now – picture the scene: the Pharaoh's court about three hundred years after the Pharaoh, the real Pharaoh, died.'

'I'm pretty certain,' Benson said repressively, as Johnston's flippant tone irritated him, 'that the current Pharaoh would not take kindly to being called a fake Pharaoh.'

'The current Pharaoh,' Johnston repeated thoughtfully, 'now there's a conundrum if you like them wrapped in mysteries. Bear with me. So, the Pharaoh is dead and the court that has grown up around him starts jostling for position. Everyone starts calling in favours, starts looking for the rewards they thought they deserved, starts forgetting all the people who helped them succeed. Everyone is secretly hoping to become the centre of power, or at least to be nearer the centre of power than everyone else.'

Johnston selected some of the newspaper articles and put them in a line together so Benson and McCabe could read them.

'Not everyone,' he said. 'For every ten people who clambered over their friends for a shot at getting into the throne room, you had one who stood to the side and let them pass. These people had real sense. They knew the odds were against them. The Pharaoh had controlled everything, personally. With the Pharaoh dead and the Empire waxing and fattening and whatever else empires do when they are getting bigger and stronger by the minute, they knew that someone was going to have to take over, not the throne, but the administration. Most people in the Empire would see the Pharaoh once in a blue moon, once in a lifetime, maybe. But how did they know about the Pharaoh's power?'

He tapped the articles.

'Through the people who actually ran the Empire. People who built the schools and trained the teachers, and ran the factories and businesses where people worked, who ran the councils and the committees. Who ran the newspapers.'

'By starting more humbly,' McCabe said, picking up one of the articles to frown over it, 'they hid the signs that they had started climbing the greasy ladder to success in the court itself.'

'The biggest – well, not the biggest, but the one with the most tentacles,' Johnston said, 'is Apeteh. It has the smallest number of people actually running it, but it has influence everywhere.'

'How, if it's the smallest?' Benson asked disbelievingly.

'By choosing their positions very well,' Johnston said promptly. 'It is less important to them to be the person in power; they want to be the people upon whom the powerful depend. Whether they know it or not.'

'The apprentice,' said McCabe, 'knew Apeteh.'

Benson and Johnston looked at each other, and then back at McCabe. Neither of them knew anything about Salmon, other than that she had lived in the Outland and after being orphaned there had been given refuge in Muinbeo. Any attempt by them to find out more from any quarter had failed, with varying degrees of politeness.

'I can talk to her when she –' Benson said, and jumped a little, as he always did when McCabe turned his head right around so he could look behind his back.

'Don't, Benson,' McCabe said. 'I am telling you this so that you will both know not to ever mention Apeteh to her. Either directly or indirectly, Apeteh is to blame for the death of her – well, her parents.'

Benson and Johnston looked at each other again. They had not been expecting the Pharaonic imperial war to come creeping into Muinbeo like this.

'She gave us a name,' McCabe said. 'Pothinus. Theo Pothinus. Apparently he is a man of some significance and power within Apeteh.'

'That's putting it mildly,' Johnston said immediately, 'Theo Pothinus.'

'Who he?' Benson asked.

'Who knows?' Johnston replied and Benson made a snorting, dismissive noise. 'He has some rubbishy title, Special Advisor, Executive Chairman of Apeteh Corporation, I can't remember. But if the court and the Empire depend on Apeteh, then Apeteh depends on Pothinus.'

'But what does he do?' Benson insisted and Johnston shrugged.

'He is Theo Pothinus,' Johnson said, 'he does whatever the hell he wants.'

'This is what he looks like,' McCabe said, handing a newspaper photograph to Benson. 'The apprentice recognised it. It isn't a good picture but a lot of people working for Apeteh are very camera shy.'

He tapped the photograph of a thin-faced man with wiry hair brushed back from his face, and long eyes hidden in folds of skin.

'Remember Theo Pothinus,' he said. 'Now we have some more news. I had an iris yesterday when I was in talking to the quaestor. And you will never guess what the *luchrupán* said to the Deputy Khipu-Camayacos.'

Chapter 9: Saturday

The Wolf Star rising

Chlovis Aornis

Maccarrill complained and groused the entire way from Knotty Down to Chlovis Motte. In the early hours of the morning – already a bad start in Maccarrill's eyes – Salmon bundled herself into her warmest clothes and wheeled out her bicycle from the shed. The bicycle had been given to her by Great-grandfather Peregrine and, for an inanimate object, it had a faintly knowing – even mischievous – air about it. The quickest route to Cluancorr was by the canal. This did, of course, involve just a couple of little instances of trespass. *But,* she said to herself as she pedalled briskly through Miss Aquinas's pasture and the Munroes' ploughed field, *it is very nearly official guardian business.*

Seeing the motte in the foggy morning twilight, she understood why the aornis was uncanny. It emanated silence and its crowning thatch of trees was dense, unwelcoming and monumental. Maccarrill flew up ahead of her. Salmon propped her bicycle up against a small hazel tree on the southern side, which was the easiest path to climb. In the midst of the trees, and watching where she was placing her feet on the shadowy and uneven ground, Salmon did not notice the wave of a small lantern at the edge of the motte.

Even with her compass, and even with her portal landscape

clear in her mind, Salmon took a few minutes to get her bearings. She moved softly, but in the dense, uneasy quiet among the trees she could hear every footfall, every breath. Maccarrill startled her, a wraith, silent among the stark branches. She climbed on, stumbling on frozen tussocks, her feet slithering over fallen branches. Salmon was on edge. She felt terribly clumsy. The ground seemed to resist her, becoming suddenly oily, marshy or iron-hard by turns. Brambles tangled in her feet, and she fell. In the flittering shadows it seemed as though the branch she reached for had moved out of her way. She stopped for a moment and looked behind her. Like a steeplejack making a mistake in looking down, she was overwhelmed with sudden panic. The forest let in no chink of moonlight, the trees seemed tightly packed together and towering. The air was freezing. She put her hand over her mouth, suddenly too frightened to move forward, and too afraid of being seen – though by what she could not have said – to retrace her steps. She almost shrieked when Maccarrill was suddenly beside her, circling her.

'Since you've dragged us out here,' he said grumpily, landing on a nearby branch and eyeing her twitchily, 'we may as well get on with it.'

Hearing Maccarrill's rasping voice made the world shift back to its normal shape. Salmon took a deep breath. It was a forest before dawn. That was all. She strode forward and in short order had found the plateau just below the western peak of the motte, and there were the dead tree and the rock. So pleased to realise that she had been right, and that the tell-tale Whedon Lights that Dr Darwin had described could be seen glimmering above the rimy ground, Salmon did not hear Maccarrill's warning squawk: she rushed forward and the portal, confused and unstable, pounced.[62]

The portal on Chlovis Motte was more than erratic, it was damaged. Shut down centuries ago, it had been illegally reopened, by someone who did not know that 'erratic' also means 'very nearly sentient', who only knew modern techniques for managing tame portals. Salmon, having never seen a portal move, froze.

The first few seconds were dizzying, there was something wrong, a little mound of earth that had not been there a moment before was shimmering, quaking. An emptiness appeared at its centre and the portal flung itself outwards, in a spray of angular spirals that shot up into the air, high as the trees, and crashed to the ground, grabbing at the frozen earth like hands with no sight to guide them. A tangled dome of hazy air, a jangled geometry of planes surged out from the emptiness at the centre, violet and gold light rippling and spinning and swirling chaotically. The dome spread like water, trees bent fantastically towards it, their branches pressing down on Salmon as she scrambled away. She could sense the gravity field before it touched her, and she clung to the branches, clawing her way in inches along them in the hope that their deep roots would help anchor her to the earth. The air was

---

[62] Erratic portals are uncommon and everything is a bit of a mess – random instructions are pulsing about: electricity, magnetic waves, scattered crumbs of magic, clashing atoms, bits of computer code. There is no pattern or tidiness, it's all ragged, things are exposed that should be covered, there's noise, and heat, jagged light and chaos. That might be your idea of fun, but we'd rather just sit in with a good book.

full of sound, shattering and booming, and Salmon had barely breath enough to scream when she realised the tree to which she was clinging was being ripped out by the roots.

The flashing brightness that surrounded her served less to show her what there was to be seen and more to show her how deep and dark were the shadows in which the dangerous things lurked. The ground was vibrating and the air full of distant roaring like the noise of the ocean trapped in a conch-shell. The earth had cracked and frayed around the mouth of the portal and the jumble of branches and tree-trunk became jammed; Salmon struggled to lie in the lee of the tree and find a secure place into which she could wedge her feet. All around her loomed vast wheels, a pendulum north and south, cogs and cams, etched in faint white on the blackness, like scratches on old wood. Salmon felt the dreadful wrench of falling, the air lurched and the tree was free. She did not register the sudden drop in the strength of the portal's pull but as she lost her grip on the tree, someone, or something, grasped her firmly by the back of her coat, and pulled. She struggled, kicking and flailing against it, unable to see which way she was being dragged. She was suddenly released, she tumbled forward and something very hot and soft hit her hard in the face, throwing her to one side. As suddenly as it had pounced, the portal let her go. Salmon scrambled away, and from a safe distance saw the portal suck itself back into the ground, invisible once more.

Salmon lay on the freezing, silent ground, waiting for her heart to stop trying to escape her chest. She was wondering about the bizarre whooping noise – was it the portal? Or swans overhead? – but no, that was impossible. No birds could fly over the aornis. She began to roll over. She realised that it was she herself who sounded like a distressed goose. She hastily sat up, catching her breath in a more decorous manner. Maccarrill was parading up and down in front of her, picking up his claws daintily and eyeing her as though he didn't know whether to hug her for being alive or clip her across the ear for being so reckless. Behind him stood a woman holding a small lamp who, Salmon knew from the cinder-grey cloak and the coloured beads, was a sombrist, but whom otherwise she did not recognise. And beside the sombrist stood McCabe.

The sombrist said, 'That's some parrot you've got, apprentice. Disappears for three seconds and comes back with a vampire.'

Maccarrill preened.

'And that's some little lantern you have there, madam,' said Salmon, 'if you got an erratic portal under control with it.'

'It is all down to what makes the light,' said the sombrist, rather cryptically, but then sombrists tended to talk like that. 'I was able to make the portal move back a little but it is really McCabe you need to thank. There is nothing like a vampire to make a portal remember its manners.'

'Perhaps,' McCabe nodded. 'It was Maccarrill who made the portal finally release you, but there are not many humans who will risk getting as close as Madam Gulliver here did, in order to get you out.'

Salmon struggled to her feet and, not knowing what else to do to thank someone who had saved her life, stuck out her hand. Madam Gulliver looked at it, and, clearly uncomfortable, straightened her cloak. She had a wide, flat forehead with a small face beneath, with high, round cheekbones almost hiding her grey eyes. She had an air of rather grim calm, as though she were accustomed to adversity.

She said, 'Sombrists do not usually shake the hand of a non-believer.'

McCabe said briskly, 'True, Madam Gulliver, but sombrists do not usually go into places that are forbidden to them by their own beliefs, such as the motte. And yet here you are and I see no sign about you of a twisted arm. So this morning seems to be a morning of exceptions, does it not?'

Madam Gulliver looked at him. She pushed her hood off her head, revealing a neat cap of greying black hair, rolled in a bun at the back of her skull. As though expecting worse to come as a result, she took Salmon's hand and shook it.

Salmon said, 'I'm pleased to meet you, Madam Gulliver. I have heard Hunter Sessaire often speak of you.'

Madam Gulliver said, 'And I suppose that now you and your despotes think that either I opened the portal or that I killed the unfortunate Maguire?'

Salmon sidled forward as Madam Gulliver was looking at McCabe, and she sniffed deeply.

McCabe said instantly, 'And so what is the verdict of the ever-so-discreet sniff-test?'

Salmon went pink and said, 'It was not she on the motte the night Fallinish and I were here.'

'Apparently Salmon's nose has you off the hook as to the murder,' McCabe said to Madam Gulliver. 'As to the portal – well, we will soon know.'

McCabe and Madam Gulliver picked their way over the churned-up earth and the scattered trees to look more closely at the ground beneath the flickering lights.

Madam Gulliver said, 'There are ways of opening portals, and there are ways. You can be light-fingered, like a thief picking a lock. Or you can do the equivalent of taking a heavy object and smashing it to pieces. If I were trying to repossess a portal, I would have done a far better job. This portal is in tatters.'

McCabe replied, 'The security engineers will find the culprit. I am surprised that a sombrist, especially you,[63] would know so much about portals, and be interested enough to be up on the aornis looking for them. I thought that sombrists thought portals were evil and the aornis little better.'

Madam Gulliver looked at him gravely. 'Evil is a big word,' she said finally. 'Some people don't know how to use it.'

McCabe looked at her, equally gravely, then he sighed and nodded, and she pulled her hood back up.

'Good morning, then,' she said, turning away.

'And don't worry,' McCabe said as she began to walk down the side of the motte, 'we won't mention anything of this to your elders or the Komnenos.'

Madam Gulliver raised her hand but did not stop walking.

'Unless we have to,' McCabe said to Salmon.

He set off down the aornis with Salmon.

'I will take you home,' he said, 'I gave Cotton Donovan some of those names you found in Marl's – Boll's – apartment. He has

---

[63] This isn't really a good time to go into detail about the sombrists, and their hierarchies and their sometimes virulent debates and disagreements about belief and the nature of the world. Suffice it to say that Madam Gulliver is an abbess, and therefore her job description includes 'not standing any nonsense', and 'having the final say', but also 'is in deep professional horse-pucky if found doubting The Discipline'.

had himself a field day, building up his story of the conspiracy. So Senator Albright is going to have a busy morning – I am going there now to arrest him, but I hear he is due at Cotton Donovan's trial this morning too.'

'Then why am I going home?'

'You are going to get some sleep,' he said. 'You think you are fine, but you were very nearly killed. Don't argue with me, Farsade.'

McCabe called her Salmon or 'apprentice' most of the time, but Farsade when he was pulling rank. She took a look at his ice-blue aura, and gave in.

'Sir?' she said as they reached the foot of the aornis and he picked up her bicycle. 'Sir, about rogue werewolves? You said that rogues thought that they were above the rest of us when it came to what was right and wrong, or just or unjust.'

'Yes.'

'What happens when the rogue is right and the rest of us are wrong?'

McCabe steadied the bicycle, and beckoned to Salmon to take the handlebars.

'Then *eble vi vivas en interesa fojoj*,' he said, 'which means, "May you live in interesting times".'

Guardian questioning room, Senate Chambers

Quaestor Finney was sitting in the secure interview room of the guardian station, resting his arms on the table, his long thin fingers intertwined with each other. He had been at the opening of a new wing of the Swanhill Library – the only wing without its own ghost – and was in full ceremonial robes, so getting through the door of the interview room had been something of a challenge. It was testimony to Finney's unshakable poise that he had managed to dress himself in full regalia while responding to dozens[64] of irises sent from the Forum. Two large guardians stood on either side of the door looking as burly as they could manage and two more guardians had been armed with tranquilliser guns; one stood like a monument between the interview room and the exit, the other was outside, blowing smoky breath into the freezing air.[65] Opposite the immaculately dressed quaestor, the normally dapper Bassett Dunne was dishevelled, barefoot and wrapped in a blanket. He needed to shave, his black curly hair was bushy and flecked with dead leaves and grass, his blue eyes were bloodshot and he was shaking.

'So, you escaped from the hospital under the influence of the moon, which I understand, and you spent the time – on Gallagrene Bog?'

'Yes,' Dunne said, rubbing his face. He just wanted to sleep. 'I was very confused,' he said. 'I went into one of the tunnels and found a little corner to sleep in.'

'You were lucky you didn't freeze to death,' Finney said but Dunne shrugged.

---

[64] The collective noun for irises in flight is an *interrogation*. When they are nesting in their banks they are a *gleam*.

[65] In case you think this was a bit hard on him, the guardian who was standing outside in sub-zero temperatures was the size of a bear so had plenty to keep him warm. Besides, he was an Outlander from Oymyakon in Russia, and didn't notice the cold until after most people had frozen and crumbled to dust.

'I don't know. It was OK – the peat probably keeps the tunnels warm. And animals are not afraid of a werewolf, apparently. Some nights I had a dog with me, one night there was a little roe deer. It was OK. Anyway, the Wolf Lodge found me near Ciplacti's Ear. They took me in and looked after me.'

He stopped, trying to recall not so much the sequence of events as the sequence of his own reasoning, but much of it was cloudy and opaque. Finney pushed the mug of tea that had been given to him over towards Dunne, and Dunne drank it gratefully. The shivering began to ease.

'But before that, you escaped the hospital ward, and you came back to the guardian offices on the night of the gairm.'

'Yes. I was trying to find someone to put me in a cell so that I could be somewhere familiar. The hospital ward upset me when I changed, I was frightened of it. So I came back to where was familiar to me. But everyone was gone. I was wandering around when I changed, and then Benson and McCabe turned up.'

'Then you tried to eat Geoffrey Ballantyne Logan,' Finney prompted.

Dunne's face brightened.

'Oh, yeah, that's right. Is that who he was? I had no idea. Well, you see,' he continued, as Finney was clearly waiting for more, 'as I said, I was trying to find someone but I began to change because of the moon. I could smell McCabe but I couldn't find him. I was walking through the corridor to the interview rooms. But I don't know why Logan was at the station.'

'McCabe had brought him in for questioning. Dunne, how much do you know about what has happened recently?'

Dunne shook his head.

'I'm sorry to have to tell you this. Fen Maguire has been murdered.'

Dunne stared in silence for a few moments. He had known the amanuensis slightly, enough to be shocked at her murder but not enough to be personally upset. He took a mouthful of tea.

'McCabe has brought Silvanus Hughes in for questioning –'

'She was murdered by Silvanus Hughes?' Dunne said, unable to believe the idea. 'I thought Hughes was that trout-faced historian, the one who laughs like he is trying to remember who you are.'

Finney shook his head.

'No, no. Drink up your tea and I will tell you the whole story.'

Dunne was exhausted and upset, so it took a while for him to understand why Logan and Hughes ended up in the guardian station for questioning.

But finally he said, 'Well, that explains what he was doing there, I suppose.'

After a moment, Finney said, 'Yes, but it doesn't explain why you attacked him.'

Dunne twirled his cup. 'I know that Logan is the pet popular academic of the Outland,' he said, 'and that everyone is peachy-pleased because he is from Muinbeo and is the respectable face of a peculiar place. But that *cur*[66] is the werewolf who bit me. He's the rogue. Moonlight used only

---

[66] That is not the word he used. But we can not possibly repeat what Dunne actually said. We have been delicately reared. We are gentle ... men.

to conjure up images of romantic encounters by rose-lined garden lakes, and now I can't look at it without everything going haywire. All because of *him*.'

Finney's mouth fell open, so discreetly that only the security guardian noticed. 'Logan? *Logan?* Ye gods.' Finney got to his feet as fast as he could, considering his clothes, but Dunne waved him down.

'If Logan has two marbles of sense,' Dunne argued, 'he will be gone out of Muinbeo by now. You can't do anything about him in the Outland. It's not like here. They find it hard enough to believe in werewolves at all, they won't understand about a rogue.'

'You are sure it was Logan? You are positive it was he?'

'I could smell him,' Dunne said. 'There's no doubt about it. I don't know why he attacked me – I suppose that it didn't matter who.'

'How did your paths cross?' asked Finney.

Dunne frowned, trying to remember. The days since he had been attacked ran together in his mind, full of heat and confusion and pain. He could barely tell day from night, he slept heavily, but was as wracked with exhaustion as though he had been sleepless for a week; he was so tired it hurt. All he could remember was the moon. It was so insistent, dominating his frightened mind, that he could almost hear its still presence. Then the wolf leaped out and he was unable to control any part of himself. He was suddenly immense, a weight he felt unable to carry. His whole being was crowded with hot fur, slitted eyes and a long snout making the world unrecognisable. His mind was overwhelmed by the thousands of scents in every inch of the world. He felt like Alice in Wonderland, suddenly pitched down a rabbit-hole, big and tiny by turns, coping as best she could without any map or guidebook.

'It was like being an adolescent again,' Dunne said resentfully. 'All of a sudden everything boils over and you have no clue what is going on.'

Finney, whose own adolescence had been smooth as a mill-pond, made sympathetic noises.

'I was in the Grand Hotel Abyss,' Dunne said, trying hard to remember. 'I was there because …'

He puzzled over it. He did not usually go to the Grand Hotel Abyss, insofar as he could remember what was usual. It had been about a month ago, Finney had told him. He had been working – he was sure of that, at least. He recalled the feeling of keeping out of sight, and not wanting to be seen. Pressing his hands to his eyes, he retraced his steps. Then he brightened up.

'That was it,' he said, in great relief. 'I had had a phone call, from a chap said he was a journalist. He said that he'd heard some rumours that there were senators bringing Outlanders in. Not refugees or anything, but some sort of shady business deal. Something to do with building a research facility that the Outlanders wanted to build. He said I should go down to the Grand Hotel Abyss that evening and see if I could spot anyone that I didn't recognise. I went in, I waited a short while, I saw a few senators in the foyer. That's not unusual. Woudes. Albright. One I didn't recognise, he was talking to Logan.'

Finney did not interrupt Dunne and made a tiny gesture to Johnston to be quiet also. Johnston was casting about in his mind for the significance of this bit of news; Finney could tell by the rapid blinking, the restless darting of Johnston's eyes. Logan had told Hughes that he would be in Muinbeo 'on business' and McCabe had told Finney about Theo Potinus and Apeteh. Was that, then, Logan's 'business'? Indeed, was that the secret of Logan's phenomenal success? Being useful to those upon whom the Pharaoh's court depended?

'I didn't want them to see me,' Dunne was saying, 'so when I saw one of the staff that I knew coming down the stairs, I turned around and went outside in case he came to talk to me. I thought I'd come back in later. I took a walk around to the back, near the stables, I stopped for a cigarette. And that's where it happened. I thought it was a dog, but it was huge.'

Dunne's hands began to shake again, and Finney said, reassuringly, 'OK.'

'There is no possibility that I would not remember that scent,' Dunne said, looking up at Finney. 'No earthly way. I didn't know who Logan was when I saw him in the corridor here, I just remembered the attack. And – well. I returned the favour.'

Johnston fished in an inside pocket, and drew out a photograph cut from a newspaper. 'Have a squint at that,' he said, sliding it across the table to Dunne. 'Recognise anyone?'

Dunne listlessly scanned the photograph of Theo Pothinus and nodded without hesitation. Johnston winked at Finney.

The Forum

The Forum was built near the southern town walls, below the Ardgorm Hill. It is a large amphitheatre of golden-brown brick made near the northernmost border of Muinbeo, where the copper yew trees grow. Most of the covens have their headquarters and meeting rooms there, as do many guilds, including the Guild of Horticulturalists, who use the gardens at the front of the Forum as a training school for their apprentices. The result is that the Forum snaps into action on the dot of eight o'clock each morning. The major public meetings take place in the Forum – trials, elections, public announcements, funerals of public figures – and it is also used, when the weather is good,[67] for theatrical productions. The seating for the audience can hold many hundreds of people, and the amphitheatre itself was designed in such a way as to ensure that everyone, regardless of where they sit, can hear everything.

Late in the morning of the Saturday that had very nearly been Salmon's last, there was to be a public meeting held in there, when the conclusion of Cotton Donovan's libel case was announced. Last thing the night before, one of the judges had called the Forum scribes and the assistants together and told them that three senators – Woudes, Albright and Richards – had been called upon by the quaestor to appear. The scribes were very cheerful about the news, as it made things more exciting and they would hear how senators were questioned – the most complicated legal tangles could be created by failure to observe protocol. But the assistants were not a bit cheerful. This meant a lot more work preparing the Forum, and an awful lot of work to try and keep the crowd, and the senators, in line.

------

[67] The weather in Muinbeo is much the same as in Ireland. So you can work out how often these theatrical productions were arranged.

The first thing McCabe, Benson and Johnston noticed was how tidy Albright's office was. Any time they had visited before, the desk was piled high, the drawers of the filing cabinet were open, there were small columns of papers by the side of the desk – in fact, the office showed every sign of being occupied by a shirker impersonating a hard worker. Now McCabe would not have been surprised to see suitcases by the door. Albright greeted them with the same crushing handshake, made eye contact for exactly four seconds – he had read somewhere that this was a sign of honesty – and waved them to their seats with the same gesture as McCabe recalled. Johnston was with them because protocol demanded someone from Finney's office if a senator had been called as a witness in court. Also because Johnston knew how to listen out for the kind of thing that, diplomatically, Finney needed to know. McCabe had the same skill but did not, Finney suspected, care enough to use it.

'Mr Albright,' McCabe said benignly and Albright smiled at him, 'we have a few questions.'

'Coast, Hal, call me Coast.'

'Mr Albright, we should keep this conversation formal. All things considered. Johnston?'

Albright's face fell like a stone and he glanced at his filing cabinet.

'Mr Albright, thank you for sparing some time to speak to us.' Johnston glanced around the office. 'Although you seem to have cleared your in-tray with remarkable success. We wished specifically to ask you about Scarlet Woudes, Berliner Richards and one Theo Pothinus.'

'I'm not sure I know any of these people well enough to be of help,' Albright said smoothly.

'Well, let us be the judge of that,' McCabe said. 'Just to give you a little context, our investigations into two murders leave us with some questions to ask about the defilement of the Gallagrene Bog, at Ciplcati's Ear.'

'Two? Have I missed something? I knew about poor Fen, of course, but –'

'Two murders,' said Johnston. 'Marl Fitzwilliam was, as the quaestor announced at the press conference, also murdered. I don't know if you knew Marl?'

'No. No, I don't think so. Couldn't make it to the press conference. So much to do, so much to do.'

'But you did know Marl, really, Mr Albright. You once wrote a letter to him. Or at least to his editor.'

'A letter?' Albright looked at McCabe, bewildered. 'His editor?'

'Marl Fitzwilliam was not his real name. His real name was Boll Mason. He was an investigative journalist and on one occasion he investigated you, Bull McCann and another –' Johnston checked his notes '– an Outlander called Jeffrey Honeyman.'

Albright blinked rapidly several times.

'Honeyman,' he said. 'An Outlander. I did not know that you kept so up to date on crimes in the Outland. If there *was* a crime, because, as I recall, Honeyman was never convicted.'

McCabe said, settling back in his chair, 'When an errant son such as yourself comes back to Muinbeo and takes up politics, quite a lot of information goes into your civic file.'

McCabe waved the minuscule phial onto which Registry of Records had copied the file in question.

'Of course your file states that you were merely associated with Honeyman and his property development company,' he said, 'and were only questioned, as all of Honeyman's even most distant associates were questioned. You were never investigated or charged. But still. It's the kind of thing we like to know.'

'And you are quite right that Honeyman was never convicted,' Johnston added. 'The investigation, as I am sure you will remember, was into a series of unexplained fires at certain buildings in England and the other countries of Celtic Saxony. Strangely, all of the buildings were on land that was ripe for property development, but couldn't be put on the open market because the building had been declared historically valuable or maybe there was an ancient tomb or a medieval village there. Building gets burned down, heritage site gets mysteriously destroyed and before you know it, Honeyman, Honeyman and Pothinus Developments buys the land and builds on it.'

'So your attitude to the ethics of acquiring land that you can then sell could do with a little polish,' McCabe said. 'And with the help of the Central Registry and the Deputy Khipu, as well as our apprentice going through Marl's papers, we find that you were involved six years ago in what was called the Cluancorr Group, which tried to strong-arm the allotment-holders away so that you could acquire the Cluancorr field and the motte. Along with a number of others, including Berliner Richards, who –'

'It was never proved that he was a dimorph,' Albright said sharply.

'And it is irrelevant whether he is or not,' Johnston replied, very nearly convincingly. 'Being a dimorph is not a crime.

Neither is negotiating business terms with Outlanders, though the senate, as I think you will discover, takes a very dim view of that sort of thing altogether. It *is* a crime to be involved with the reopening of an erratic portal that was sealed generations ago to stop smuggling from the Outland. Especially a portal as notorious as the one on the top of the aornian hill, a portal that has killed people.'

'We also know for sure and certain,' continued McCabe, arranging himself comfortably in the seat, 'that infecting and defiling public land, especially an area that many consider to be sacred, is a crime.'

'And that,' Johnston added, 'is even before we include the crime of pretending to build a convalescent home when the truth is that you were getting paid to let Outlanders do research here.'

'Incidentally,' McCabe finished, 'what kind of research was it that was illegal in the Outland but you thought might be legal here?'

'I want my lawyer,' Albright said instantly.

'And I want your files,' McCabe said, springing to his feet. 'The quaestor's permission to search was posted publicly this morning, along with the notice that you and a select few other senators are to be witnesses in Cotton Donovan's libel trial, and the Deputy Khipu's apprentices have already seized Senator Woudes's office. In fact –'

McCabe and Johnston turned as the door opened. Butter McKenzie and Honour Looby, Dr Boru's most senior apprentice archivists, came in, looking simultaneously apprehensive and excited. Johnston could see Velvet lurking behind them, waiting for the apprentices to call her and the swarm of imps and *luchrupáns* that would search the office.

'Excuse me, Senator Albright,' McKenzie said. 'Please stay in the office and don't touch anything. I have the quaestor's search warrant if you want to read it. Honour,' he said over his shoulder, 'can you take the book-loom?'

Albright stood up and backed away from his desk as though he was afraid Apprentice Looby would lift him bodily and put him in a box.

'Where's your *eolas*?' McKenzie asked.

'I don't have one.'

McKenzie, still reading his list, beckoned behind him and three sturdy *luchrupáns* led the march in, each with a glimmering orb in its hands. Everyone in Muinbeo knew that, in theory, anything that made information visible was in itself a source of power and the *luchrupáns*' orbs acted in the same manner as dowsing sticks near a source of water. Albright rubbed his mouth nervously as a *luchrupán* fished out a bag from under the desk and carefully lifted out a fragile mechanism; the *eolas* was a complicated and delicate complex of cogs and dials and vibrating quartz which could search the world's written information on any subject. Albright lunged forward to grab the *luchrupán*, and then shrank back, wringing his hand and clutching his shoulder.

'It doesn't do to try to manhandle the staff,' Looby said mildly. 'Dr Boru doesn't like it.'

'Is there no invasion of privacy that damn Boru woman has not thought of?' Albright growled, as the orbs flashed and crackled at every corner and the *luchrupáns* pulled out drawers and the unread books from Albright's shelves. 'One of these days she'll get her tongue cut out.'

'I don't think that's very likely,' McKenzie said, almost soothingly. 'If you'll just put your hands on the wall, senator.'

At the Forum, during the libel case against Cotton Donovan

Early though it had started, the exciting bits of Cotton Donovan's trial for libel, which led to the unmasking of the Gallagrene conspiracy, did not really get going until the town bells had just begun to chime midday. By that time, Salmon was awake again and pleaded with her foster-father to let her see at least some of the first event where Rainbow would be there in his new role of apprentice. Mindful of McCabe's instructions that she should not have more excitement that day, but virtually unable to refuse anything his children asked, Archer compromised and said she could go in for an hour, and then straight home again to bed. They sat near an exit, where they wouldn't be too obvious. Salmon instinctively ducked down when she saw McCabe arrive and seat himself on the opposite side of the Forum.

When called to give evidence, Senator Woudes stuck to her original line of denying all knowledge of the Gallagrene Group or of Pothinus, Ribiero or Whistler or any of the other names on the list found in Marl's flat. But Sugar Henry was called as a witness and said that, some days ago, the quaestor had requested that the Possible Institute investigate the opening of a sealed erratic portal on the Gallagrene Bog. The portal connected with the Outland, and they had tracked the reactivation to Albright's office. The quaestor, Sugar added, had also asked them to perform the same investigation at the Viking motte near Cluancorr. A note was passed to one of the judges to the effect that Senator Albright could not appear because he had just been arrested, but it was not until Sand Butler came forward that Woudes really accepted that the game was up.

'I cannot excuse myself on the grounds of ignorance,' Sand said very shakily. 'I did not ask what was in the flasks that I was told to empty into the bogland near Ciplacti's Ear. I did what I was told to do because I was afraid of the consequences of refusal. And for that, I say that there are many of you must share the blame.'

The crowd went very silent, taken aback. Sand licked his lips and glanced between the orators.

'I was blackmailed into doing this,' he said, 'because … because I am a dimorph.'

The crowd started making noise again, some hissing, some shocked noises, quite a lot of *What? What did he say? He's not! Well, did you ever? He looks normal and everything. Though I always thought that Apples McGinty's youngest looked too much like a chihuahua to be entirely human. Of course you know Apples McGinty. You do, you do, from out near Cronna?*

'I was told to take the job helping the Ghillies of Demeter with their survey, and, when I was on the bog, to empty the flasks into the ground near the Ear. Otherwise they would tell my fiancée. And that is why I say that most of you are partly to blame. If it were not for the prejudice against dimorphs, I would never have been forced into doing this!'

Scattered through the crowd, a very few people began to clap.

'Who asked you to empty the flasks?' asked Donovan's lawyer. 'Who blackmailed you?'

'Kale Lake,' answered Sand, without hesitation.

The crowd gasped.

'She is a distant cousin – though not distant enough. She found out. She blackmailed me once before, and I stole money but I was caught. When I became engaged to be married, it started again.'

Senator Woudes put her head in her hands. Salmon and Archer stared at each other, and then looked back into the crowd. As Salmon looked back, she saw that McCabe had already gone. Just behind where McCabe had been seated, and directly opposite Salmon, the space between two people flickered and then steadied. She caught a glimpse of a disappearing aura.

On McCabe's advice, Cotton Donovan's defence replaced the witness who had been attacked by the rogue werewolf with the maître d'hôtel at the Grand Hotel Abyss, Puck Welsh. He was an elf; though creatures of air in the land of the *sidh*, elves were more Atlas than Ariel in the earthier Muinbeo. Puck loomed over the humans and even over McCabe, his eyes bigger than saucers and red as a bull's, his double-jointed fingers long as piccolos. The bright green suit he wore complemented the gold of his skin but even this overwhelmed the unaccustomed humans and made them think, trying not to stare at elfish arms and legs, of some gigantic tropical insect. He recounted that the three senators had had a number of meetings with two men, and when he was shown some photographs he chose, without hesitation, the photograph of Theo Pothinus.

McCabe was not investigating the defilement of Gallagrene Bog, nor the attempt by three of the senators to illegally allow an Outland corporation to set up business in Muinbeo. His contribution to the court that morning – apart from sending an iris to Donovan's lawyer suggesting that Puck Welsh be shown the photograph of Pothinus – was to tell Donovan what Salmon had realised in the middle of the night: that what Cluancorr and Gallagrene Bog had in common was erratic portals.[68] But McCabe's job was to find out who had committed murder, not who was guilty of greed.

In the afternoon of the day that the scandal of Gallagrene Bog first broke, and when Salmon had recovered from having almost been devoured by an erratic portal, McCabe, Benson and Johnston pored over the memory theatre in McCabe's cluttered office, not only seeking new evidence about Fen's and Boll's murders, and the evidence of ideas newly brought together, but testing their conclusions, seeing if their arguments were convincing. Fallinish sat patiently with them, his head on his paws, dozing occasionally.

'I think we have enough to go on,' McCabe said eventually, 'but I am not sure we know why he did it.'

'Because Fen found out about the Gallagrene Group?' Benson said, but McCabe shook his head.

---

[68] The problem with erratic portals was not just that they opened and closed randomly and sometimes killed people. You have to understand – Muinbeo flakes away from the Outland, like a stamp coming off a letter, and the main reason that it has been safe from the Pharaoh's court, and the war, is that no one could get in. This is why the Pharaoh's court pretends that Muinbeo does not exist: it is too embarrassing to be unable to find it. So two open and unprotected portals could bring a lot worse into Muinbeo than a few greedy corporations.

'I don't think that she did,' he said. 'That iris slough we found in her house – the Deputy Khipu and the Possible Institute worked out how it was done. And they think that there was only one way. Someone who had access to all of the information but who was not restricted by having to use any of the systems we have. If you look at the slough, there are no names at all – we don't know who sent it, but we don't know either who was supposed to receive it. We assumed Fen, because we found it in her house. But there is no name.'

Benson shook his head. 'Then how did it get to her house? Why, even, did it get to her house?'

'Who found it?' McCabe said, and answered himself: 'Salmon. Remember?'

Johnston and Benson looked at each other, astonishment growing on their faces.

McCabe said, 'Boru had the idea. The Possible Institute measures the alignment of the Medon with the stars and planets. They have some machine that's all cogs and brains, and all it does is measure the Medon. Boru asked them to look at the alignment at the time you were in the Mirror House.'

'Which told them what?' Johnston said.

'That the Khipu-Camayacos itself sent the message, and it sent it to Salmon.'

Benson's jaw slackened and Johnston's eyebrows went up. They both turned, still looking astonished, as Salmon knocked and came in.

'You're supposed to be in bed recovering,' McCabe said sternly.

Salmon shut the door and said, 'I know, but I'm afraid I went to the Forum this morning. And then I had to come in

– I saw something. Do you remember, when we first found Fen's body, I went off with Fallinish because I saw a trace of an aura? Like a scent?'

'Yes,' said McCabe, 'that was how you knew that it wasn't Madam Gulliver.'

'I saw the trace again at the Forum. It was Valerian Hobbs.'

'Where was he?'

Salmon was surprised. 'Right behind you, sir,' she said. 'He was looking right at you.

McCabe's face often lapsed into vampire configuration when he was thinking. Now, his fangs began to descend, and his brow corrugated. He recalled thinking he had seen someone out of the corner of his eye. He remembered thinking the same thing after the press conference in the wake of Marl's death. Perhaps Valerian Hobbs was able to spend a lot of time at the corner of people's eyes.

'Sir?' Benson said. 'I found out something about that, from Mack Amberson. About Valerian Hobbs. Even Apeteh know very little about him, but Marl – Boll – had been investigating him for years, it was practically an obsession. Apparently Hobbs spent a lot of time in remote parts of the Amazonian Kingdom, the Inca countries, and especially in the Manchurian Empire. He has a lot of tricks up his sleeve, learned from extremely unusual people and one of these tricks is to be able – I haven't the foggiest idea how – to hide from ordinary sight.'

'How does Mack know this?' asked McCabe. 'I didn't know he was friendly with Marl.'

Benson allowed himself a rare smile. He had been certain that Mack was hiding something about how well he had known Marl, and Benson had finally worked it out.

'Mack has an incurable habit,' he said. 'I found an old guardian file on him. He goes trout poaching in the Outland. Marl found out, showed him a new spot, and they got talking. He never said he was a journalist, just that he was anti-Pharaoh, anti-court.'

'So it was Hobbs who knocked you down,' McCabe said to Salmon, 'on the night of the gairm.'

'Why was Hobbs knocking down apprentices?' Johnston asked. 'I thought he was one of these smooth lifestyle-guru types.'

Benson said, with the gusty sigh of one explaining the obvious to a novice, 'He had bribed Carbon Smith into opening the erratic portal so that he could bring into Muinbeo all his unsavoury Outland friends, like Theo Pothinus.'

'The only way in is the only way out,' Johnston said, putting the pieces together. 'There's been a murder, Pothinus wants out. The night of the gairm is safe, because so many officials were at the gairm. Though even *Hobbs* hardly expected the Patriarch. And then he finds the apprentice there too. He has to think fast, think of something to get her right away from the motte. So he gives her something to chase.'

'And knocked her down in the process,' said McCabe. 'Well, we'll settle that with him later.'

'Sir, it doesn't matter,' Salmon said.

McCabe said thoughtfully, 'I don't like people knocking my apprentices about, all the same.'

'Anyway,' Benson said, 'now that the group has been discovered, he's probably run off back to his institute. He won't come within a hundred miles of Muinbeo for a very long time.'

'Then it is as well, though not for Hobbs, that vampires live for a very long time,' McCabe said rather grimly.

Salmon felt oddly pleased at the thought that McCabe would remember a wrong done to her. It was reassuring.

Then his fangs snapped back and he said, 'Why does it matter that Hobbs was on the motte on the night of the murder if he didn't kill Fen? He was in the Gallagrene Group, but we think that Shear Amberson killed Fen, and he wasn't in the group.'

'But the Khipu-Camayacos thinks that the group was involved,' Benson said. 'Why else would the Khipu – the *Khipu* – have sent the iris, if the group wasn't important?'

'Important for what, though?' Johnston said thoughtfully. 'The Khipu does not normally involve herself in everyday affairs – why is the Khipu concerned about finding a murderer?'

'I don't think so,' McCabe said. 'The Khipu lets everyone get on with life without interference. But I think that there are certain things that Khipu watches; certain places, like the Great River, or Uisneach, or the Swanhill Library. Maybe some people too. So I think – this is just a guess – I think that the Khipu was protecting the Gallagrene Bog itself. Protecting Ciplacti's Ear.'

There was a pause while his companions thought about that. Then Benson, ever practical, got back to business.

'Though Shear wasn't in the group, he wanted to join Valerian Hobbs's institute. And Hobbs – along with Kale Lake – *was* in the group. Shear probably knew about their plans, but said nothing. Pachamama's courses are expensive, and he probably wanted to become a favourite, Hobbs's pet.'

'Is that why he killed Marl? Boll, I mean? Because Barl – Moll – I mean ... the journalist was going to find out something about the institute?' Johnston wondered aloud. McCabe reached behind him and pulled out a battered file, the edges tied with scarlet ribbon. 'Hobbs is not the only one who can play about with time and space,' he said modestly. 'Look what I found in Hobbs's house before he shut up shop.'

He opened the file and took out a newspaper. Benson took it and Salmon and Johnston stood beside him, reading over his shoulder.[69] They read the same article that Rainbow had shown to Cotton Donovan: Marl's exposé of dangerously poor hygiene practices in a chain of Outland restaurants.

Salmon riffled through the file. 'Hobbs was digging up as much information on Marl as Marl was digging up on him,' she said. 'There is nothing that Hobbs didn't know about Marl, it seems.'

Johnston took the paper and read out a few sentences.

'"An example of the dangerously poor standards in Dr Hobbs's chain of restaurants in Londinia is their attitude to customer health. Each time I ordered a dish of food, I asked the waiter if any nuts were used in preparation. Each time, he assured me there were not. Yet my lips were tingling and my eyes itching and streaming by the end of the night, a sure sign that he was wrong. Luckily, I have only a mild allergy. But when I was in Manchuria, another customer was not so lucky. Assured by the Grim Reaper in the form of a waiter that there were no shellfish in the 'local speciality', the woman went into

---

[69] Or, in Salmon's case, over the crook of his elbow.

anaphylactic shock and died almost instantly. Her death was never reported in the newspapers – owned by Dr Hobbs – and no charges were ever brought. Dare we ask the relationship between Dr Hobbs and the local magistrate?'"

'So Hobbs had a long-standing grudge,' Benson said, 'as well as worrying about Boll's current investigation.'

'And now we know how anyone, including Hobbs, could have known that Marl/Boll had an allergy,' Johnson said. 'He mentioned it himself in a newspaper! Though if it was only a mild allergy, as the article says, I don't see how it could have been used to kill him. And anyway, Hobbs wasn't even *at* that dinner of Shearwater's.'

McCabe looked at him quizzically. 'He didn't need to be there,' he said. 'Think about it. And remember, Hobbs can hide in plain sight.'

'I see,' said Johnston, 'and he knew where Marl lived, of course – everyone knew. He had opportunity galore to steal into Marl's flat and add the histamine, bit by bit, to his food – until the next time Marl ate food naturally containing histamine and the inevitable happened.'

'If Hobbs was on the motte,' Salmon said, 'he *might* have seen Shearwater kill Fen. Then if Boll Mason was being too inquisitive, Hobbs might have insisted that Shear … do something.'

'That leaves us still not knowing why Shear killed Fen,' Benson said gloomily, 'or even being certain that he did. The business with the scarf that the *luchrupán* told Boru about only really proves that Shear lied about when he last saw Fen. Can we even prove Shear had the weapon? Maybe the apprentice can go through Cullen's invoices and order book to check?'

'Well, Cedar Cullen already confirmed that only one person ordered a Mercurian cutlass,' McCabe said. 'And it wasn't Shear, it was Fen. Besides that, we spoke to all the school-friends who were supposed to dine with Immo and Fen. Fen's party piece was a traditional baked cutlass.'

Benson picked up McCabe's train of thought. 'And if Fen's fish disappeared and Shear has a speciality fish that he didn't order, it is reasonable circumstantial evidence that he stole the fish. We already know that he used the sword on the fish to kill Fen. He destroys the evidence by making a fish curry out of it. He was planning eventually to eat the murder weapon.'

'But what does our clever boyo do instead?' McCabe asked, rhetorically. 'He doesn't trouble himself to get a new weapon when he finds himself with someone else to kill. No, he just feeds the old one, plus a dose of histamine, to his next victim, for whom of course the histamine was poison. I believe that is called recycling.'

There was a knock on the outer door, and Johnston went to answer it. McCabe pored over the notices on the theatre puppets.

Benson looked at Salmon for a while and then said, 'A word of advice, apprentice. About Valerian Hobbs. Don't be telling people you can see what other people can't. It might be dangerous.'

Salmon did not know how to respond. Generally, Benson just seemed irritated by her, so she didn't know if it was advice or a warning. Or a threat, she wondered, as the door opened, and Johnston brought in the Witch Sackville.

A private house, near Roanoake Cross

In a lonely and well-appointed house near Roanoake, the murderer is catching up on the sleep that had failed to come at night, but wakes, suddenly and violently. There is no sound. There is a little sighing in the snow-laden trees outside, but otherwise there is silence. The murderer gets up, and goes to the kitchen table.

I sat up in the dark, chilled and afraid. I could hear the Thanatos chant but he was not chanting the right words, he was chanting my name. I was hallucinating, so wracked with the awe of what I have done that I could see things that were not there; not clear, identifiable things, not like those stupid plays, the Scottish play we did in school where a man hag-ridden with remorse and terror can name the phantom that appears to him; this is a knife, its handle toward my hand, this is the gashed face and gory locks of my friend. I could see, but I could not tell you what it was that I saw. It was not the figure of Fen's face, it was as though all the air and life had been sucked from the room, and there was nothing left but her absence, what I saw was the hole I had ripped in the world by killing her. I have never been so paralysed with fear. It was, I think, the words of the Patriarch. No one had expected the Patriarch to be there. His presence was not occasioned by Fen's importance, but because of the outrage done to the acceptable order of things. And suddenly this thing has a life outside the action of my hands, a life outside the explanations of my head. What have I done? By vengeful Sekhmet, what have I done?

Immo Harper's house, near Cluancorr

Whoever Immo Harper had expected to find on her doorstep, it was not Winter Sackville. She was not sure how she felt about the sight of the harlequin glasses and white cap of hair but, apart from anything else, she could hardly be rude to a Smoke Coven witch, and the senior one at that, so she stood back with as friendly a smile as possible. Winter did not seem particularly comfortable either. They both made a reasonably good show of pretending that neither one of them recalled that Winter had raised objections to Immo becoming the landlady of the Wooden O.

It was never personal, Winter thought defensively. *I just felt that the person I recommended was better.*

On the other hand, Immo thought, *Interfering old biddy. Just because she likes hammers everything has to be a nail.*

Winter walked briskly into the kitchen, and Immo took her coat, hanging it up on the back of the door while Winter rubbed her hands beside the fire. When they had exhausted the weather as a conversation piece, Winter made a few complimentary remarks about how cosy the house was and what a nice view. Immo turned off her radio on which she had been listening to the reports from the senate court. Upon receipt of a cup of tea, Winter got to her point.

'I came to see how you were,' she said, with a faintly belligerent air, and looked at Immo as though expecting a reaction.

'I'm fine,' Immo said, surprised.

'You found a corpse on your doorstep,' Winter said, 'and Death can stand between you and its sister, Sleep.'

Immo turned away, nodding. There was a pause.

Winter twirled her cup gently in her hands and said, 'I don't want to interfere, but I wondered whether you had seen anything … well, odd.'

Immo realised that she had been expecting someone to ask her that question. She had, after all, been on the scene of a dead body, and she was the nearest neighbour, as it were, to the erratic portal on the motte.

But she had to shake her head. 'I wish I had,' she said. 'I wish I could help. I always take a quick walk round the houses and by the edge of the woods in the evening, to make sure everything is OK, and I saw nothing.'

'And when did you last see Fen herself?'

'Actually I was in the Rowan Tree with Fen and Sand the night before she died. You were there yourself – you must have seen them?'

Winter rolled her eyes and laughed, to Immo's surprise. 'You may guess how often I will be found in a pub. But Honesty Williams and his Blue-Furred Bluegrass Band were playing. I'm his sponsor and promised that I would be there. Apollo's teeth, the noise!'

Winter had never really known why Honesty's mother, Widow Williams, had asked Winter to sponsor Honesty when he was born. They had not known each other well, and Winter sometimes wondered if it was a way to associate Honesty with someone respectable. Refusing to sponsor a child[70] was to court bad fortune so even if she had not had a soft spot for the rackety Widow Williams, Winter would have said yes. Honesty was a likeable, kind-hearted boy but she had not realised her duties would include attending musical events in pubs.

Immo laughed at Winter's expression. Then she stopped laughing, and a frown began to gather around her eyes.

'Do you know,' she said, 'it's the oddest thing. Remember the look on Fen's face when someone switched on the radio for the news?'

Later, when Winter Sackville had set off, as agreed, to go to the guardian house and tell McCabe what she and Immo had remembered, Immo sat back down at her kitchen table, with her account books and a calculating imp. But she did not take up her work again. She went upstairs, and from the front guest room looked out over the motte. It was still and silent, but she could see some of the Outland Watch making their way up the wooded paths. They were on duty tonight. Immo wandered out, pointlessly checked the rooms that were always available

---

[70] Many people in Muinbeo believe that it is important to give a new baby a sponsor – someone who will promise to look after the child if something happens the parents. Happily, it is not usually necessary to do so, and a sponsor's duties are usually limited to expressing intelligent interest in the hobbies of their fosterlet (as the child is called) and being imaginative when it comes to birthday presents.

for guests and decided that perhaps a cup of tea might settle her nerves. Winter Sackville's visit had upset her, and more than anything she wished that if she had been unable to prevent Fen's death, at least she could have helped to catch the killer.

As she was waiting for the kettle to begin to sing, she absentmindedly picked up a letter from Outland Watch, enclosing a list of the dates on which, every fortnight, they would cross her land to go up onto the motte. She wondered if Carbon Smith was with them or if finding the body … Immo stopped in her tracks. She turned around and looked at her calendar.

Guardian rooms, Senate Chambers

'And you are quite certain about this?' McCabe did not look around from where he was adding a note to the Fen puppet.

Winter stood behind him, watching him in fascination. 'Well, Immo and I both recalled that the radio was on and someone turned it up so that they could hear the news. And that Fen went white, I mean completely white. Sand Butler noticed it too, I remember him putting his arm round her, asking if she was all right.'

'Apprentice, wind up the telephone there and ask the Deputy Khipu's office to send us round a transcript of the news broadcast on that night.'

In a very few minutes, the postal pipe belched and a sheaf of papers, neatly rolled and tied with a sturdy scarlet ribbon, was puffed out onto the floor. Salmon opened it, and scanned it quickly, reading out some of the headlines. Then she stopped. The headline seemed to throb gently, a darker shadow rippling over it.

'Excuse me, sir,' she said.

She grasped the handle of the phone and wrung the lever so vigorously that even several floors down they could hear the complaints of the exchange imps and their exhortations to have a bit of patience, would you not? Salmon asked to speak to Velvet, Winter and McCabe looking at her in some surprise as she said firmly that she didn't care where Velvet was, she could shout through the cubicle door, couldn't she? A few moments after Salmon hung up, the postal pipe belched again and a much smaller roll of pieces of paper fluttered out. Salmon picked them up, and examined them closely, then read the transcript again.

'Felicitas,' she said looking up at McCabe. 'Oh, Fel-ic-it-as.'

'What are you up to, apprentice?' McCabe demanded.

'Balor's iron eye. They won,' said Salmon, staring at the screen, and then swinging her chair around, stunned. 'She was only after winning the Outland lottery, sir. Look.'

She gave the papers to McCabe and then stood at his shoulder reading them out to him as though she thought he needed help.

'Look. Velvet Corbuse found a file in Fen's desk. Dr Boru disapproved because it had been called *Miscellaneous* and she thinks that's a hanging offence, but it really was miscellaneous, just random bits of stuff Fen needed now and then. But look. Fen had a lottery ticket, that's it there, and that's the date on it. The day before she died. Look at these. She did the lottery most weeks but not all. Look at this. List of dates, each one initialled – two sets each time. Look at this. The radio transcript for the night before Fen died – an announcement that the lottery prize had been won, on one ticket. They read out the numbers too.

Look at them. And now look at Fen's last lottery ticket. That's what Fen heard on the radio in the pub.'

'What do we think, apprentice?'

'We think that we should go to talk to Velvet Corbuse and the Deputy Khipu to see if they can confirm whose initials these are. Fen and Shear must have bought the tickets together, and the initials are to show that they had both paid the money. They would have shared the money if they won. The *F.M.* must mean Fen Maguire. But what about *S.A?* Who was her friend and who do we now think needed money? Who lied about when he saw her? I think Shear Amberson became greedy.'

But when Benson, McCabe and Salmon went around to Shear's house that evening, they found that he had also become suspicious.

A private house, near Roanoake Cross

The crossroads at the Old Mill Field was a sprawling and lopsided one. The main road straggled and wandered off towards Cluancorr and Cassidy's Bridge, while a thin, overgrown road, which looked as though it had evolved rather than was built, ran between the Mill Field and Roanoake Corner, around which the sombrists all lived. The last path led up to Shearwater Amberson's log house. There was only an ivy-covered ruin of the mill now and, beside it, the log house still looked shiny and recent. The roof of the house was covered in grass and small plants, and in what spare time he had, Shear had cultivated some of the acre or so of land he had, mainly with brassicas and squashes.

He kept no pets, and inside his house there were no walls.

A staircase in the centre of the house led to a gallery and the upstairs bedroom. The kitchen was separated from the sitting area by a marble-topped island, and anything in the house that was not wood was chrome. It was airy and attractive, with big windows and a large hearth by the open fireplace. Even before they searched the house, both McCabe and Salmon knew that Shear was gone. Fallinish had loped round once, sniffing, but returned to McCabe's side, looking up expectantly as though awaiting a more interesting order. The wardrobe in the downstairs bedroom was open, clothes pulled out and hangers strewn about the floor. All his walking clothes and hiking boots were gone. There was no money and no keys. Salmon and McCabe searched in silence, then came together again in the kitchen. McCabe shook his head, his hands on his hips. Salmon was staring in puzzlement into the cold-room at the back of Shear's pantry.[71]

'Nothing,' McCabe said. 'No trace.'

'I found this, sir,' she said, and held up a small flat rectangle of ruby glass. 'In his room. But I can't open it up. It is locked closed.'

She was holding a tabulet, a quasi-magical device made of glass, wrought silver and a kind of thin, almost invisible ink which was reputed to have been invented by the Fir Bolg. It was used principally by the senate, to publish information, but individuals sometimes also used them in order, strangely enough, to hide information. The writing in this ink was so fine and delicate that it could slip through the atoms of air,

---

[71] No need for a fridge-freezer when you've got a cold-room.

which was how, by using screens filled with another kind of ink, it was possible for the words to appear.[72]

'Can't open it, eh?' said McCabe, and took off his hat.

Salmon set the tabulet down on the marble island-top, and McCabe withdrew from the crown of his hat a long thin needle with what looked at first like a bulb of thistledown at one end. He slid this with infinite gentleness along the closed lip of the tabulet. It looked less, Salmon thought, as though the tiny filaments of rare metal found a lock and fitted in, and more as though they made the lock appear, that the shape of the key drew the lock out of the glass and silver. When McCabe lifted the lid, the tabulet immediately unpacked itself, and a word-frame like a loom, so light and delicate that even the glass seemed to waft in the gentlest breath of air, appeared. McCabe clicked impatiently. The screen remained blank, and as he saw Salmon look hopefully at his hat for further solutions, he shook his head.

In the same way that the tabulet could make information available to many, it was possible for those with secrets to lock the words in by using a code or cipher to bind the tiniest atoms of ink securely within the atoms of air. McCabe could unlock the tabulet but there was nothing he could do to unpick the words it contained. None the less, he tucked it under his arm.

'How did you find it?'

'I was looking for it, sir,' Salmon said. 'I've often seen that Shear writes short accounts of what has been found on the bog, tells people what has been happening with the survey

---

[72] It is a little bit like writing using invisible ink, or lemon juice, and then using heat to make the writing appear.

of wildlife. It occurred to me that he must have a tabulet, and if he has a tabulet – well, who knows what he might be putting into it.'

Salmon, Fallinish and McCabe went out, McCabe pondering on the nature of hidden information. Many in Muinbeo believed that not even a thought existed without the *actual* Khipu-Camayacos knowing about it. He thought about how that might work, and the possibility that some whisper had been sent into the ether that only the writer, and the Khipu, could read. And that as a result the Khipu did the impossible and sent an iris with no name. What Shear had tied up could be untied, McCabe thought. He had the greatest faith in Copper Boru.

The Senate Chambers

When they got back to the senate buildings to find Dr Boru, he found she was looking for him. As soon as he stepped up from the tunnel, an imp met him and told him that Dr Boru would be very happy if the guardian would go, now this minute if not sooner, to the senate canteen, where she and Velvet Corbuse were waiting.

'And not patiently either,' said the imp, 'so if I were you, vampire, I'd get a shunty on.'

The Deputy Khipu and the apprentice amanuensis were sitting at the back of the canteen.

'I have something for you,' he said, and nodded at Salmon, who took out the tabulet and passed it over the table.

'Locked and ciphered,' said McCabe, and Boru looked fondly at the codex.

'Not for long,' she said. 'Now. Velvet has remembered something.'

Velvet in turn pushed a sheet of paper towards him and, unexpectedly, she put her face in her hands. McCabe stared at the top of her head. He wondered for one insane moment if she was going to confess to Fen's murder.

'Shear Amberson,' she said. 'I can't believe it.

'Why do you think Shearwater Amberson is involved with Fen Maguire's death?' McCabe said, just to be absolutely sure everyone was talking about the same thing. He recalled from many years ago an occasion when –[73]

'Because,' said Velvet, 'I think that she gave him the murder weapon. She asked him to go and collect the fish for her, from Hopper Bryce. She orders a fish. He picks it up. She gets stabbed and the fish is nowhere to be seen.'

McCabe said, 'And you are sure it was Shear she said was getting the fish for her?'

Velvet nodded.

'She told me, but I didn't understand. I could only remember very roughly what it sounded like because I didn't understand when she said it. Hoprasinos. That's what she said. That's who she said was lifting the fish for her. I didn't understand it. It was in the back of my mind the whole time. Then the other night, we were in the Weavers' Lodge at the dinner and Cedar – Cedar Cullen – was being asked about the unusual orders he

---

[73] No, no. We couldn't possibly. We have been sworn to secrecy. And bribery won't work either. Though we are partial to – no, no, what are we saying?

gets and he said, oh, the most unusual food is usually ordered by … Hoprasinos. I looked through all Fen's old papers, and I found this, so I went in to Cedar's shop today again to ask him.'

She pointed at the paper. McCabe was looking at a note written in Old Greek. He had known, but hadn't thought about, Greek being Fen's second language. He turned the paper over and saw that it was an old memo requesting delivery of ink. It was years out of date and Fen had used it to leave a note for someone to say that she would be 'in the canteen round 1'. McCabe flattened it and read Fen's salutation using in Greek the nickname that many people used for a popular Ghillie of Demeter.

'Hoprasinos,' Boru repeated. 'It means that which is green, a green thing, or a green man. Lots of people call Shearwater the Green Man Amberson.'

Dr Boru looked at Velvet, and from some hidden pocket Boru flicked out a watch on a chain.

'Velvet, you have had a shock – you used to get along well with Shear. Go and get something to eat. Did you send an iris, like I told you to, to have someone meet you?'

'I'm going to meet Night in the Ravenous Raven,' Velvet said, with a loud sniff. 'I sent an iris, and he is there now.'

'Well in the name of Athena do not breathe a word of this anywhere you might be overheard,' McCabe warned her.

'Come on,' said Dr Boru. 'I will walk with you. McCabe, I will come back in this evening to crack our little code, so come to my office tomorrow morning.'

Velvet made a gesture of protesting that she did not need to be accompanied to the restaurant but in fact discovering that she had lunched with someone, laughed at the jokes of someone, had even socialised with someone who would end a life for the sake of money was bewilderingly shocking to her. She could not really take it in: her mind was shying away from the thought with such terror that it could not focus on anything else for fear that any other subject, however ordinary, might also suddenly sprout tentacles and fangs. She was grateful for Dr Boru's tactful company, but feeling so thrown off kilter and in consequence in such confessional mood, she did not want to speak for fear of what might come blurting out of her mouth.

Dr Boru was as shocked as Velvet but did not have such strong reactions. She tried to think of neutral things to talk about, and Velvet replied calmly enough. The only mistake Boru made was when Velvet started to fret about how much time she could have saved if she had understood the name that Fen had given her.

'It wasn't your fault,' the Deputy Khipu repeated. 'How many people know more than their own second language? Very few. It was just chance. It's just the luck of the draw that you're not Greek-speaking. What is your other language, out of curiosity?'

Velvet drew in a deep breath, stopped in the street, looked up at Dr Boru. Tears streamed suddenly down her face. The normal second speech for her was Raven, and though she did not blurt that out, she was too distressed to remember what else she spoke. She finally stammered, 'Mozarabic.'

Boru had stopped when Velvet stopped. As Fen in the office on the last night of her life, so Boru on sleety, windy Belvedere Street – a quick sweep of her eye took in the very faint facial marks, the line up the side of Velvet's nose, around her eye and into her hair with its odd-coloured burnishes.

'Hmm,' she said, eyebrows up and mouth down disbelievingly, and then, opening her eyes wide, said in perfect Raven, 'You will need many skills to be my apprentice.'

Velvet stared at her and Dr Boru laughed.

'Raven is not one of my strong languages,' she said, 'so I hope I did not accidentally say something terrible.'

'But you are not a dimorph,' Velvet said.

'Well, I hope you won't hold that against me,' Boru replied briskly. 'Dreadful thing, bigotry.'

Copper Boru's rooms, the Senate Chambers

McCabe knocked on Dr Boru's office door an hour or so later and told Salmon to stop smoothing her hair.

'Any luck with our Mr Amberson's tabulet?'

Boru smiled at him and said, 'Come in. Hello, Salmon. Nothing to do with luck, McCabe. I've done this kind of code-breaking many times.'

'Have you ever been caught? Oh, dear. Sorry, bad question.'

It was a particularly gloomy day outside, so Dr Boru had acquired some tall lamps with glass shades designed to look like trailing birch trees or the pebbled floor of a trout-brown river. The mellow lights now made her office look less like an office on a rather lowering winter's day and more like a wet sunny dawn in an overgrown glade.

Arrayed on the window-sill of Boru's office – a much deeper sill than McCabe remembered – were about a dozen thin, shining strips of a metal McCabe could not quite recognise. The lock-picks were so thin that from certain angles they were invisible. Some had a plain shaft and some had little bumps or branches, and the end of each pick was different to the others. Some looked very functional and ended in a point or pincers, one had a fringe of thin spikes, one had what looked like the smallest compass in the world, one had a minuscule but complicated arrangement of spheres linked to each other, and when McCabe looked more closely he realised that he was looking at a chemical structure.

'Thus you unlocked what Amberson had put into the tabulet,' he said. 'And what did you see then?'

Dr Boru touched a button and the screen filled with a steady tide of shapes that did not, to McCabe's eye, represent any natural language.

'What are we looking at?' McCabe asked. Boru shook her head a little.

'Turbulent clouds,' she said, 'and a still lake turning choppy. Swans flying low. We are looking at storm warnings, McCabe, make no mistake. This code he used is ancient. It is also infamous.'

'Which begs the question of why he used it.'

Boru gave him a look that told him he had missed the point.

'Which begs the question,' she corrected him, 'of who taught this to Amberson. This is not a code that you can learn from a book over a weekend. I don't need to remind you, for example, of the code in the Book of the Blind Harper.'[74]

---

[74] We would much rather she didn't, either. We admit we felt a little shudder at the mention of the Book of the Blind Harper – a book that made the Voynich Manuscript look like an infant's alphabet. There was a reason that harper was blind, believe you us.

McCabe said nothing. Boru was not easily alarmed but he could tell that she would rather not even have had the tabulet in her office.

'*Tia feliĉego estas kompreni,*' he said and Boru shook her head.

'Not necessarily. This is what Amberson wrote.'

Boru took back the sheaf of papers and took out one of the pages from the back of the pile.

'It says, *It is an amazing thing, but I had briefly forgotten that I had killed Fen. I awoke early, feeling completely refreshed, very calm and very aware. It was as though I had recovered from a long illness and had at last purged the infection. I could not remember why it was that I felt so buoyant and then I remembered Fen. For a second I was frozen; I did not mean to take any joy from her death, I should not feel happy that her life was ended. Animals do not kill for pleasure, they kill for necessity. Survival of the fittest. But her death is in the past, she no longer exists, that reality is over. In a peculiar way, I am her future.*

'*These notes that I am attaching to the research form have given me an idea. In the same way that in nature nothing is wasted, I do not want any aspect of Fen's death to go unobserved; if the unconsidered life is not worth living then that too is true of the unconsidered death. I will watch the investigation closely, learn what I can about those who hunt the hunter.*'

Boru stopped and looked up at McCabe. McCabe looked at Salmon.

'What do we think, apprentice?'

'We think that this is the smell of someone's goose being cooked.'

Salmon had accompanied McCabe to the guardian offices in the morning. She had not, she comforted herself, exactly promised that she would go from there to the school library. But she knew that the only reason that Archer had not come to fetch her home yet was that her foster-parents were under the impression that she would take one of the guardian horses to the school. She had fully intended to go. She had brought her demonstration project notes, but as McCabe and Boru trawled through the diary that Shear Amberson had written after committing the first murder, Salmon went to McCabe's office to get all of the paperwork in order. Quaestor Finney did not like there to be any gaps in the evidence being sent to the courts and it was one of the jobs of the apprentice to write up the administrative report. This described each of the steps taken in the investigation and noted where in the case papers the judges should look for a reason why the step was taken and what evidence was found as a result. In the middle of the afternoon, McCabe came in.

'Apprentice,' he said, preoccupied and worried, 'I think I know where Amberson is. No,' he added, as she got up from the desk, 'you are not coming. No buts, it is too dangerous.'

'But I'm — '

'Not yet, you're not.'

'You don't know what I was going to say,' Salmon said indignantly.

'If it was anything that was grounds for claiming you could come looking for a dangerous man on a bog that you don't know and that doesn't know you, then, *not yet, you're not.* Stay here. I mean it. If you dare to disobey me, Farsade, I am telling you now that you will be on the wrong end of some of the things that I keep in my hat.'

Salmon looked at him, looked at his hat and looked back at him. His voice (and the fact that he called her Farsade) said he meant it but his aura – a kind of frosted green that she now recognised – said he was protecting her.

'Don't leave without telling Dr Boru,' he added, 'and always take Maccarrill with you.'

He shut the door, and Salmon heard his footsteps echoing away. A few minutes later, though, McCabe's head popped up through the floor, just beside Salmon's feet. He had forgotten that she had never seen him bend time and space in this way.

'Sorry,' he said, when the echoes of Salmon's full-blooded shriek had died away. 'It was quicker than coming back up the regular way. I meant to say, don't go out to get lunch. Ring the Fooderie and get them to deliver. I will leave Fallinish here. And if anything – anything – happens, you know where the panic button is.'

Maccarrill found himself comfortable perches at different points in the room. Fallinish sniffed the puppets and pushed them about at Salmon's request with his snout, or by elongating his telescopic front left elbow until he could reach the puppets with his claw. Between them they worked for a few hours, reminding each other of things they had forgotten or new things they had been told, like Immo Harper's realisation about Carbon Smith and the timetable for the Outland Watch. Salmon had felt very daring as she added a new puppet to the motte, with a metallic question-mark pinned to its back.

'Immo's right,' Maccarrill said. 'There is no reason for Carbon Smith to have been up on the motte. The Outland

Watch is only on duty every second week and she had been up the week before. She should have been at home. And where on earth is the Fooderie with your lunch? I'm famished. It should have been here by now.'

Dr Boru may not have been the world's friendliest being but she could read humans as easily as a farmer or a sailor reads the sky. When Shearwater Amberson came into her office as the sun passed the meridian, she knew from the moment she looked at him that he had every intention of committing another murder if he thought that it was required. He was wearing the stolen uniform of the Ravenous Raven Fooderie, and underneath, he was neatly dressed in a dark Aran jumper, dark corduroy trousers and hiking boots, but it was clear he had been sleeping rough.[75] He opened the door almost silently and stepped in, then stopped as he saw Dr Boru. He stared at her for a moment and then his glance flickered around the room. Boru wondered about her best course of action.

'Dr Boru,' he said politely, 'you have something that I need.'

'Mr Amberson,' she said, 'what is it that you think I have?'

She had in fact expected him to have realised that it was she who had broken the code of his diary. Instead, he began looking through the files on her desk. Boru watched him for a moment.

'Fen had a file – personal things. Ordinary, everyday bits, routine information. No use to anyone.'

---

[75] He looked rough. That's how you could tell.

He seemed to expect an answer, so Boru said, 'They are often the most interesting kind of information. But all of Fen's records have been either given to the guardians investigating her murder, or they have been registered in the archives.'

'Well, find what I am looking for and unregister it.'

Boru laughed, and regretted it when Shear looked at her.

'Mr Amberson, things cannot be unregistered. They are with the Khipu-Camayacos. You cannot change the tides.'

Shear nodded slowly.

'That,' he said agreeably, 'is just not good enough!'

Shear was strong and as fast as a snake. Boru had no time to react. Shear's weight knocked her over, and instantly his fingers tightened into her flesh.

'I need the ticket,' he said, through his teeth, his knuckles white around Boru's throat, 'and I need it now. Thank you.'

As Salmon was coming to the end of her task, Maccarrill flew out of the building to make sure that it was safe for her to leave once she had Dr Boru with her, and Fallinish went to check the inside of the building. Within a minute Maccarrill was back, just as Salmon realised that the noise she heard was not silver trays falling down a cliff, but Fallinish barking.

'You have a panic button that will call McCabe?' said Maccarrill. 'Well, it's time to panic. Then get back here and lock the door.'

Salmon dashed to the wall and slammed her hand against the orange panic button that any of the apprentices could use if they were in trouble. She ignored Maccarrill's order to return to the office and instead sprinted up the stairs so fast in the wake of his tail feathers she almost overshot the Deputy Khipu's office. Fallinish was barking fearsomely and throwing himself against the door but the door, though it was now considerably dented, had been built to withstand much more than one reconstituted dog. Salmon was not as strong. She did, however, have opposable thumbs, so she picked up a heavy fire extinguisher, lifted it as high as she could, and let it drop onto the handle and lock. The wood splintered and Fallinish crashed through the door.

Shear was reeling back, whirling his arms like a windmill to try to keep his balance. As he staggered around, clutching his blackening eye, Dr Boru struck him once more with her quarterstaff, neatly behind the knees, and knocked him to the ground. But Shear was back on his feet in a second. As Salmon ran to Boru and Boru strode forward to keep between Salmon and Shear, Shear took out a knife with one hand and with the other he hurled a large paperweight. Boru crashed through a chair and lay still. Salmon did not alter her stride. Her foster-father had told the truth and this was the day that the ghost-fencing made sense: she measured her stride, launched herself at Shear and delivered a perfect kick in his solar plexus.

'Would you look at that,' said Maccarrill, as Salmon landed and Shear staggered to his feet again, clutching his stomach and breathing in dreadful, dragging gasps. 'I'll have some of what this boyo has been eating, you just can't keep him down. But don't you touch her, now, or I will have to hurt you.'

He folded his wings like a falcon, and plummeted into the back of Shear's neck. Fallinish clamped his considerable jaws around Shear's arm and clung on, his metal paws braced and a low rumbling growl, like a distant steam train, echoing in his chest. Salmon dodged under the wings, the whip-like tail and flailing fists, and helped Boru to her feet. To her immense relief, Salmon saw the door open and, as Maccarrill flew up out of the range of Shear's slashing blade, McCabe, shedding particles of light and regaining his composition after using his talaris,[76] took a gigantic step forward. Fallinish let go, and McCabe locked Shear's arms behind him. He looked down to where Boru was conscious again and sitting up.

'There are procedures for requesting files, Shearwater,' Boru said, tenderly feeling her skull and checking her fingers for blood.

Shear's face was expressionless and set.

'You might not think that what I am looking for is mine,' he said, 'but it is.'

'What are you looking for?'

Shear ignored McCabe's question. He pulled himself out of the vampire's grasp and returned to the drawers of cards in the immense cabinet in the centre of the room. McCabe let him go because he wanted to see where Shear would go first. There was a tension in his movements that made McCabe wary. McCabe wondered if Shear already knew that Valerian Hobbs had shut down all contact with the Pachamama project. McCabe turned and waved Boru and Salmon towards the corner by the window. He tapped Fallinish on the top of the head, and the dog obeyed, positioning himself in front of Salmon and Boru. He glimmered faintly and did not move.

'You're under arrest, Shear,' McCabe said.

---

[76] See footnote 33.

Shear did not react for a moment, and then he looked up.

'You are under arrest for the murders of Persephone-Fen Maguire and Marl Fitzwilliam, otherwise Boll Mason.'

Shear dropped the pages he was holding.

'You wouldn't be looking for a lottery ticket, would you?' McCabe said, 'because it won't be there. Registry of Records has already sent it to the guardians as evidence.'

Shear stepped away from the cabinet and moved towards McCabe, fluid and determined. Fallinish growled thunderously, but remained where McCabe had told him to stand.

'You killed Fen so that you would get all of the money that was won by the lottery numbers you and she had chosen. You helped Hobbs to kill Marl because Hobbs persuaded you it was to protect the Pachamama Institute, and, since Hobbs had seen you kill Fen, you couldn't refuse. Boll was uncovering Coast Albright's little conspiracy to allow Pothinus and the Apeteh Corporation to duck Outland laws forbidding certain medical experiments on humans, by providing Apeteh's research company with their own little laboratory in Muinbeo. And Hobbs wanted the conspiracy to stay covered up.'

'What nonsense is this?' Shear stopped in his tracks. 'What rubbish are you talking?'

'You stabbed Fen with a Mercurian cutlass fish, Hoprasinos. You took the fish home and cooked it. Then you found out that Valerian knew that you had killed Fen. We had a very interesting conversation with Carbon Smith after Immo reminded us that Carbon had no reason to be on the motte. And it was your bad luck that, once Hobbs persuaded Smith to break open the portal for a fee, she decided to earn the money on the same night that you murdered Fen. It meant that Hobbs was on the motte too, watching Smith to make sure that the portal worked – no access to the Outland, no money for Smith. When Hobbs realised who Marl Fitzwilliam really was, he remembered that Marl was investigating Apeteh and the associated institutes – he and Marl had crossed swords before, so I understand from Cotton Donovan, who, now that he has his own apprentice, agreed to do a little research for me. Hobbs told you what he had seen, he … persuaded you to change your dinner menu, and to serve fish, and every other kind of food that contained histamine, so it looked like Marl died of an allergic shock. But when we tested Marl's body, we found such high levels of histamine in it that it could not have occurred naturally.'

Shear looked as though he were about to be sick.

'That meal was cooked far in advance!' he said. 'Mack had to call round to my house to take it out of the cold-room after Marl invited himself to dinner!'

'Where did you get this fish to curry? The remains of which had that violet-coloured flesh that only one species possesses? Our apprentice here went through the butcher's order books and till receipts with a fine-tooth comb. Only Fen ordered one of those in the last six months. Where is the fish that Fen bought? Why would anyone make a curry of a Mercurian cutlass, when the usual thing to do is bake it to show it off? Why, when we examined your cold-room, did we find the most peculiar liquid there, that I am very certain will turn out to be the sword of a Mercurian cutlass fish, boiled down into gelatine? You had made a chicken casserole that would, according to the apprentice when she saw it also in your cold-room, have fed an invading army. Why did you defrost your fish curry just because Marl was coming? Marl ate meat.'

'That does not prove I killed Fen.'

'That is not our only evidence against you, Mr Amberson. Even the fact that you claimed not to have seen Fen since the morning and yet in your description of her you mentioned that she was wearing a red and green shawl that she had not in fact acquired until later that afternoon – even that is also not the only evidence we have.'

McCabe was relieved to hear the footsteps of Johnston and Benson coming up the hallway. Everyone stood aside while they seized Shear's arms but they were almost tossed to the ground as he struggled against them.

'You are under arrest,' Benson managed to say as they struggled, 'and you do not need to say anything. Anything you do say can be used in evidence, for or against you.'

'I need to find the ticket.'

'If you do not have a lawyer, one will be found for you.'

'I need to find the ticket. It is not the proceeds of crime.'

'If you cannot afford legal advice, any coven or association to which you belong will pay.'

'Even if you claim I am a murderer, the ticket is mine, bought and paid for. The money is mine. Winning the lottery is no crime.'

Shear broke free and dug his knee into Johnston's stomach so that he fell heavily against the wall. Shear swung around and punched Benson hard in the face. Benson staggered but before he and Johnston could grab Shear again, McCabe stepped in. He seemed to increase in height, Salmon thought. He seemed bigger and bulkier and his arms seemed unnaturally long. He seized Shear around the waist and shoulders and twisted him in opposite directions.

'Don't throw people about, Mr Amberson,' he said, 'and stop fretting about your ticket. You can't claim anything on it. That ticket is for the Outland lottery, in a part of the world that does not believe Muinbeo exists. You can't claim the money.'

'That's a lie,' Shear said. 'That's a lie.'

But he stopped struggling and stayed very still.

'You never checked, did you, you greedy little stoat? The rules are clear. You have to own a home in that exact part of the Outland. They won't pay up if you come from even a different part of their world. They certainly won't pay into Muinbeo.'

'Valerian –' Shear began, and stopped.

McCabe set him down.

'Oh, yes, Valerian,' said McCabe. 'Valerian Hobbs, with his neat little camouflage tricks learned in the Outland jungles so he can hide himself in plain sight. When the Deputy Khipu-Camayacos kindly cracked your cipher for us, we found your notes about how he said you could use the address of the Pachamama Institute, the organisation that you thought was going to change your life by putting you through a few courses. The bank account number he gave you was not the institute's. It was his personal bank account on an island that is outside the reach of all financial laws. That is where all the Pachamama money has gone. You would never have seen a penny of what you won. And you would never see Valerian Hobbs again.'

Shear, through the streaks and smears of peat, had gone a ghastly shade of muddy pale. He didn't move. All of the tension went out of him, and his shoulders sagged. He wiped his hand over his moustache and looked around. He looked so stricken and disbelieving, his black eye swelling till it was bigger than a duck's egg, that Salmon very nearly felt sorry for him until McCabe spoke.

'There is no money for you. You killed Fen for nothing. You stabbed your dear friend through the heart and left her to despair and death, you left her alone and betrayed, afraid and in the dark, for nothing. Nothing. That is what you have done. By vengeful Sekhmet, that is what you have done.'

Shear looked around as though he did not know what he was seeing. He shook his head. His knees gave way, and he crumpled on the floor. Putting his hands over his face, he began to cry.

Chapter 10: Two weeks later, the end of January

The Twin Stars[77] rising

The Forum

As it happened, the demonstration for that year's crop of apprentices was held the week after Shearwater Amberson was tried for the murders of both Fen Maguire and Marl Fitzwilliam/Boll Mason. Shear pleaded guilty, at which point the guardians closed the borders and the lawyers went grumpily to the pub, deprived of their chance to show off their oratorical skills. The case was heard in the Forum, and Shear's voice was steady as a rock when, in response to the judge's question about his plea, he admitted guilt. In the words of the enraged Coast Albright, Shear sang like a canary. The senators' careers evaporated before their eyes, as he gave the courtroom every detail of the plan to have the Gallagrene Bog destroyed and cut away so that the long-departed Outlander Pothinus, representative of the Apeteh Institute of dubious repute, could set up a research facility. Shear had never known what the facility was researching. He had simply agreed to go along with it because he wanted to help Valerian Hobbs. He wanted to join Hobbs's Pachamama Institute, which he understood was now defunct. He had

---

[77] Bran and Oisín; Castor and Pollux are elsewhere.

admired Hobbs greatly, his unflinching attitude to the nature of the world, his ability to take charge of nature, to make himself into an extraordinary man. Name after name echoed around the Forum. Carbon Smith bribed to open the sealed portals in order that Theo Pothinus and other Outlanders could come and go unobserved. Kale Lake, who was a microbiologist, had prepared bacteria. She had blackmailed Sand Butler into introducing this noxious mixture into the bog over a period of time. The only time that Shear showed any emotion was when the judge asked where Shear had gone between the time that Salmon had realised that he had killed Fen for the lottery ticket and the time he had tried to kill the Deputy Khipu-Camayacos.

'I went onto the Gallagrene Bog,' he said. 'Out beyond Ciplacti's Ear. I thought I could live there. That is what Hobbs's Institute was all about – how to live without all this human pandering and weakness, how to be strong and self-reliant, like an animal.'

The judge said caustically, 'Animals have many admirable characteristics, Mr Amberson. But perhaps you should have tried harder to maintain your humanity.'

'Humans are weak,' Shear recited. 'Animals do what they need to do. Look at Geoffrey Logan as he calls himself – for years he rejected his werewolf nature, until Hobbs taught him to celebrate it.'

A murmur of shock rippled round the Forum, and the crowd shifted as the alpha werewolves hurried out, signalling to their pack to follow. Outraged, Hellebore Postmaa, the lanky red-haired Wildlife and Landscape senator sitting among those waiting to give evidence, stood up.

'The next time you go off on a tangent about getting back to nature red in tooth and claw, you moron,' he said, ignoring the Forum assistants who were trying to maintain protocol,[78] 'just remember that wolves will care for orphaned cubs belonging to other wolves. Penguins protect each other from brutal weather. Crows watch over their dying. Polar bears have no natural predators and even they do not slaughter each other for a stinking lottery ticket.'

Shear gripped the edge of the podium he stood behind, as Postmaa sat down with a thump.

'I went out onto Gallagrene,' he said, 'and it was hostile to me. All I have done is ripped up the earth, poisoned the water, by taking Fen out of the world. The Gallagrene is not what I thought it was. If there was any justice I would never have come out again.'

The Goldsmiths' house, Marvaan

When, at home that evening with the Goldsmiths, Salmon mentioned that her demonstration was in five days' time, Rainbow was disbelieving.

'How can they want more demonstration of you being a good apprentice than the facts of the investigation about Fen's death?' he said. 'You helped to catch a murderer!'

'I don't think it works like that, Rainbow,' Salmon said rather sadly.

---

[78] That is to say, they were trying to get him to sit down and shut up.

She was dreading the demonstration. Being wonderfully single-minded, she had given it very little thought while she was working with McCabe, but now that the case was over, it was looming in her mind like a bad dream. She had begun to hope, much as Rainbow was saying, that the events spoke for themselves. Her work and her ideas helped to catch the killer and she had, after all, helped to protect the Deputy Khipu from Shear Amberson. But McCabe, casually, disillusioned her. She repeated to Rainbow what McCabe had said.

'The demonstration isn't just about whether you are a good or bad apprentice,' she said. 'I mean that's some of it, they have to know that you are suited to it, but that's only half the story. They have to make sure that you are learning to look after yourself, that you are learning to be a grown-up, to maybe become a despotes yourself. If it was only about the job I could just get the court transcripts and go to the apprenticeship board with it. And tell them everything I did. But that isn't all they want to know.'

She looked so apprehensive that her foster-family immediately tried to think of things to do for her.

'Tell you what,' Archer said, 'you get your portfolio finished up, and then we'll play a game of Beggar My Neighbour. You choose the cards.'

Archer knew she loved looking through the designs and samples he had from the Guild of Cardmakers.

'If you give me the photographs you took of the vegetable patch,' Marigold said, 'I brought back some good off-cuts from the vellum framing course last week, I can make you some presentation frames for them.'

'When you've finished the demonstration, we can go fishing,' Rainbow said, looking at Berry, who nodded.[79]

'Come on, pet,' Berry said, giving Salmon a hug in passing and ruffling her bright hair. 'I'll go through the portfolio with you, and we'll get you as well prepared as we can.'

Being president of the Guild of Weavers, Berry had sat through many, many apprenticeship demonstrations, but each one was slightly different and every apprentice coped differently. McCabe had, in his brusque way, advised Salmon very well as to what the board really was looking for – evidence, however faint, that the apprenticeship was only a stage that would last until the apprentice was able to take charge of their own job and their own life.

After Berry and Salmon had looked through the apprentice portfolio which the board would examine the next day, Salmon was not entirely comforted by Berry's assurances that all seemed in order to her. Naturally, it included the court transcripts, with little stickers to indicate the places where Salmon was mentioned. She had included the routine notes received from Registry of Records to confirm registration of all her records of her work, including her doodles, questions and marginal notes, and she had a certificate signed by Dr O'Buachalla to say that she attended, and quite often attended to, her tutorials.

---

[79] Just to clarify, Rainbow did not mean, sit by a trout-filled river with good fishing rods, and actively try to catch one or more fish. He meant *fishing* as in taking a picnic down to Millstone Pond, and sitting in the sheltered lee of the bridge chatting and eating, while every fish in Muinbeo brought the sprats along to have a laugh at their unconvincing bait.

Marigold was taking care of the photographs Salmon had taken (with Nefertiti's assistance) of Knotty Down's orchard and vegetable garden, since the board would take a dim view of an apprentice who had no idea how to feed itself. As part of the practical demonstration, Salmon was taking the Spider, the copper oven that most apprentices used, to show that she could take it apart, clean and repair it, and put it back together again. Maccarrill had made her practice till she could have possibly done it blindfold, had such a bizarre necessity ever arisen. There would be a ghost-fencing exercise, which she was still dreading, but less so since she seemed, in Dr Boru's office, to have found some kind of rhythm in her movements.

There would be a general knowledge test for which McCabe, Johnston, the Goldsmiths, even Benson had helped her prepare by throwing random questions at her. At odd moments, they asked her to explain place names or asked for a list of the planets and stars. They asked her about geological time, about Outland politics, the appearance of extinct species, how to recognise and prepare mushrooms, about sporting records and notable events in history. They asked her anything that popped into their heads and that, therefore, might pop into the head of a board member.

'What is it that is really worrying you?' Berry said eventually. Salmon was turning a photograph over and over in her fingers.

'It's the Witch Sackville,' she said. 'I don't think that she wants me to be an apprentice.'

'Why? I mean, do you know why she doesn't want you to be an apprentice?'

'I think she wants the coven to look after me.'

'Would you mind that?'

'I don't want to be looked after.'

She was staring at her hands, trying to follow Winter Sackville's train of thought.

Suddenly she said, 'I think she thinks I need to be looked after because I used to live in the Outland, and she thinks everything in the Outland terrible and that I must be fragile because of dangerous things happening around me. She thinks that it was always war, always awful, all the time.'

She looked at Berry, quite surprised at what she'd realised.

'And you don't agree?'

Salmon looked around at the notes, the transcript, the photographs, the Spider.

'There were good parts to living there. And nothing will change the bad things that did happen,' she said. 'Looking after me, thinking I'm fragile, would just mean that all the fear, people being killed, my parents, their friends, all the running away and hiding, all of that just – well, it stays as a horrible part of life. No good comes of it. It was sad and frightening but I learned a lot. So actually I might be a better guardian because of it.'

'If it comes to it,' Berry said, after a moment's pause, 'say that to the Witch Sackville.'

Salmon nodded, unable to imagine doing so, but glad to know that Berry understood.

The next day was bitterly cold and very bright. Thin, trailing clouds smeared the blue sky, and the high, small sun was surprisingly warm. The demonstrations took place in the great hall of the Grand Hotel Abyss, and all of the Goldsmiths travelled in the carriage with Salmon, though they were not permitted to attend. Archer kissed her on the cheek.

'If you get stuck just bite your thumb,' he said. 'Aren't you the Salmon of Knowledge itself?' and she was so nervous that she thought it was the funniest thing she'd ever heard.

'Remember – we'll be waiting down in the Ravenous Raven Fooderie,' Berry said. 'As I recall, after my first demonstration I could have eaten a buttered donkey.'

Salmon climbed out of the carriage and went up to the entrance of the hotel. She hitched the strap of her portfolio up a little higher on her shoulder and walked into the foyer. At the top of the stairs she could see Hunter, Nefertiti, Bracken and a little knot of apprentices chattering, fiddling nervously with their portfolios. As she closed the door, McCabe emerged from the shadows. He raised his hat, and they set off up the stairs.

Time and place?

Presumably

So there you have it, the whole grim story of how one woman got to be slain by her friend, who loved an image of what he could be like more than he loved his friend. Now, you can't say that we didn't warn you – we said right from the start that there were things you would not find out. No, go on, have another glass, and look, you won't get that quality of chocolate too handy anywhere else. You seem a nice enough … person but we can't just tell you straight off what the Patriarch said, or what the Khipu-Camayacos looks like, or why a rook might turn into a raven. Even Salmon's foster-family don't know her full story, and every time that McCabe walks onto the bogs in Muinbeo he knows – he can practically feel through his feet and through the pores of his skin – how much past there is down below in those ancient depths. And the past is not as far away in Muinbeo as anyone might think. Someone as old as McCabe knows that the past eventually reappears in the future. McCabe knows more than most, of course, and he knows that eventually, regardless of the Witch Sackville and her coven, it will be up to him to let Salmon see what it is her *freaky eyes* are built to see. No, now, we won't hear another word about it. You're very welcome, we were happy – happy! – to be able to help out a poor stranded traveller. That's why we leave the lamps in the windows. There are many travellers up here, and few places to stay, especially when the weather turns so treacherous, like it did today.

You're not by any means the only guests we have here, not by a long chalk. We tell lots of stories to lots of people and we hear many stories back. There is no need to even think about leaving yet. That snow is in for the night and you can hear for yourself the way that wind is howling. No, it is the wind. Honestly. It just sounds like that, since we're so high up here, and there are so many peaks and plateaux and ravines but that won't bother you, when you're settled in cosy by the fire. Dinner will be along soon, we're always glad of the company and a chance to chat, the chance to tell a few stories from beyond the Great Way.

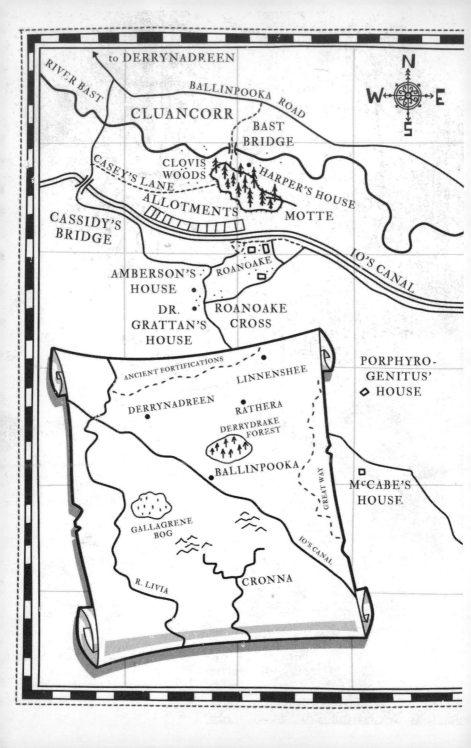

About the author

Susan Maxwell studied English and History in University College Galway before training as an archivist in Dublin. She has worked in a variety of organisations as an archivist but currently works with the United Nations in The Hague, where she is also undertaking a PhD. She has had short stories and poetry published in *The Stinging Fly* and *The Three Spires*, but this is her first published novel.